ARIZONA

By

Clarence Budington Kelland

BOOKS, INC.

New York

By arrangement with Harper & Brothers, New York

CHAPTER 1

PHOEBE TITUS walked the length of the Plaza de Armas, and passed into the Calle Real through the gap that Guillermo Tellez had cut through the ancient wall that defended the Old Pueblo of Tucson. Tellez had found it easier thus to breach the aged adobe than to go around by the main gate, but Phoebe was not grateful for the short cut. Other matters occupied her mind.

In her brown right hand she carried an enormous Sharps rifle, which, in turn, carried a slug that would have knocked over a buffalo. In her left hand she grasped the handle of a whip such as skillful drivers of Conestoga wagons were accustomed to use to impart enthusiasm to four and six horse teams. The lash dragged behind her like some slender snake.

On her head, covering her reddish-chestnut hair, was a black and dusty man's wide-awake hat. On her feet were masculine boots which must have been sizes too large. On her slender but sturdy body she wore a faded pink calico dress which was unable quite to conceal the gracious lines it was intended to adorn.

At the time of this grim progress under the platinum glare

of Arizona's June moon, Phoebe Titus lacked three months and eleven days of being twenty.

She walked purposefully along the Calle Real until she came to an open door giving into a noisy and smoke-filled room where Hoosus carried on the trade of a gambler. This was just beyond the Callejón del Herrero. She entered without pausing, accompanied by the Sharps and followed by the lash. There was a monte table at the left, and at the right a faro layout, presided over by Hoosus himself.

All the Americans in Tucson called him "Hoosus." They did not know his last name. Indeed, they did not know that when they called him Hoosus, they were making an inaccurate effort to pronounce in Spanish his given name, which was "Jesús."

Phoebe cuddled the heavy Sharps with a gesture which bespoke readiness, and let the whip drop to the hard earth floor. The lookout spoke to the dealer, who paused in slipping a card from the case. Hoosus lifted his obsidian eyes and stared at Phoebe.

"Tom Longstreet," said Phoebe, "and you, Timmins, turn around," she said, and placed her back against the adobe wall beside the door. There were perhaps twenty men in the room. Honest miners in red shirts, prospectors, a man or two of other respectable occupations, and a balance of riff-raff for whose presence Tucson was indebted to the activities of vigilantes in San Francisco and the harrying of sheriffs in Texas. They all stood perfectly still, but stared at Phoebe.

"Longstreet," said Phoebe, "you and Timmins just stole eleven hunderd and fourteen dollars in gold and silver and two hundred and eleven dollars in Tubac money out of my house."

"Me? Me and Timmins? No sich thing."

"If you didn't," said Phoebe, "you're goin' to wish you had. Because you're a-goin' to lay thirteen hunderd and twenty-five dollars on that faro layout."

"We hain't got no thirteen hunderd dollars," said the Texan, Timmins.

"Then," said Phoebe, "there's a-goin' to be two holes dug in the new cemetery outside the wall that you'll just fit."

She shifted the big gun upward and her finger crept inside the guard and around the trigger. "Commence countin' out," she said grimly.

"You can't prove we stole a cent. You can't prove we was near your house."

"I heard some of the citizens of this town say they wa'n't no law in Tucson," she answered. "So I don't have to prove. Start to count."

"Better you count," said Kee-soos in his soft voice.

Longstreet and Timmins commenced to disgorge coins and the curious money of the town of Tubac with its animal emblems on the table.

"You add it up, Kee-soos," said Phoebe.

Hoosus fingered the spoils and announced a total of eleven hundred and fifty-six dollars.

"You counted it, so it must be right," said Phoebe. "They been a-playin' faro with you. They hain't had time to spend none. So you got the rest. So you kin just add your share."

"I no win theese mooch," protested Kee-soos.

"If you didn't, you would of," said Phoebe inexorably. "I'm a-waitin'."

Kee-soos added his contribution to the pile.

"You, Bill Dakes, you're a fool, but an honest man. Scoop up the lot, but don't get in the road of this gun."

While Dakes was carrying out this command, Phoebe addressed the room.

"That money," she said in a level voice which did not betray the fury that stirred her, "I earnt by standin' over a hot cookstove in the b'ilin' sun. I earned it bakin' pies for you riffraff. I hain't tradin' on bein' a woman. What I'm sayin' is I earned that money honest, which is more'n most of ye ever done. I didn't stop off in this town of yourn because I wanted to, but because pa was sick and wa'n't able to go on to California. I never see or dreamt of sich a filthy hole. I never dreamt a place could be lived in by so many off-scourin's and scum. The only man I've seen since I come down through Apache Pass was an Injun. I'll venture them towns of Sodom 'n' Gomorrah wasn't a patch on the filthy britches of Tucson." She paused and patted the stock of her rifle. "You make your brags the' hain't no law. Wa-al, you kin figger that suits me. What law I need I'll make whenever I git ready to use it. Like now. . . . Got all that money, Bill Dakes?"

"Yes'm," said Bill.

"Step over to the other side of the door. Now I'm notifyin' everybuddy I won't tolerate no more depredations. I calc'late to go on a-makin' pies and sellin' them fur a dollar apiece. I calc'late to go on keepin' the money in my house. . . . Hoosus, you kind of figger to be an important man around here."

The gambler made no reply, but his black snake's eyes neither moved nor spoke.

"I got my pa to tend. I got my four hosses to see to. I got my bakin'. So I hain't got no time to be chasin' thieves. . . . Hoosus, the' hain't a-goin' to be no more thieves."

"Ver' nize," said Hoosus.

"Because," said Phoebe, "the next time anybuddy molests my money or my proppity, I'm a-goin' to take this here Sharps 'n' blow a hole through you, Hoosus, that a body kin drive a team of Army mules through."

"Me. I ain' steal."

"You'll see nobuddy else does," she said. "It's a law I'm makin' and layin' down. If somebuddy steals from me, you git shot. Be I plain 'n' clear?"

"Sí."

"Now, Tom Longstreet, you 'n' Timmins git through the door. Out into the moonlight where ye kin see good 'n' plain."

The two furious men marched past her and into the street. Phoebe followed them. "Bill Dakes," she ordered, "give Long-street this here whip."

Dakes obeyed.

"Now, Longstreet, lemme see ye tan Timmins' hide, 'n' don't lay on light. I know when a man's usin' a whip in earnest. Put a snap into it. I hain't funnin' with ye." She shifted her rifle. The lash curled through the air and caressed Timmins, who danced and cursed.

"One," counted Phoebe. . . . "Two. . . . Three. . . . Four. . . . Five." And so on up to twenty. "Now you, Timmins, give Longstreet as good as he give you."

She saw to it that twenty lashes were administered, and

then she faced the augmented crowd. And a motley collection of human beings it was. A couple of debauched, degenerate Apaches, who had sunk almost to the state of scavengers; a couple of unsoldierly looking members of the First United States Dragoons, who had taken possession of the town a couple of years ago, when Mr. Gadsden had purchased a strip of land from Mexico. There were a few Pimas and Papagos, industrious, agricultural people, and friendly with the whites. Scattered about were naked terracotta Mexican children; Mexicans in tall, wide-brimmed, conical hats and serapes, a few hard-working and honest miners and freighters, and if anything were needed to add a touch of the bizarre, there was a company of buffoons from Sonora, who, lurid in the costumes of their trade, had followed their audience as it melted away to see what was going on.

"I aim," said Phoebe, "to be left alone."

With that she turned, followed by Dakes, carrying her whip and money, and retraced her steps up the Calle Real and through the rapidly dwindling wall of the only walled city ever erected within the confines of the United States, and so to the miserable adobe hovel on the Plaza de Armas where her ailing father awaited her return.

"I got it," she said tersely, "and I ain't goin' to hide it again. Anybuddy kin come steal it that wants to."

She put away her rifle and went to bed in her curtained corner of the stifling room. This miserable erection, whose adobe bricks were composed now of equal parts of sun-baked dust and filth, had been the best residence she could acquire when her journey from Freeport in Illinois to California had been interrupted by her father's sickness. It consisted of one room, and that possessed of but a single opening, the door. Its roof slanted upward toward the rear, where it had formed a platform against the antique wall for long-dead Spanish defenders to fire down upon besieging Indians. The darkness of the place seemed weighted with heat. In such a room the chances for a sick man to regain his health were slender indeed. It was oppressive, stifling, buzzing with mosquitoes and gnats. But it was the best that Tucson afforded. There was no hotel, no inn. If one could not possess himself of a house, he must, perforce, satisfy himself with the famous Tucson bed, which consisted of lying down anywhere on your stomach and covering it with your back.

Phoebe undressed in her curtained corner and lay down on her pallet and slept. She slept, unconscious that she had made history, and that she had emerged a personage with whom Arizona, then nothing but a part of Dona Ana County of the territory of New Mexico, knew it must reckon.

Next morning, as if she had played no part in an epoch-marking event, Phoebe went about her trade. A square of canvas that once had been the cover of a wagon kept the June sun from beating down upon her chestnut hair as she stood over her cookstove. One side of this canvas was affixed to the old wall of the city; a second side was secured to the wall of her adobe hovel. Along the two exposed sides was a rude counter formed by resting unfinished boards upon barrels. Within this space, this place of business, Phoebe baked pies which the men of the town were eager to buy at the price of one dollar per pie.

Phoebe muffled her hand in her apron and opened the hot oven door. She clanged it too quickly and stepped back from the heat, though it could have been but little greater than the heat of the summer air. A thermometer would have registered a hundred degrees in that spot.

" 'Most baked?" asked a sergeant of dragoons.

"When you see me takin' them out of the oven," she said tartly, "you'll know they're done."

"When a man pays a dollar for a pie," said a trooper disconsolately, "he ought to git some friendliness with it."

"When I sell anything," snapped Phoebe, "I deliver jest what I sell, neither more nor less."

A fat man with a shaven chin, a dilapidated wide-awake hat and an open vest ambled up to the counter. A Navy pistol, holstered, flapped against his enormous thigh. His nose was not that of an abstemious citizen.

"This here batch all sold, Miss Phoebe?" he asked.

"All eight of 'em, judge."

"Seems like a duly elected justice of the peace ought to have him some special rights," complained Judge Bogardus. "How long'll I have to wait?"

"Maybe an hour," said Phoebe. "Who elected you a justice?"

"Oh, some of the boys," said the judge.

"In a mescal shop," said Phoebe. "What right did they have?"

"Wa—al," said the judge, scratching his ear, "who's got a right to say they didn't have no right?"

This being unanswerable, Phoebe walked to the door of the hovel to gaze into its murky depths.

"How you endurin' it, pa?" she asked.

A voice, feeble but not querulous, came from the pallet in the corner, "Calc'late I feel some better today, daughter."

She went to him, lifted his head with strong, calloused hand, and gave him a drink of water. Then she returned to the stove.

"A hull hour, ye say?" asked the judge.

"Mebby more," she replied.

"Guess I kin sort of utilize the time by callin' court. I believe Satan finds work fur idle hands to do. Might's well have the session right out here in the open air where it don't stink quite so much. Anybuddy see Mike Briggs around?"

"Here I be," said a long-nosed individual whose eyes were so close together that they narrowly escaped merging into one.

"You're the defendant, Mike," said the judge, nodding in a friendly way. "Jest step over here close into the jurisdiction of the court. Huh. Prisoner at the bar, the charge agin ye is that you up 'n' blowed the head plumb off'n a Mexican by the name of Solano Pechecho, contrairy to the statute in sich case made 'n' pervided. In consequence of which said shootin', the said Mexican is deader 'n' blazes. Be ye guilty or not guilty?"

"Jedge," said the defendant, "I jest can't deny shootin' that feller. Everybuddy see me do it."

"What in tunket made ye act like that, Mike?" asked the judge.

Mr. Briggs appeared sincerely to search his mind for a reason, and found one that, apparently, satisfied him. "Jedge," he said earnestly, "after about two-three drinks I jest can't stummick Mexicans."

"That there," said the judge, "raises up a p'int of law, and with questions of law I'm amply able to cope. . . . Gentlemen, the facts is clear. This here feller citizen of ourn blasted the tarnation head off'n this Mexican. Which fetches us to the law covering the matter."

He reached into an inner pocket of his vest and extracted a grubby and dog-eared pamphlet. "This here," he said, holding it aloft for all to see, "is the cornerstone of the basis of the law of the land, bein' as it is the Constitution and the Declaration of Independence of the United States of America."

He opened it and laid it on Phoebe's counter. "This mawnin', gentlemen, I read her from sody to hock. Mexicans hain't mentioned in it. And more particular as bearin' on this case before the court I don't find no word in it declarin' or statin' that killin' Mexicans is illegal."

He shut his law library, replaced it in his pocket and faced his auditors. "Therefore," he said, "the verdict of this here court, this here trybunal, as ye might say, is that Mike Briggs is fined the sum of five dollars fur firin' off a firearm and creatin' a disturbance of the peace, and court's hereby adjourned to the closest bar, where the said fine'll be duly disposed of."

Phoebe Titus, lifting hot pies from her oven, listened to this trial of a cold-blooded murderer, and something within her resented it. That such a thing could take place was incredible, appalling.

"Sometime," she said, "the law's a'comin' to Arizony, and half of you'll git hung."

"Madam," said a gentleman in black hat, skirted black coat, black trousers tucked into shining black boots, and a snowy-white shirt, the uniform of the border gambler, "you wrong an enterprising community. Not half, Miss Phoebe. You belittle us. Not half of us, ma'am, but ninety per cent at least."

"The decent folks here, if the' is any," said Phoebe with cold fury, "could take example from San Francisco."

"Ma'am," said the judge, "we don't aim to have no Stranglers here."

Phoebe placed her pies in a row on the counter and popped another batch of eight into the oven.

"Law's bound to come," she said. "Mebby the government back in Washington has forgot us. Mebby it's too busy fightin' 'n' squabblin' about what territory shall be slave and what free even to remember the' is sich a place. But law'll come."

"Miss Phoebe," said a red-shirted miner, "there hain't no more law in Arizony than there is clean spots on an Injun. And there won't never be none. We're too fur off. We'll jest have to scramble along the best we kin."

"Scramble along! To be sure, scramble along! With a murder a night, and no man's property safe that he hain't strong enough to pertect. Sure, we got to scramble along, and make this country, and tear gold 'n' silver 'n' copper out of the hills with our fingernails. The decent ones of us got to scramble along preyed on by scalawags that the Vigilantes drove out of Californy. It's the decent ones that allus has to scramble—but they allus manage to do it. That's what gives folks hope to keep a-goin'—because bein' honest 'n' able in workin' your fingers to the bone allus comes out on top in the end. When the rasslin' match is over 'n' the dust settles down law'n order'll be shovin' your faces in the muck."

"Not in Tucson," said the gambler.

"It's a'comin' as sure's sunrise," she said, and her shoulders straightened and her eyes glowed. "The Overland Stage is carryin' thro' the mail from St. Louis to San Francisco twice a week. The's even argyment over a railroad." She swept her arms widely. "Look at them mountains bulgin' with gold 'n' silver 'n' copper. Look at this here ruined 'n' devastated land capable of raisin' harvest the like of which a body never seen! Where wealth lays a-waitin' men'll come to git it. Come in droves. Bringin' law 'n' order with 'em. We'll force Congress to give us organization as a Territory 'n' then we'll git to be a state! Right where ye stand, right where this filthy, crumblin', ornery corner of hell is reelin' 'n' roarin' 'n' robbin' 'n' killin', there'll be a city—and wimmin 'n' homes 'n' streets 'n' churches."

"You 'n' me won't never live to see it," said Judge Bogardus confidently.

"You won't," retorted Phoebe, "because you'll be hung. But me, I'll live to see this town as peaceful 'n' prosperous as Boston. And when I do I'll go a-ridin' to the buryin' ground where you're a-layin' with your boots on and tell ye about it."

"What fur d'ye care what happens to Arizony?" asked the judge. "You're jest stoppin' off because your pappy's sick. You're Californy bound."

She turned away and pretended to feed the fire in her cookstove. That cookstove that had ridden with her in the bed of her Conestoga wagon over hundreds of miles of plain and desert and mountains, from clement, civilized, settled Illinois. For some reason, the question jolted her. What did she care, indeed? What did Tucson and the whole broad empire of Arizona matter to her?

CHAPTER II

THROUGH the burning months of the summer, Phoebe Titus not only maintained herself but continued to add to her hoard of gold and silver and Tubac money. Virgil Titus lingered, but did not improve, even with the cooler weather of October. He worried constantly about his daughter.

"What's goin' to happen to ye, Phoebe?" he asked constantly. "When I'm gone, what's goin' to become of ye?"

"Don't you fret, pa," she told him.

"Be ye goin' on to Californy," he asked, "or be ye goin' back to Illinois? Ye can't stay here. 'Tain't fit for a woman."

"When the time comes," she said, "I'll make up my mind."

But her mind was being made up for her. A pattern was being woven of which she was an integral part. A pattern consisting of occupations, opportunities, interests which already held her in its threads, and some of whose threads she was holding in her fingers with an increasingly firm grip. Money was to be made in Tucson if one was willing to work, and Phoebe was determined she should have money. For nineteen years her father's shiftlessness and good-humored incompetence had kept the family in a state close to the border of poverty. She was determined that she never would experience poverty again. So she reached out for money, caring nothing, in her young strength and vigor and restless energy, what labor she spent to obtain it.

But that was not all. A driving ambition that was almost masculine forced her to undertakings. Little of the pleasure of youth had been hers, and little of it was obtainable in this environment, even if she coveted it. So she found a recreation in toil and a pleasure in ability to accomplish.

There were few of the inhabitants of Tucson to whom she showed other than a harsh, forbidding exterior. At a time of life when other girls in more normal surroundings were making themselves amiable and charming and beautiful to attract men, Phoebe was giving equal thought to repelling them. In that whole community of eight hundred people there were not twenty who could be admitted to any decent home, not twenty who did not bear some criminal taint or who were not so vicious in character and habits as to make any association with them unthinkable.

So Phoebe built a character for herself which was rapidly becoming herself. She was tart, abrupt, acid. Instead of laboring to please as a young woman should do, she labored to displease. She imitated the cactus of the desert, thrusting out defensive spines, sharp and barbed. She smiled little and laughed so rarely that it surprised even herself when she did so. This was not because she was unable to understand the joy of life, and to look forward to living. It was not because she did not see things to laugh at, or because she had no store of laughter. It was because she feared to let down her defenses even for an instant.

"If you don't git out of here," Virgil asked her, "how be ye ever goin' to marry? How be ye ever goin' to have a husband and children and a home, like a woman ought to have?" He sighed and stirred restlessly on his pallet. "Don't ye want them?"

"I want what every woman wants," she said.

"I wisht you'd promise me to go back to Freeport," he pleaded with her.

"I couldn't ever be content in Freeport ag'in," she said. "I wasn't ever contented there. I guess, pa, I hain't the kind of woman to git along in easy, settled places."

"I wisht I hadn't fetched ye here."

"You didn't," she said. "I fetched you." In her mind she was saying, "I fetched you and mebby I killed you doin' it."

In spite of herself, however, the forbidding shell in which she felt compelled to encase herself failed sometimes to perform the duty she imposed upon it. The Phoebe Titus whom she sought to conceal from all human eyes, even her own, occasionally came briefly to view. When it did so she hastily concealed it, or disguised it with brusqueness—and for days afterward would present an even more grim and harsh aspect to the world.

There was, for instance, the slight matter of little Estevan Ochoa, least fortunate of the Ochoa brood who huddled together in a hovel on La Plaza Militar. He might have been eight years old, though in his nudity he seemed an ill-favored little gnome who might have been ageless. His brown little face in which were beautiful, liquid brown eyes, was no higher from the ground than the top of Phoebe's counter— and because his legs were wizened and there was a great lump between his shoulders he made sport for the other children. And his parents wished for him that someday he might use his malformation to be the clown in one of those dreadful traveling companies of mountebanks which came sometimes to add to the merriment of Tucson.

In the beginning, when Phoebe was baking, he would come often to stand and gaze with a concentrated curiosity, and to sniff when the oven door opened with a hopeless wistfulness. He annoyed Phoebe with his queer, sad face and great angel's eyes, so that she would not look at nor notice him. She would not even give him the attention it required to drive him away. But Phoebe and her pies exercised some potent fascination over the lad so that he came, day after day and stood entranced as at some notable performance.

Out of her somber eyes Phoebe noted the juvenile cruelty of the other Mexican children; noted too that Estevan's older brothers and parents made no movement of protection.

So, one day, trying to conceal the act even from herself, Phoebe found a very small dish and in it baked a very small pie. She set it out to cool and when it could be touched with the bare hand she pushed it ungraciously across her bare-board counter to Estevan.

"Take it and scat!" she said, looking about to see that none had observed the gift.

"For me?" little Estevan asked in Spanish, for he had no English.

She understood that much. "For you. Skedaddle."

"Wherever the Señorita goes," he said with a strange gravity and courtliness, "I shall twice daily pray that she goes with God."

Even yet, because of disbelief or because of instinctive good manners, he did not touch the dainty, but gazed at Phoebe with suddenly born adoration.

"To serve the Señorita in all things," he said, "will be the labor of my life."

These two sayings Phoebe did not understand, for her Spanish had not yet come to her, but it would have been impossible not to comprehend their purport, and she was embarrassed.

"Git," she said sharply.

Estevan smiled at her, for now he understood. He understood what was hidden from every other soul in Tucson—that this strange Englishwoman was gracious even as the saints, and good even as the Madonna.

"Is it permitted to eat it here?" he asked. "The big ones will steal it away from me."

Somehow she understood this—perhaps it was the eloquent pantomime that accompanied it. She jerked her thumb toward the hovel where her father lay.

"If anyone tries to take it away from you," she said savagely, "I'll skin 'em alive."

And this, strangely too, Estevan understood, and of it he boasted to the other urchins.

"The Señorita," he said, "has become my patron. She will drink the blood of any who lays a hand upon me."

And so Phoebe Titus made her first friend—a friend that was eager to be her slave.

Of the few worthy citizens of Tucson the one with whom she formed some bonds of friendship was Solomon Warner, who, bringing in a stock of goods across the desert by mule-back, had been the first American to undertake a commercial enterprise in the Old Pueblo. She and Solomon had this in common, that neither had an eye for anything but business. They talked trade, mines, cattle, opportunities.

"Take Poston," he said to her, "down to Tubac. Makin' money hand over fist, and his town growin' so it's bigger than Tucson—and better. Lives like a nabob with wines on his table. And why's his town better? Because everybody's dependent on Poston. He's the law. He pays the wages. He gives the work. He furnishes the money. Tubac ain't any Sunday school, but it's some milder 'n Tucson. Even prints his own money, and it's better 'n' safer than United States greenbacks."

"Funny what folks'll use for money," said Phoebe. "Now take these *boletas* of Poston's." She shuffled a dozen of them in her strong hand. "Nothin' but scraps of cardboard, but they're as good as gold."

"That's because Poston's good as gold," said Solomon.

"Look at this shilling one with a pig printed on it," she said. "It ain't actually wuth a hundredth part of a shilling— but you can buy with it."

"Poston's smart. He puts animal pictures on 'em so the most ignorant can tell 'em apart. A pig for a shilling, a rooster for fifty cents, a horse for a dollar. And every one of 'em good jest because Poston's good."

"I been a-thinkin' why goods cost so much here—why ye got to pay two shillings fur one needle."

"On account of the cost of gettin' it here to sell," said Solomon.

"It don't cost much to make a needle," said Phoebe, "but it

sells for a quarter. If the needlemaker could get a quarter for all he makes he'd git awful rich."

"Most of the cost is in the carryin'," said Solomon.

"Then," said Phoebe, "seems to me it's a better thing to do the carryin' than the manufacturin' or the sellin'."

"Calc'late so," said Solomon.

"I've been studying over it. All we get to eat and wear and use is freighted up here from Guaymas down in Mexico, or from Fort Yuma—or else they have to lug it overland clean from St. Louis."

"To be sure."

"I can make a sight of money bakin' pies," said Phoebe, "but it's hot labor. I got to do it all myself, burnin' my fingers and wearin' myself out. I could make more money freightin', and somebuddy else would have to do the hard work. Hosses or mules or oxen, and hired men to drive 'em."

"Ye have to own the teams 'n' the wagons," said Solomon.

"I own a Conestoga wagon," she said, "that's fit to haul any-thin' anywhere, and I own four hosses. But I been so busy tendin' pa and bakin' that I hain't had time to think about 'em. And I'm storin' up money that'll buy more."

"There's the Injuns," said Solomon.

"Because there's Injuns ye kin git more for freightin'," she said. "I'm a-goin' to go into it."

Warner, who was a careful man, and one to sit and think things out before he decided, puffed on his pipe and made clucking noises.

Presently he spoke, "You 'n' me think alike, Phoebe. We both got confidence this country's goin' to grow. I didn't drive no mule teams acrost here with every cent I got in the world onto their hurricane decks without figgerin'. People's comin' in. Houses'll be built. More mines'll be sunk. And all they eat and wear and set on and sleep on has got to be freighted in. To say nothin' of machinery."

"That's my way of lookin' at it," said Phoebe.

"But one wagon, mebby two, would allus have to be waitin' for a train to set out. Wouldn't be safe to go alone. Say four wagons with good men 'ud be sure to git through."

"I can't raise the money fur it," said Phoebe.

"The two of us could," said Solomon, "if we was to go partners."

"Mr. Warner," said Phoebe, "you've made a trade."

Next morning, while her first batch of pies was baking, Phoebe looked up from her stove to see a strange young man regarding her both wistfully and quizzically. He was very tall, six feet, two inches, she guessed with swift appraisal. He was also broad of shoulder and long of leg. As he took off his hat when their eyes met, he smiled, not diffidently but not boldly. It was a natural, spontaneous, boyish sort of smile, and Phoebe responded to it involuntarily. His hair was light and long, bleached by sun and wind, and his eyes were brown. His mouth was large and his teeth were white which was novelty enough in itself to cause remark in Tucson, which knew no toothbrushes and could count its yellow fangs by hundreds.

"Good mawnin', Miss," said this stranger in a soft, throaty drawl. "Is that thar contraption a cookin' stove?"

"Does it look like a plow?"

"No'm, it don't scarcely look like no plow. It don't smell

like no plow neither." He lifted his head and sniffed. "Ma'am, would I be forgettin' my manners if I was to ask what gives off that smell?"

"Pies," said Phoebe.

"Pies!" exclaimed the young man. "What would a feller have to do to git to taste one of them thar dainties?"

"He'd have," said Phoebe, "to own a dollar."

"If I didn't have but one left, ma'am—and I reckon I hain't got many more'n one—I'd jest natural have to squander it." He looked around him. "My! My! I don't never recollect seein' sich a town as this here one. What's this here mud wall fur?"

"The Spaniards built it to keep out the Injuns," she said. "That was hundreds of years back."

"They'd 'a' had to build it a sight higher to keep me back from them pies," he said. "Injuns bother you much?"

"Apaches allus a-raidin' around and killin' ranchers 'n' runnin' off stock," she said. "They most ruined this Santa Cruz Valley. If 'twa'n't fur the friendly Pimas and Papagos fightin' 'em off and chasin' after 'em with war parties 'n' lickin' 'em, I dunno but what this town 'ud have to give up."

"We seen Injuns when we come through, but they wa'n't hos-tile none. Jest rode back a piece and scared the livers out of us. I hear tell they don't never attack if folks is ready to fight back."

"But ye dassen't wink an eye," said Phoebe, who had fallen into this conversation without in the least intending to do so. It was, perhaps, the first wholly natural thing she had done since she arrived in Tucson.

"We seen the big chief of them all," said the stranger.

"Mangas Coloradas."

"That wa'n't his name. Cochise, the agent to the mail station back in Apache Pass said he was. Come in with some of his tribe to sell wood."

"What'd he look like?" Phoebe wanted to know.

"Six foot high, about middle age, I'd reckon. Kind of a sad, serious sort of a face on him, and a head shaped like what a senator's head ought to be. Kind of noble. Didn't have much on but moccasins that come up to his knees and turned up at the toes, with a button on the tip, and a cloth around the middle of him and a head band. I'd hate to have to rassle with him."

Phoebe turned to her oven, and finding the pies baked to her satisfaction, removed them and set them on the counter to cool.

"I never see you before," she said tentatively.

"Come in with a wagon train last night. Me 'n' my pappy 'n' my mammy is headin' fur Californy. Stopped off a day to kind of vittle up 'n' do some blacksmithin'. You live here?"

"I don't know but what I do," said Phoebe. "Anyhow, I'm here."

"Bakin' pies," said the young man.

"Bakin' pies," said Phoebe, "and nussin' my pa, that's sick."

"My name," said the young man casually, "is Peter Muncie."

"Dew tell!" exclaimed Phoebe. "Any sheriffs lookin' after ye?"

"I hain't contrived no depredation yit to excite a sheriff," said Peter, "but if it'll help, I'll see what I kin manage."

Phoebe flushed and blamed herself for leaving this opening.

"Mebby you didn't notice, but I said my name was Peter Muncie."

"I hain't deaf."

"Whar I come from, if one says his name, 'tother says her name back to him."

"You're pullin' out tomorrow," she said. "What good'll my name do ye?"

"So," he said, with a glint in his eye, "I'll know who to ask fur when I come back."

"Be ye comin' back?"

"I be," he said, "if that thar pie turns out to eat as good as it smells."

"You better eat your pie 'n' skedaddle," she said, but not with her accustomed sharpness.

"Kin I borrow the tin?" he asked. "I want to carry some to pappy 'n' mammy. Mammy'd sure relish a slice of pie. My mammy," he said, "is nice lookin'. When she was a gal, I venture she was full as nice lookin' as you be."

"My name's Phoebe Titus," she said, for some reason not clear to herself. "And fetch that tin back quick's ye kin. I got to use it."

"Don't they have no dances nor nothin' here?"

"Yes, but they ain't very nice. Jest the ones the Mexicans give amongst themselves, where the mothers come along and look after their daughters. Mexicans is awful careful of their daughters. You don't scarcely ever see a nice Mexican gal out of the house."

"If the' was one tonight, would you go to it with me?"

"No."

Suddenly he slapped his thigh. "Gosh almighty," he said, "you hain't the gal that made them skunks give back the money they stole 'n' then made 'em larrup each another? Be you her?"

"I got my money back," said Phoebe.

"And I figgered that gal 'ud be rawboned 'n' humbly! Miss Phoebe, seems like you're overpowerin'. Fust-class cook, with a crop full of sand, and perty as a little red settin' hen. I wisht I wa'n't goin' to Californy."

"Quit talkin' nonsense," said Phoebe.

Suddenly he leaned his large, long-fingered hands on the boards of her counter. "Miss Phoebe," he said, "Californy's a long ways and heaps kin happen betwixt 'n' between. But I got a feelin' I'll be comin' back someday. I got a feelin' I'll have a hankerin' to come back. Miss Phoebe, if I was to write ye a letter from Californy, would ye answer it?"

"No," she said.

"I'll bet ye would," he said, and grinned broadly. "I kin play the banjo 'n' I'm awful comical company. Folks says so fur miles around. Yes'm, soon's I git settled in Californy I aim to write you that thar letter."

"Save your postage," she said, "to buy potato seed."

"When you git it," he said, "and see 'Peter Muncie' signed to the end of it, you'll know it come from me."

"And when I never git it 'n' no name's signed to the end of it," she said, "I'll know I been a-listenin' to one that jest goes around talkin' to hear the sound of his own voice."

"Would ye like to hear from me, Phoebe?"

"No."

"I like wimmin better that sticks to the truth. I'll fetch back this pie tin in less'n an hour. And we kin talk some more."

"I'll be busy," said Phoebe.

"Don't forgit the name," he said over his shoulder. "It's Peter Muncie."

CHAPTER III

FEW besides Solomon Warner and little Estevan Ochoa knew of Phoebe's gentleness and patience and devotion to Virgil Titus during his illness; and none besides these dreamed of her grief when he died on the eighth of November. He knew the end was at hand, and the prospect of leaving Phoebe alone in this frightful spot made his going an unwelcome release.

"Phoebe," he said again and again, "I wisht you'd promise to go back when I'm gone. I fetched you here. I'm allus accusin' myself. I shouldn't ever 'a' come."

"You didn't fetch me, Pa," she said, and took his wasted hand in hers with a gentleness that Tucson would have thought incredible. "I fetched you. I grabbed you up and jerked you away. It wa'n't any of your doin'." She paused and her lips set to still a possible quivering. "I hadn't no business to drag you off out of civilization, but somethin' was a-draggin' me, Pa. Somethin' drug me and I couldn't withstand it. And you wa'n't never fit for sich a life, Pa. I shouldn't 'a' drug you."

"I never was much of a man," said Virgil, "just a one to set around in a store and swap stories with fellers like Abe."

For an instant his eyes brightened. "Call to mind how Abe used to set on a cracker barrel in the store to Freeport with them legs of his'n a-sprawl?"

"Jest a sharp, schemin', humbly politician," said Phoebe, for she knew how her father loved to argue about the man who had been defeated for the senatorship by Steve Douglas, the Little Giant.

"Steve licked him," said Virgil, "but Abe outsmarted him. Yes, sirree, he fixed it with that there question so's Steve never kin be President. Right in Freeport, the day of the big debate, he done it. And Steve he up 'n' uttered the Freeport heresy. Wonder what's become of Abe 'thout me to come in and advise with him."

"He's aimin' to be President, Pa. And that'll be a sight fur sore eyes."

"I dunno," said Virgil. "I dunno. The's a heap of distance betwixt the top of Abe and the bottom of him. Folks don't grasp him like I do." And then he fell silent and his mind was vexed by thoughts of his death and of his daughter alone in this hovel in a city of hovels. "Ye won't hold it agin me, Phoebe, fetchin' ye away out here?"

"No, Pa," she said.

"Phoebe," he said after a minute, "ye hain't kissed me since ye was a mite of a gal. Seems like I kind of forgit what a kiss feels like. When a man nears his end he kind of thinks about kisses and folks he's fond of. Phoebe, the's times you seem kind of set and harsh-like. The's even times when I feel as if you didn't like me. I'd go a sight easier if I knowed it wa'n't so."

It was not an easy thing for her to do—to demonstrate her

affection—but she leaned over him and kissed him on the lips. "I hain't neber had but what was kind thoughts of ye, Pa," she said.

And after that, until the night he died, Phoebe Titus made it her practice to kiss Virgil before she retired to her pallet. Virgil would say to her, "It's good fur ye, Phoebe. Mind, daughter, that ye never forgit how to kiss. A woman that hain't eager for the kiss of her man hain't fit. She's lackin'. I been a-watchin' ye and a-listenin' to ye, Phoebe. You're one that's in danger of forgittin' how important a kiss kin be."

So, in November, Virgil died, and Phoebe concealed her mourning in the darkness of the mud hovel which was her home. She let no tear run down her sun-tanned cheeks, but she sat in silence, hands clenched in her lap, and reflected with self-accusation that it was her ambition, her restlessness, that had brought this gentle, shiftless, kindly man to his death. There was no woman in Tucson to sit by her, for she would have none. There was no man to be her confidant. It was a Gethsemane in which she must sit alone. It was a grief and loneliness which no human being would ever know had rested so heavily upon her.

She prepared his body, and, kneeling alone beside him before he was carried out to the new cemetery just outside the walls, she kissed him on the forehead, for she knew that he would be happy to have it so. Then Solomon Warner and others carried him out and disposed of him, and Phoebe was alone.

Sick though he had been, Virgil was a protection. His presence in the hovel which had been their home was a defense to Phoebe. Now it was possible to continue her journey to

California and to escape from this dingy, dilapidated, sun-baked straggle of mud boxes. Now she could go away forever from this naked, parched unwholesome spot of sore-backed burros, coyote dogs, and broken-down corrals. But she did not go, because she had taken root.

Her restless energy had compelled her to take root. A force within her that compelled her to industry, a tireless, grim ambition that forced her to seek out opportunities, had bound her to this soil. Her labor and her hard-earned money were now invested in Arizona, and she must stay to husband and to increase it.

With Solomon Warner, she owned four teams and wagons —her own four horses and Conestoga wagon and three six-mule teams. These were busy, for it seemed, toward the end of 1859, that the boom had come to Arizona. Poston's mines were flourishing in and about Tubac, wrenching silver from the mountains in fabulous quantities. The Heintzelman mine smelted ore that yielded the astounding sum of $950 a ton. Seventy-five miles south of Tucson was the Patagonia. For the reduction works it was necessary to freight in stamps, retorts, furnaces, engines and lumber. For the men who worked in the mines it was necessary to freight in supplies.

Even though the mines and works must be operated at times with an implement in one hand and a rifle in the other to repel Apache raids, Arizona roared and surged and prospered. But in the sky to the east was a cloud that no man heeded, for all men in this outpost of civilization were too busy to heed it.

With every arriving overland stage came disquieting news from Washington. Rumblings, rumors. Secession was in the air. What opinion there was in Tucson was overwhelmingly with the South.

Phoebe, although the freighting business proved profitable from the first, continued her pie baking. She wanted more capital, always more money with which to make more money, to avail herself of new opportunities, to expand.

"Mebby we better pull in our horns and sit tight for a spell," suggested Solomon Warner. "If it comes to a war betwixt North and South, there's no tellin'."

"Money's to be made in troubled times," answered Phoebe, "if ye know how to use them. What I come to see you about, Solomon, is this: A man named Tarbox got into town yestiddy with a party of lumbermen from Maine. He's lookin' around."

"For what?" asked Solomon.

"To find out if any money can be made cuttin' lumber. Lumber's needed, Solomon, and the's plenty of it down in the Santa Rita Mountains."

"I don't know anything about cutting timber."

"Neither do I, but I can find out."

"And while these men is choppin down trees, what's goin' to stop the Apaches from choppin' them down?"

"If," said Phoebe, "they hain't able to protect themselves, they more'n half deserve what they git. It's a chance."

"What kind of a chance?"

"I hear Poston's in town from Tubac. Maybe we could make a dicker with him."

"You're gittin' too many irons in the fire, Phoebe. Better leave this alone."

"You don't want to go into it?"

"Not for a penny," said Solomon.

Phoebe did not argue. She set off in search of Charles D. Poston, of the Heintzelman mine, and found him at the flour mill.

"How are you, Miss Phoebe?" he asked genially. "You never come down to Tubac to see us. We'll show you civilization. Finest and most flourishing community in America."

"I don't git to travel much," she said; and then, "Mr. Poston, you need a sight of lumber to the mines."

"We certainly do."

"What's it wuth to ye?"

"I'd be willing to pay as high as a hundred and fifty a thousand."

"Put it in writin'," said Phoebe.

"Where are you going to get it. And how?"

"I calc'late to throw a party of men into the Santa Ritas. Injuns is the drawback."

"And quite a drawback they are," he said, smiling all over his broad bearded face.

"Here's what I thought," she told him: "You got standin' with the Injuns. Now, couldn't you call in some of the chiefs and make a bargain with them, Mr. Poston? They go raidin' down betwixt here and Tubac into Sonora. How if you was to make a dicker that none of us would meddle with their Mexican raidin' if they agreed to leave my lumber workin' alone?"

"Might be done," he said.

"Is it a deal?"

"They say you always finish what you start, Miss Phoebe.

A hundred and fifty a thousand is the figure, and I take all you can cut."

"I'll git it down to the Tubac-Tucson road, mebby about halfway betwixt. Haulin' to Tubac'll be extry at regular freightin' rates."

"You don't figure to lose money, do you?" Poston asked, with another smile.

"If ye can't make a decent profit," said Phoebe, "what's the good of goin' into it?"

"Good luck to you," said Mr. Poston.

Phoebe left him and found Tarbox and a number of his men against a bar.

"Your name Tarbox?" she asked.

"That's what they call me."

"Lumberman?"

"Out of the state of Maine."

"My name's Titus. Ask about me if you got a mind. I keep my bargains and pay when it's due."

"What d'ye calc'late to pay me fur?" he asked.

"Cuttin' down trees 'n' whipsawin' lumber."

A chunky man who had been standing beside Tarbox at the bar turned his head. "You're jest a half hour too late, Phoebe," he said.

"Meanin' what?"

"I just hired Tarbox and his party to log fur me."

"And who, Lazarus Ward, d'ye calc'late to sell your lumber to?"

"Poston," he said.

"He'll be ridin' back from the flour mill," said Phoebe. "Better go ask him if he wants any more lumber."

"Why wouldn't he want lumber?"

"He does. I said more lumber. I jest contracted with him to supply him all he kin use."

"I'll see about that," said Lazarus, and he turned and strode out of the barroom. Presently he returned and his eyes were angry.

"You stole a march on me," he said furiously.

"Didn't neither," she said. "I jest took a-holt of the right end of the string fust. You made a grab at the wrong end."

"I got these men hired," he said. "You can't cut no lumber 'thout 'em."

"And you can't sell no lumber. And if ye can't sell no lumber, ye can't pay no wages," she countered.

"Seems like the lady's got an argymint there," observed Tarbox.

"How about throwin' in together?" asked Lazarus.

"I don't want no partnership with Lazarus Ward. I don't like your ways of doin'."

"Then ye don't git no lumbermen," said Lazarus.

"I got suthin' to say about that, seems as though," said Tarbox. "How you a'goin' to pay wages if you can't sell? Me 'n' my party don't calc'late to work fur nothin'. This here leetle lady's got ye whipsawed, Mr. Ward. So our deal's off. . . . Miss, you've hired you a mess of lumbermen."

"And I'm pushed out of this here deal that I thought up?" demanded Lazarus.

"Clean, plumb out of it," said Phoebe.

"You'll rue it," said Lazarus. "Sure's I'm born, you'll rue it."

Phoebe faced him, but did not smile. "Mebby so," she said. "Any time ye git ready to start a rumpus with me, jest turn loose your dog. . . . You, Mr. Tarbox, come along with me. We got things to talk over."

Two days later the party rode out of Tucson, accompanied by a wagon filled with supplies and tools. Phoebe accompanied them. It was the first time she had left Tucson since she entered it with her sick father so many months before. They journeyed southward unmolested, until they came to a suitable spot on the south bank of the Santa Cruz River convenient to the Tubac road.

"We'll build a house 'n' a corrall here," she directed. "Better keep a watch. Mr. Poston's makin' a dicker with the Injuns, and see to it you keep your part of it. If you leave them alone, they'll leave you alone."

"We hain't got no hankerin' for traffic with Injuns," said Tarbox.

Phoebe remained until the work was under way. Then she joined a party, mostly Mexicans, who were driving a pack train of eighteen burros to Tucson. The little beasts trotted along patiently, bells jingling pleasantly, bearing upon their backs luscious fruits and other articles of commerce from fertile Sonora—none of which had paid its duty at a port of entry.

"Phoebe," said Solomon Warner, when she arrived at home, "I dunno if I'd of treated Lazarus Ward so. He's a vindictive man. And he hain't one that would scorn to stoop to anythin'."

"If ye go in business," said Phoebe, "ye got to take risks. In this kind of a country, men like Lazarus is jest a natural risk to be expected."

"He's been talkin' loud," said Solomon.

"The louder he hollers, the better I kin hear him," said Phoebe.

"Don't figger he's jest a skunk, Phoebe. He's a feller that's able. And sure as shootin', he'll do you a spite."

Phoebe was not worrying about any man's spite. Her confidence in herself was boundless. It was not vanity because it was deeper and higher and wider than vanity. It was certainty. She simply was aware that Phoebe Titus was a person who could look out for herself. This was when she thought about it at all. Usually she simply took it for granted. She was too young yet to appreciate that she was not an ordinary human being; it may be that personages do not realize they are personages but think they are like the run of people with whom they come into contact. It is events, happenings, trials and tests, victories and defeats that cause an unusual individual to realize at last that he is unusual. As for Phoebe, she simply knew she was Phoebe Titus and that she was afraid of nothing.

Since that afternoon when she had met him over her pie counter, Phoebe had thought, when she found time for thinking, of Peter Muncie. Sometimes, just before she went to sleep, she wondered if he remembered her. She wondered if her face was as distinct in his memory as his face was in hers, and if he could recall the movement of her features and gestures of her hands as she could visualize his. She did not protest to herself because she thought about him. It was a queer pleasure. He had gone on to California, and she never would see him again, but it was pleasant to recall his voice and his youth; to realize that such young men existed in the world. As the weeks and months went past, he represented a genus instead of an individual. She did not say to herself that she wanted Peter Muncie, but that she wanted a man of the sort that Peter Muncie exemplified. But even so, she wondered if he would write to her as he said he would, and if he should write, what she would reply. If she replied.

So in planning and in labor passed the remaining weeks of that year and the early months of the next. The country was becoming more vexed. Tempers were quickening as the cleavage between North and South became deeper and wider. Even in Tucson it manifested itself as mail and papers arrived from the East. Men quarreled in bars. Strangers meeting on the trail bickered and separated in enmity. A pall of uneasiness overhung the remote little community, as well it might. For if a nation at peace with itself scarcely bothered to remember the existence of Arizona, what would a nation at war do for it?

Sparsely settled Arizona hung on now only by the skin of its teeth and because there was no definite war with the Apaches. A meager handful of troopers, widely separated, was all that saved its ranchers and miners from destruction. If war should come and the army should be withdrawn to fight elsewhere, what would become of everybody?

The spring of 1860 passed and Phoebe had been in Tucson a full year. In that year she had become a person of affairs and responsibilities. A person of note in a tiny community. She was prospering.

Late in May she rode down to Canoa, as her lumber camp was called. It had been doing excellently. Lumber had flowed down from the hills and been hauled to Mr. Poston in Tubac, who had paid for it promptly in silver bullion of standard fineness, and then had used it for building houses, for strengthening the workings in his mine and for such other purposes as presented themselves. A hundred and fifty dollars a thousand feet, Phoebe received, and the lumber cost her nothing. It was cut in the mountains, which were no man's property, and its cost to her was merely the cost of the labor expended upon it. As the profits mounted, she bought more mules and horses and wagons. At the present rate of progress, it would not be long before she would be the most important freighter in Arizona.

She arrived at Canoa in midafternoon. As she approached from the north, a small cavalcade of Mexicans came up from the southward. Sitting on their horses, they asked for Tarbox, who came out and stood by the corral gate.

"The Apaches," they told him, "have raided our ranches. They have driven off our stock and stolen our property. They have carried them off over the Baboquivari Valley. They travel to the north and will cross the Santa Cruz between this place and Tucson."

"Now, that's too bad," commiserated Tarbox.

"There is a great wealth of livestock, cattle, horses, mules," said the leader of the Mexicans. "We are few. The Americans are great fighters. We come to you asking your aid."

"Careful, Tarbox," warned Phoebe.

"We ask aid of Don Charles Poston in Tubac, but he has refused. So we have come to you. But we do not ask this aid for nothing. We are generous."

"For what reason did you come to Canoa? What made you think you could get help here?" asked Phoebe.

"An American said it would be given. He told us the men

of Canoa would ride with us eagerly, both for love of battle and for love of gain."

"What man was this?" asked Phoebe.

"A broad man that smiles with his teeth," said the Mexican. "His name is Lazarus Ward."

"Again," said Phoebe to Tarbox, "I tell you to be careful."

"If you will come with us in a *corrida*—a cutting off of these Apaches before they can cross the river and hide in their mountains—we will give you one half of all the stock and the property we can recover. It is of great value."

"I forbid it," said Phoebe.

Tarbox leaned against the poles of the corral, considering. His men had labored hard and steadily. Lumber was piled by the roadside—more than a week of hauling could carry away. They deserved some fun. They deserved a little holiday, and if it could be made a profitable holiday, so much the better.

"Do the men good," he said to Phoebe.

"But we got a treaty with the Apaches. We weren't to interfere with their Mexican raiding and they weren't to tamper with our lumberin'. Our word was give. So was Poston's."

"Aw, shucks! It'll be jest a little picnic fur the boys," said Tarbox.

"I'm a-payin' your wages, and I forbid it," said Phoebe.

"You kin boss us when we're a-workin' fur ye," said Tarbox, "but when we're a-layin' off, our time's our own 'n' we kin do with it what we've a mind to."

"Decent folks don't break treaties," said Phoebe.

"It's Poston's bargain, not our'n," said Tarbox. He turned to the Mexicans. "Light 'n' rest your hosses," he said. "The men'll be in by sundown. I calc'late we'll go along with ye."

Phoebe saw it was useless to protest. The men were in a mood for a frolic, and this they viewed as some sort of merry-making. And she owed it to Lazarus Ward. As Solomon had warned her, Lazarus would do her a spite when the opportunity came—and it had come.

When the men came in, Tarbox told them of the offer of the Mexicans. They were delighted at the prospect of excitement and of gain. They quickly ate their evening meal, armed themselves and rode away with the Mexicans. Phoebe remained behind.

The party of forty or more Mexicans and State-of-Maine men went up the river to a spot where the Apaches must ford with their stolen stock, and there, among cacti and rocks, they laid their ambuscade. Phoebe, next morning, could hear the sound of their guns as the unsuspecting Indians rode up to the river, and blind rage shook her. Not rage that she had been disobeyed, not rage that Lazarus Ward had done her a meanness; but rage because a pledged word had been broken. She could attend to the disobedience in her good time, and to Lazarus' spite, but a broken pledge never could be repaired.

The Apaches, surprised, fled at the first salvo, deserting the stolen stock. It was driven back to Canoa—cattle, mules, horses, a splendid herd of them. And there the Mexicans divided fairly and honorably with the lumbermen. There was a drinking of mescal in celebration, and the Mexicans rode off with their depleted property to the southward.

"Now," said Phoebe, "that you've busted the treaty and got all this here stock, what d'ye propose to do with it?"

"Drive it to Tucson 'n' sell it," said Tarbox.

"Be a sight of trouble," said Phoebe. "Ye hain't herders 'n' ye don't understand drivin'. You'd lose a hull lot of 'em. The mischief's done, and I calc'late I'll be the chief sufferer by it. So I might's well derive what profit I kin. I'll buy this here stock—cows, hosses 'n' mules."

"Fur a fair price?" asked Tarbox.

"Fur more'n you deserve," she said.

She went out to look at the animals in the big corral, and offered a price. There was haggling, but in the end Tarbox accepted. Phoebe rode back to Tucson, hired Mexicans and Indians to help her, and drove the animals back to Tucson again. From them she culled out such horses and mules as she desired to keep and sold or bartered the rest.

"Wa-al," she told Solomon Warner, "I got twenty-two prime mules, sixteen hosses, and the rest I sold fur clost to two thousand dollars. Mebby Lazarus done me a meanness. That remains yit to be seen. But so fur I come out of it perty good."

"So fur," said Solomon gravely.

Less than thirty days after this profitable ambuscade, word reached Tucson of happenings at Canoa. A *vaquero* came riding into the town, his horse nearly foundered, himself exhausted, and only able to cry out the word "Apaches!" He fell from his horse and was restored with mescal. Canoa had been attacked by Indians.

A party was swiftly organized, and reached Canoa a little after sunrise. Phoebe rode with them. The house was a mass of blackened, smoking timbers; three dead men had been thrown down the well head foremost; seven other men were presently buried in a row inside the corral—the corral that looked as if it had been struck by a hurricane. And from Canoa and neighboring ranches the Apaches had driven away three hundred head of cattle. Canoa had ceased to exist; the lumber-men had ceased to exist; the lumber business with Phoebe's investment in it was deleted so thoroughly that it might as well never have existed. Nor was it ever to come again to life.

Phoebe commented on it to Solomon Warner. There was no discouragement in her voice and not a trace of rancor. She spoke calmly, almost placidly.

"Looks like Lazarus got the best of it," she said, "fur the time bein'."

CHAPTER IV

PHOEBE had hired Mexicans and built herself a three-room adobe house as far south of the city as it was safe to go, and she had given up the baking of pies. The country depended upon transportation. Three-ton boilers must be freighted from Lavaca in Texas to the Rio Grande, and thence to Tubac or Patagonia, a toilsome, dangerous road of twelve hundred miles. By the time the boiler or engine arrived at its destination, its cost was greater than its weight in the silver it was to aid in gouging from the earth.

But law did not accompany capital and machinery as it flowed in. To the south, the rich and fertile state of Sonora was devastated and its citizens starving, for there was no hand to hold the Apaches in check. Arizona was in slightly better case because there was an inadequate pretense of Army protection. The inadequate soldiery in Tucson neither drilled nor threatened, but devoted itself wholeheartedly to the business of indolence and drunkenness. Van Tramp, who knew what he was talking about, called Tucson a paradise for devils. No man but went armed to the teeth, and it was rarely you met upon the street one who was neither gambler, thief, murderer nor renegade. Yet, in spite of this, Arizona trembled upon the verge of a boom; perhaps even recognition by Congress and a territorial government. It remained, however, possibly the one spot on earth owned by a civilized government where every man was his own judge, jury and executioner.

Yet, in these conditions, a woman, alone, Phoebe Titus existed and prospered. True, even among cutthroats of the border breed there was some prejudice against molesting a woman. But Phoebe did not depend upon her femininity.

It was just before the massacre of Canoa that a letter came by overland mail from California. It was the first letter Phoebe ever had received. It was from Peter Muncie, ill-spelled but irrepressibly gay. It was not long, but in its every line it spoke of the character of the tall young man who had bought Phoebe's pies. It made him stand before her eyes. In no sense that could be detected was it a love letter, but beneath its blitheness and apparent irresponsibility, it was a solid nugget. "I sad I war going to come back to that thar Tucson," it said. "By Judas, you hang holt of yore hosses long enough and I'll be thar."

Phoebe pondered long whether she should reply, but in the end she scrawled a short answer:

"I am well and I hope this finds you the same. If I ever see you in Tucson, I would rekollect yore name was Peter Muncie."

Unwholesome rumors spread across desert and mountain, undermining confidence, giving birth to terrors, destroying the friendship of man for man, and destroying that trust which all citizens must have for the government under which they reside.

"Man was in the store today," Solomon Warner told Phoebe, "that says it's common talk that Colonel Loring and that Colonel Crittenden is doin' their dumdest to git the troops in the territory to side with the South. This man says these officers aim to seize all the guns 'n' ammunition 'n' supplies."

"But Colonel Roberts is workin' jest as hard t'other way," said Phoebe. "If it comes to a war, Solomon, how d'ye calc'late Californy'll go?"

"South end fur the South, north end fur the North," said Solomon.

Phoebe slapped the dust off her boots. "In times like these," she said, "folks has got to make guesses. I'm a-goin' to guess that if the's a war back east, they're goin' to want all the soldiers they kin git. And that'll mean they'll be sent fur out of Arizony."

"The government couldn't do that!" exclaimed Solomon, aghast. "They wouldn't leave us to the mercy of the Injuns!"

"Most likely the government ain't thinkin' much about Injuns just now," Phoebe said. "If them troops is called away, the's a-goin' to be a mess. The Apaches'll go sweepin' through this country like a flood down a dry wash. Solomon, while it's possible I'm goin' to Santa Rita and Tubac."

"For what, for goodness sake?"

"To git contracts fur haulin' everythin' that's movable from the mines into Tubac 'n' Tucson. The' won't be wagons 'n' mules enough to do it. It's goin' to be a case of everybuddy save what he's able, and the man that starts savin' first'll save most."

So she set out for Tubac and the Heintzelman mine, but before she left she said to Solomon, "Git rid of every piece of

Tubac money we got. Git silver fur it, or gold, or things to sell that folks'll need. And don't take in no more. Tubac money hain't a-goin' to be wuth the cardboard it's printed on."

"Poston's good. He'll stand back of it," protested Solomon.

"Poston's honest. He'd stand back of it so long's he's got anythin' to stand with. But if these troops git withdrawn, there's likely not to be no mines, and no Tubac and no Poston, neither. You do like I say."

Poston received her in his hacienda. His broad face was grave, but he declined to believe that troops would be withdrawn from Arizona. "The War Department couldn't do it. It would be inhuman. Whatever they do, they'll not leave us defenseless."

"Mr. Poston," said Phoebe, "mebby they won't, but mebby they will. You can't defend the mines. You got hunderds of thousands of dollars' worth of supplies and things that kin be moved. Suppose the troops stay. Ain't it better to move that property to where it can be defended till ye find out?"

"And give you a neat contract for freighting?" he asked with a smile.

"My business is freightin'," she said, "but a good freighter knows when and where to freight."

A Mexican servant appeared in the door with a soldier at his heels.

"Come in. Come in," said Poston. "What can I do for you?"

"Message from Lieutenant Chapin from Fort Buchanan," said the orderly.

"Let me have it. Juan, see this man has food and drink."

He opened the message, read it swiftly and passed it to

Phoebe. "I enclose for your attention," it said, "an order from the commanding officer of the military department."

The order was brief:

Santa Fe, June, 1861.

Commanding Officer, Fort Buchanan:

On receipt of this, you will abandon and destroy your post, burn your commissary and Quartermaster's stores, and everything between the Colorado and Rio Grande that will feed an enemy.

March out with your guns loaded, and do not permit any citizen within three miles of your lines.

Major General Lynde.

Phoebe got to her feet. "I calc'late I'm goin' to be a busy woman," she said. "Anythin' I kin do for you, Mr. Poston?"

"Teams and wagons," he said.

"Send a messenger to Tucson. I'll write an order to Solomon Warner. I'll have six wagons 'n' teams sent here. I'm sendin' as many to the Santa Rita. I'm a-headin' for there now."

"Miss Phoebe, you mustn't. Forty miles across country. The news will be out, the news of this indefensible crime. You never would make it."

"It's business," said Phoebe. "I got to."

With a small escort, she set out upon that forty-mile ride. Fortune was with her, for they encountered neither Apache nor outlaw Mexican, reaching the mines in the afternoon of the next day. She found Pumpelly, the metallurgist, and Grosvenor, the superintendent, in conference. News of the withdrawal of troops had not yet come to them.

"I've ordered six wagons 'n' teams to come here to freight your stuff to Tubac," she said without preamble.

"Why should we freight to Tubac, Miss Titus?" Pumpelly asked.

"Because," she said, "the War Department has ordered all troops out of Arizony."

"Impossible! No sane government would do such a thing!"

"With my own eyes I saw the order from General Lynde," she said.

Pumpelly and Grosvenor looked at each other in silence; then Grosvenor spoke.

"She's right," he said. "We won't be able to hold out. But"—he turned to Phoebe—"we're in a tight place. Our Indians quit work in the mines. We're out of money. We owe our Mexicans and what few American workmen we have. We simply haven't been able, since the Indians quit, to take out enough ore to pay. And we haven't a shilling to pay for transporting property to Tubac."

"There's money owed us," said Pumpelly. "Poston owes some. If we can get in some debts."

"Jest now," said Phoebe, "I hain't worryin' about pay. Maybe I'll be paid, and maybe I won't. I'm thinkin' about the future. If Arizony's cleaned out, the' won't be any future. If we can save what's to be saved till these times is over, we'll have somethin' to start up with ag'in. If ye can collect enough to pay me, all right. If ye can't, I'll haul ye and wait for my pay."

"We'll ride over and see Poston tomorrow," said Grosvenor.

Before dawn they started. Phoebe again faced that forty-mile ride, and again traversed the perilous country in safety. But Poston had no money. He had, however, silver bullion, and this, together with some flour and calico, Pumpelly and Grosvenor accepted in payment. It was loaded on a wagon and dispatched in the charge of a couple of trusted Mexicans who seemed to have less than the ordinary regard for the safety of their scalps. The wagon set forth immediately, swaying and creaking under the weight of its treasure. Pumpelly, Grosvenor and Phoebe slept that night in the hacienda, and in the morning, leading the horses they had ridden before and mounted upon fresh ones, they started upon their return.

The loose horses were troublesome and the journey slow, so that nightfall found them still some miles from their destination, but, in a hostile Indian country, night is far safer for the traveler than the light of day. There was little moon, and the inadequate light from the stars serves only to stimulate the imagination. Indians seem to lurk behind giant saguaros; the erect shafts of century plants or Spanish bayonets become the lances of lurking Apaches. Nerves grow tense, and one becomes dependent upon the instinct and the more delicate sensitory organs of his horse. Even the motion of a horse's ears becomes significant; eyes strain ahead and behind, and peer through the gloom at the sand beneath for sign. It was eerie, nerve-racking. They spoke little, for fear their voices would carry to ears they did not wish to hear.

"It seems," whispered Phoebe, "that this is a sight of trouble to take to drum up a little business."

Before dawn they reached the house. The wagon had not yet arrived, nor had they passed it upon the road.

"Pumpelly," said Grosvenor in midafternoon, "it looks as if those Mexicans have headed for Sonora."

"One thing to do. Go and see," Pumpelly said.

"I got an interest in that silver myself," said Phoebe.

So again they mounted horses and set down the rocky defile, riding for a couple of miles before they descended a long, boulder-strewn slope to cut off a bend in the wagon road. As they crossed the arroyo to mount the opposite mountainside, the wagon swung into sight and commenced to descend.

"Looks like we wronged the Mexicans," Pumpelly said. "Better not let them see us. They might figure out what we had in our minds, and that wouldn't arouse any good will."

So they drew aside and, after dismounting and watering the horses at a spring, pushed back to the hacienda.

But the wagon did not arrive. The afternoon passed without its appearance, and it became evident that something must have occurred to delay its progress.

"Better go see. They can't be far," said Pumpelly.

"Finish your supper," said Grosvenor. "I'll take a walk down the road."

Phoebe and Pumpelly sat over the evening meal, and then, in growing uneasiness, determined to follow Grosvenor. They walked down the road; then, aware of a sound behind them, they halted, pistols cocked. But it was the house cat, tail erect and lonely, meowing as it followed them. Phoebe gathered it in her arms and soothed it.

"Hush," said Pumpelly, and peering ahead, they saw on the top of a hill beside the road the crouched figure of a man, black against the sky. Then the man was gone. They walked on, pistols in hand, eyes alert. They saw nothing of Grosvenor. Ahead lay the arroyo from which they had seen the approaching wagon at noontime; and then, turning a great shoulder of rock, the wagon was before their eyes, off the road, tilted precariously. No mules were visible. No sounds were audible. The night was silent, save for the distant howling of a coyote.

They crouched, peering, listening. Something was dreadfully amiss. Nothing was as it should be. Moving aside into the shelter of rocks and cactus, they waited, and then the moon came up, turning the heavens into a vault of silver and the desert into something mysterious, awful, perilously beautiful. They edged forward inch by inch. Something white gleamed beside the road, a little heap of whiteness. It was flour, a peck of spilled flour!

Now they were some twenty yards from the wagon, and suddenly Phoebe cried out. In the shadows of a huge boulder at the roadside, her foot had touched something soft, something dreadfully soft and inert.

It was a man, naked, mutilated, lying horribly, with head downhill and in a pool of blood that looked black as jet in the still night. Two lance stabs in the throat had all but severed the head; there were bullet holes, other lance wounds, and the body was still warm.

It was Grosvenor.

CHAPTER V

THEY crouched over Grosvenor's body, straining eyes over the broken terrain. The wagon was in full view and dark huddles indicated the presence of more bodies.

"Back to the hacienda," Pumpelly said urgently. "This might have been Apaches or Mexicans. That spy we saw on the hilltop—he'll bring them down on us."

Phoebe had seen death, even violent death, in Tucson, but never before had her eyes beheld such a horror as lay at her feet. Illness overcame her and her legs became powerless to sustain her body. The silvery world swam and became purple. She forced herself to speak.

"Shall we carry him?" she asked.

"No. We've two miles to cover. Grosvenor will be no better off with us dead."

She stood erect, drew shafts of the night air of the desert into her lungs, averting her eyes from what lay at her feet. She was ashamed, and accused her womanhood of the weakness that had overcome her.

"If it's Mexicans," she said, "we'll be as bad off at the hacienda. These murderers'll be in cahoots with your men."

"If it's Indians—and I think it is—we've a chance if we make the house. You keep watch to the right; I'll take the left."

So, in dreadful doubt, they commenced to retrace their steps. The cat ran ahead of them, tail in air. Their footfalls on the roadside seemed to thunder a betrayal of their passage to lurking enemies as yard after yard dropped behind them. Besides the sound of their own flight, no noise save the occasional howling of a coyote came to their quickened ears. They did not speak, but only hastened and hoped. The same thought preyed upon both their minds. If the marauders were Mexicans, then, surely, they were hastening to their death. And they would not know until death was upon them.

Half a mile from the hacienda, they halted, for here the road entered a dense expanse of mesquite and paloverde in which could have been ambushed a hundred Apaches or Mexicans. They halted.

"Shall we," asked Pumpelly, "skirt this in the open plain?"

"How much longer?" asked Phoebe.

"Maybe half an hour to make the circle. But that spy will have given warning."

"Stick to the road," said Phoebe, and they plunged into the thicket, almost running until they emerged in the valley and saw before them the lights of the camp. And then, from behind, from left and from right, came the terror of Apache signals given and answered, and they broke into a run. The door was before them; they reached it without hearing the war cry of an Indian or the hiss of a speeding arrow.

The single American employee was making bread; the Mexicans were sleeping in their quarters, all unaware of peril.

Pumpelly aroused them, and through the night they stood

to their arms. Before dawn a Mexican was sent to the fort and another to Tubac for aid, and with the coming of light an armed and cautious party went out to bring in the body of Grosvenor. Pumpelly's Apache boy, who had been made a captive in babyhood and was devoted to his master, read the sign about the wagon. Fifteen Indians had lurked until they could spring upon the unwatchful Mexicans and murder them. They had then cut the mules from the wagon and, a quarter of a mile away had killed and feasted upon one of the animals, leaving behind a party to waylay any who came out to meet the wagon. Grosvenor had been shot by an Indian who had crouched behind a saguaro—ten yards away the mark of his gunstock remained in the sand. They had looted the wagon, tossing to the ground as useless the silver which Pumpelly had gone to Tubac to collect.

That day, from the fort came Lieutenant Evans and nineteen soldiers, and, not long after, Poston rode in with a party of Americans from Tubac, and there was a council of war.

"Mr. Pumpelly," urged the lieutenant, "I advise your accompanying us to the fort. Abandon the mine. Abandon everything. We withdraw from this country in two weeks."

Pumpelly shook his head. "I'm in duty bound to save what I can for the company," he said. "I've got to get everything movable to Tubac. I've got to extract the silver from our ore. It's a six weeks' job. I've got to get enough bullion to pay our men. They can't escape without it."

"My wagons are on their way," Phoebe said. "Six of them."

"You," said Poston, "will go with the soldiers to the fort or with me to Tubac. You had a look at Grosvenor. Do you want to be like that?" He cursed Washington painstakingly.

"What good to the politicians are the few troops we have in Arizona? But to us they are the difference between life and death. We come here, where not one of the measley lot would dare set foot. We found an empire. We offer our lives and our money to conquer and bring into the Republic a region worth its weight in gold. And the demagogues, the Secessionists, the Abolitionists squabble themselves—and desert us to be murdered in our beds. Is either side going to win with this miserable handful of soldiers that stands between us and massacre?"

"I stay," said Pumpelly, "till my job is done."

"And I," said Phoebe, "have ordered in my wagons. I stay till they come."

"I cannot guarantee to protect you," said Lieutenant Evans. "You say it will take you six weeks to clean up. We'll be gone in two."

"Can you lend me men?" Pumpelly asked of Poston.

"Mighty few."

"Ranches will be abandoned if the ranchers have time to abandon them. Maybe I can hire some of them."

"You won't hire Briggs," said the lieutenant. "His place up the Sonoita Creek was raided. He's dead, with his family."

Once more Poston cursed Washington and all politicians.

"Hard words," said Phoebe sententiously, "dig no potaters."

"How long can you stay?" Pumpelly asked Evans.

"I ride back tomorrow," said the soldier.

"I'll go with you and see if I can't get a detachment to stay here."

"You won't," said Evans. "You won't get anything."

"I can try."

Poston, leaving two men in the camp, rode back toward Tubac to organize his own difficulties. Next day, accompanied by his Apache lad, Juan, Pumpelly went with the detachment to the fort, and Phoebe was alone with three Americans and the gang of Mexican workmen, not one of whom was to be trusted, and who, in these troubled times, might prove even more dangerous than the Indians who rode about the surrounding hills.

It was a sort of double investment; Apaches, in ever increasing numbers and boldness, held at a distance by the few Americans and the force of Mexicans: the Mexicans deterred from plundering the mine and murdering their employers only by the sleepless vigilance and the rigorous maintenance of a dead-line between the furnaces and the hacienda where silver and supplies were stored.

On the fourth day Pumpelly returned from his perilous venture and succeeded in reaching the house. On the sixth day Phoebe's wagon train arrived, bringing both reinforcements and the possibility of escape. Communication with Tubac was cut. The little community was isolated, and, but for the character of Apache warfare, it could not have maintained itself through the first night of the siege. Not that the Indians lacked courage, but they also possessed discretion. They liked to make war cheaply—to pay as little in warriors as their tactics could contrive. They would not attack boldly, but waited patiently for a moment when the besieged would sleep, when vigilance would relax, so that they could launch a surprise attack.

"Thank God for the watchdogs," Pumpelly said, after the first abortive night raid. "Those three dogs are worth a dozen men with rifles."

"How soon can you have my wagons loaded?" Phoebe asked.

Pumpelly, a cultured man who was to write his book, laughed through his unkempt beard.

"Do you ever think of anything but business, Phoebe?" he asked.

"When the time comes to think of other things, I'll think of them," she said.

"But meantime, to drum up trade, you ride your horse into the heart of Apache country. To get freight for your wagons, you let yourself be shut up in this isolated spot in hourly danger of your life. Don't you think, Miss Phoebe, that the desire for gain can carry you too far?"

It was still in the house as they stood to their arms in regular watches. Outside, the Mexican workmen slept on their arms about the furnaces on a promontory a hundred yards away. At three strategic places out in the darkness the watchdogs were tied—watchdogs who hated Indians even more than they hated coyotes.

Phoebe made an effort at self-analysis, at introspection. As she sat there unafraid, but, nevertheless, with reasonable apprehensions, she wondered just why it was she had not remained in safety in Tucson, or even in Tubac. And Pumpelly's question stirred her to look into herself and to discover why she had done such a thing.

"It's like this, Raphael," she said, "it ain't altogether to make money—though money's good. It ain't that I'm hungry for actual dollars. It's findin' a way to earn them. If I was just to set and somebody dumped a hundred thousand dollars in my lap, I don't know as I'd thank 'em. But makin' a dollar or ten dollars or ten thousand dollars in some way another person couldn't contrive or didn't dast to contrive—that's what I like."

Pumpelly nodded, for in some measure he understood. For was he not here himself?

"But you're only a child," he said, and scrutinized her brown face and slender figure in its rough and worn man's clothing. "You're a girl. You're young, and I venture to say you're the best looking woman in Arizona."

"Be I?" Phoebe asked. "Not that there's many in Arizony."

"Do you ever look in the glass to see if you are pretty?" Pumpelly asked.

"I did once," said Phoebe shortly, and her mind traveled to that tall, drawling young man who had journeyed on to California with his parents. On the night after she first saw him, by the aid of a sputtering candle she had stood, womanlike, before a small mirror and studied her face. As she undressed behind the blanket that screened her corner of the room, she had considered her body, and she had not been dissatisfied. She remembered that she had said to herself, "If what I got hain't good enough fur him, then he's hard to make content."

"Wouldn't you," asked Pumpelly, "like to study yourself in your glass every hour, as some women do? Wouldn't you like lovely dresses and little shoes and fine underwear and stockings? Wouldn't you like hats on that auburn hair of yours that would make other women jealous? Instead of wasting your youth and beauty?"

"Mebby my looks is passable," said Phoebe. "If they be they won't wear out in six months like a pair of pants. I ain't old, but a year or two won't make me much older. I hain't wastin' Raphael, I'm buildin'."

"The young years," said Pumpelly, "are the years for love."

"And jest who would I love with?" she demanded. She frowned at him. "Jest because I ride a hoss straddle with a man's hat on and man's pants and man's boots, it don't mean I ain't a woman. I've heard men I wouldn't wipe my shoes on sneerin' at me—mebby it was because I wouldn't look at 'em. Sneerin' at me and sayin' I was more man than woman." Her face, sharp-lined, young, vivid, was grave as she spoke, and she shook her head. "I ain't no man, Raphael," she said, "and when a man comes and I'm ready he'll find out."

"Don't wait too long," Pumpelly said. "Habits form. What was merely a pretense in the beginning can become real. A human being in maturity is only the sum total of his pretenses. I doubt if any man knows what his true character is— or any woman. As events require, or vanities, we make believe. We act not as we would act naturally, but as we think circumstances require, or as will be most becoming. And out of our acting emerges ourselves."

"If you're in a dangerous spot," said Phoebe, "with robbers all around ye, it might be wise to hide what money ye got."

"Yes."

"But when the danger's gone and the' hain't no more robbers, you can dig it up, and it's still money?"

"Yes."

"Well," said Phoebe, "I'm a-hidin' this womanliness you're harpin' on, because I got to. And watchin' it and guardin' it. When a safe time comes, I calc'late to dig it up."

"Don't let it be too late," he warned.

She stood erect, slender. The grace of her carriage, the graciousness of her supple, strong body was not to be concealed even by the clothing she wore. She raised her long slim arms above her head in a gesture the man was never to forget, throwing back her head and shoulders, so that her woolen shirt drew tight over her round, firm breast. In that instant she was woman, all woman, conscious of what she was and of what she had to give.

"It won't never be too late," she said, "not even if I wait till I'm forty."

Then, suddenly, startlingly, the dogs, in their distant stations flew into a frenzy. Savage yells tortured the night and there was a volley of shots. Phoebe and Pumpelly leaped through the door, rifles ready. Already the Mexicans, working at night at the furnaces, because it was safer than the daylight, were discharging their weapons toward the place of the attack. But the Apaches did not launch themselves upon the mine. Their surprise had failed, and, according to their nature, they withdrew to try again. But the foray had not been without its profit to them, for alongside the furnaces, Nelson, the chief smelterman, lay dead with a bullet through his head.

Work was pushed; men were driven. Already three of the wagons were loaded with movables, but it was necessary to continue with the smelting, and daily the store of lead planches containing the silver increased in size and in value.

"Our greatest danger," said Pumpelly, "will be when the silver is refined and we're ready to pull out. We'll concentrate as much of that as is possible into the last couple of days, and redouble our vigilance with our Mexicans."

Armed parties drudged at cutting wood for charcoal and hauling it to the mine; the liquor was gone, but rations of diluted alcohol were doled out to the Mexicans, both to bolster up their courage and to maintain in them some vestiges of good nature as they worked hard hours, patrolled, or snatched a few hours of troubled sleep. At last came fifty hours of such ceaseless driving and urging as Phoebe had not imagined human beings could endure. The Americans did not close their eyes as the silver was separated from the lead, but stood menacingly over the Mexican laborers from dawn to dawn and from dark to dark, never daring to turn away their eyes. And before the silver was cool they loaded it into Phoebe's wagons, and then, to the last portable article of the company's property, even the wooden contraption for working the blast—they abandoned the property and set out upon the forty-mile march to Tubac.

Six wagons, each drawn by six horses or mules. They rocked and rolled and jolted and creaked as their drivers cursed and cajoled. Indians rode beside them, yelling their shrill threats from a safe distance, riding in now and then to take a swift unaimed shot at the wagon train. Once, in a rocky defile, there was a semblance of concerted attack, but the train was too strong, too vigilant, too well armed. And so, with the loss of one man dead, one wounded through the arm, and of two mules and a horse killed, they rumbled at last into Tubac and safety. And once more they were in touch with the world and with the news of the world of which Arizona seemed to have ceased to be a part and to have joined itself to Inferno. Arizona deserted by the nation!

They arrived in Tubac on June fifteenth, 1861. Just two months before, Major Anderson had surrendered Fort Sumter —and the United States were torn asunder. For four years war would ravage the land, and until it was ended, Arizona, with its little handful of Americans, would be compelled to get along as best it could.

Already the graves of outlying ranchmen and their families were almost as numerous as the living who remained.

CHAPTER VI

Phoebe found Tubac a little city ridden by terror. Posten's *casa grande* was no longer the home of gay hospitality where silver glinted and wine sparkled and gay music entertained. The scores of lovely *señoritas* who had ventured up from Sonora with bright eyes and acquisitive hearts had fled southward, abandoning Los God-dammes whose laborious life they had come to ameliorate with their complaisance. Few women, and they with white, drawn anxious faces remained—Las Camisas-Colorados, despised by the dainty Mexican houris because of their honest red petticoats and their toil-worn hands.

No man dared walk a pace beyond the protection of the town, for behind every rock, every bush, lurked an Apache, watchful, ready with arrow, lance or gun. From the southward was advancing a party of hundreds of marauding Mexicans, in the belief that the United States had disintegrated and that now they would be able to recover the land wrested from them after the late war.

Up and down the valley—throughout all of abandoned Arizona—great clouds of smoke obscured the sky—the smoke of ranch houses, wheat fields, and of supply depots, the latter put to the torch by withdrawing troops lest they fall into the hands of some enemy as yet invisible. Observing the departure of the blue coats, Mexican laborers rose and murdered their employers at the mines—and the Apaches, under their great war chief, Red Sleeves, grew bolder and assembled in greater numbers as their leaders told them that their might had frightened out of the country the white invaders whose cruelty and lack of understanding had earned them only hatred.

"Miss Phoebe," said Poston, for even in these days of terror he maintained his courtliness of manner, "we've got to clear out. We can't maintain ourselves. We've all got to vamose. Arizona must be abandoned."

"How much you got invested here?" she asked.

"Around a million dollars."

"And you calc'late to skedaddle and leave it to the Indians?"

"Better leave a million dollars than our bodies," he said.

"Colonel Poston," she replied, "so long as I got one hoss, or one mule, or one wagon, or one pound of bullion, I ain't leavin' it to nobody. You men can high-tail out of the country, but the's one woman'll stay."

"No one's life is safe this side of Yuma—this side of the Colorado. It's not only the Mexicans and the Indians, it's the whites. Hatred, Miss Phoebe! If you meet a man on the road, your hand is on your revolver till you find out if he's for North or South."

"North or South don't matter to us folks here," she said. "It's jest Arizona that matters. Arizona's our'n. We're makin' it out of desert and mountain. It ain't no concern of our'n if one side wants slaves 'n' t'other don't want them. You'll go and Raphael Pumpelly'll go. You're eddicated men. You come

with money-backin' to make more money. But there's them
that hain't eddicated and that come with their bare hands to
build them a home and to dig out for themselves a chance.
Them's the ones that'll cling, Colonel. And them's the ones
that'll be here when this here war's over, stickin' to the earth
like cholla spines to your skin. And them's the one's'll reap
their reward."

"Perhaps you are right, Phoebe," Pumpelly said. "But my
saying is that only those will stay who can't get away."

"Tomorrow we'll commence loading your wagons for
Yuma," said Poston.

"Not my wagons," Phoebe replied.

"Eh? Not your wagons? What do you mean, girl?"

"Ye kin load 'em fur Tucson, and my men and my mules'll
git 'em through fur ye. But not fur Yuma."

"You've twelve wagons. They'll carry a ton apiece. I've been
paying sixty cents a pound to freight to the Colorado. Twelve
tons at sixty cents a pound. There's fourteen thousand dollars."

"I'll be no party to it," she said, "and I'll not risk my wagons
and my stock."

"I'll pay a dollar a pound in bullion."

"No." She walked to the window of the hacienda and looked
steadily out upon the valley, the fruitful rich valley of the
Santa Cruz, and her heart was a leaden weight as she saw the
desolation and ruin of it. "Colonel," she said, "I tell ye how
I feel, and what I think's honest and what I think's right. I'm a
one to make money where I kin find it. But the's ways of
makin' money fair and ways of makin' money so a decent
woman don't want it. You're in a fix. I got hosses and mules
and wagons, and I kin gouge ye. I don't calc'late to. Whatever

I do fur you will be at the reg'lar rates. But even if I thought
I could git a train through to the Colorado, I wouldn't send it.
I'll help no man to run away from Arizona, when he ought to
stay and fight fur it."

"I'm the alcalde here," said Poston. "I could use my authority
to seize your wagons."

"If I was you," said Phoebe, "I wouldn't try it."

Both men stared at her, and Pumpelly laughed. "I guess
I wouldn't try it, if I were you, Poston," he said.

"What ye better do," said Phoebe, "is git a man through to
Tucson, if ye kin—to tell them the fix we're in and ask fur
help. What happened last night? The Injuns sneak up and
cut through your adobe and ocotillo wall around the corral,
and run off nigh to two hundred head of stock. Next they'll be
runnin' off what's left of humans."

There was a silence. So close that it was not comfortable to
hear rifles detonated at intervals; shrill yells tortured the air.
The fringe of savages was becoming a wall, and the wall was
drawing nearer and nearer.

"She's right," agreed Pumpelly. "But can a man get
through?"

"A man kin," said Phoebe.

Poston studied her curiously, this girl who, grim-faced,
bronzed, booted like a man, did not look like a girl but like a
seasoned frontiersman.

"Aren't you afraid?" he asked.

"Of course I be," she said. "I ain't a fool. But I ain't so scairt
I can't use my brains. Git a man through and Solomon Warner
and Oury'll raise a party and come to git us."

Thus it was determined, and under cover of the night a

man led forth his horse to thread his way northward in a hazardous attempt to penetrate the loose lines of the besiegers. From the moment of his departure there was nothing to do but to labor and to wait, and to listen. An hour passed, two hours. There was no savage shout of triumph, and hope asserted itself. The messenger might have got through. And he did get through, for, four days later, in midafternoon, heavy firing to the northward apprized the defenders that a body of men was moving toward them, and just before nightfall Granville Oury rode into the city at the head of twenty-five mounted men.

In this manner was Tubac deserted—a thriving, happy, prosperous little city of a thousand souls was left to Mexican and savage, and with it an investment of a million, of which a hundred and fifty thousand dollars was in portable supplies for which there was no room in the wagons. Men, women and children, in a long column, riding horses, mules, perched upon wagons and guarded by mounted men, fought their way northward. Pitiful refugees, forgotten and deserted by a government that could have saved them and their property by leaving a scant couple of companies of troopers in Arizona. Let it not be wondered at that they were bitter, or that, at the first opportunity, they declared for the Confederacy. For at the moment their sole hope seemed to lie with the men of the South, and with Jefferson Davis, who proved himself not unmindful of them.

Along that hot and weary and perilous road there was a grave for almost every milestone—a fresh grave of rancher or rancher's wife or child who should not have died, victims to the distant hatred of abolitionist for slaveowner; victims of a frightened government. Once Phoebe spoke with bitterness as they drew near to the walls of the Old Pueblo of Tucson.

"It's what ye might have expected of Abe Lincoln," she said. "Prob'ly, while them ranchers was bein' murdered he was settin' sprawled out a-tellin' a funny story."

"The loneliest noise in the world," said a man, "is the crowin' of cocks on a deserted ranch."

They entered Tucson just before nightfall, a Tucson whose population had been temporarily augmented by fugitives from ranch and from mine. Gaunt animals, starved dogs, sweating, cursing, drinking men, frightened, slatternly women, made the little town more inclement, more unsightly, than it ever had been. Mescal shops and bars were doing a land-office business and their proprietors welcomed noisily the thirsty recruits from Tubac. It was hot, with a still, dry, blazing heat, and odors clung and hung, for there was no breeze to carry them away.

Phoebe stopped before Solomon Warner's store. In the doorway she came face to face with a newcomer, a newcomer in a tall, belled beaver hat, fawn-colored coat with flaring skirts, and only slightly wilted linen. She noted first his hands, for they were the most active part of him, slender, white, innocent of the stigma of toil. His face was slender, patrician, with eyelids that drooped indolently, insolently. It was the countenance of a gentleman behind whom lay generations of others who had been gentlemen. His eyes met hers, widened with surprise, crinkled at the corners with a sort of humor. He stepped aside with hat lifted and a bow that would have been a credit to St. Louis' most elite drawing room. Phoebe frowned as she passed him and entered the store. She frowned because she had felt something not dissimilar to the impact of a blow. It was as if her innermost self and the innermost self of this handsome young man with his waving chestnut hair had collided and rebounded. But her set and dusty face gave no sign of this emotion. Always Phoebe was one whose emotions must be guessed, for she did not permit them to exhibit themselves to a curious public.

Solomon sat upon a flour barrel and nodded without arising as he saw her.

"Back alive, eh?" he asked. "Fetch the stock with you?"

"Every hoss and every mule," she said.

"Wa-al," he told her, "you've done it, but I don't hold with it. I been thinking, Phoebe, since you been prowling amongst Injuns. You're too venturesome for me. I can't endure the wear and tear of it."

"Meanin'," said Phoebe, "that you want to bust up the partnership?"

"There's risks that hadn't ought to be took," he said.

"Solomon," she said directly, nodding her head for emphasis as she spoke, "I advise you agin it. You'll go farther cleavin' to me than you'll go alone."

"Maybe, but I can't eat my meals with so much recklessness sprinkled over 'em."

"Recklessness, ye call it? I call it somethin' else, Solomon. This hain't Freeport, or Boston, or St. Louis. I've seen men dead without their hair. I've seen burnin' buildin's and stock slaughtered wanton. I've seen men workin' by day and by night with a tool in one hand and a rifle in the orther, dodgin' bullets and arrows. Not because it was how they liked it, or because they was venturesome. But jest because that's how things is in this country. It's how folks has got to live. What's reckless 'n' venturesome t'other side of the Mississippi is just run o'mine here."

"I reckon you'll travel far," said Solomon, "and maybe I'd travel farther 'n' faster if I was to go with ye. But I hain't a-goin' to do it, Phoebe. I'm a slow and conservative man."

"Have it your way, Solomon," she said, and he was surprised beyond relief when her brown hand touched his shoulder almost with gentleness. "You been fair 'n' square, Solomon. Pick your half of what we own together, and I'll be content with the rest. And don't do yourself no disadvantage." Then, as if she regretted this moment of generosity, she scowled and changed the subject suddenly. "Who's the green-horn I passed in the door?"

"Name of Carteret," said Solomon. "He got off of the last stage through from the East. We hain't got no more stage line, Phoebe. No more mail. No more communication with nowhere. We're plumb cut off from the world." He paused. "He was kind of throwed off of the stage," he added. "There hain't no more Arizony. The government has throwed it up like it lay heavy on Washington's stomach."

"I hear Oury 'n' the rest is fur declarin' fur the South?"

"They be."

"Wa-al," said Phoebe, "the North don't want us; mebby the South'll take the leavin's."

"A letter come fur ye on the last stage from the West." He rummaged in a drawer and produced a bedraggled envelope, and though Phoebe had seen that uncomfortable handwriting but once before, she recognized it, and it was the second inward shock of the day. Her second letter from Peter Muncie! She thrust it carelessly into a pocket of her trousers.

"I'll be goin' home," she said.

"I better go with you," Solomon said.

"Why?"

"Wa-al, different kinds of folks has been rushin' in here," he said, and reaching under the counter, strapped a Navy revolver around his waist.

"I calc'late to be able to make out," she said. "You stay where you be."

With that she strode out to the wagon that waited for her and drove along the Calle Real, ankle deep with dust and filth, turning eastward on Calle de la Allegria and across the Plaza de la Mesilla to a small, square, one-story adobe house with a corral, on the very outskirts of the town. It was her home. She had bought it from a Mexican, settled in it with such furniture as had accompanied her father and herself from Freeport in the Conestoga wagon. And there she had lived, with an adipose Mexican woman to cook her frijoles and do her washing, until she had gone out upon this last business excursion.

As she approached she saw three strange horses in the corral, and when she stopped before the door, a man, trousers tucked in boots, no hat upon his unkempt hair, lounged from the interior and stood leering at her from the doorway. In a moment a second man joined him, and the second man was Lazarus Ward.

"What," demanded Phoebe from her wagon, "be ye doin' in my house?"

"Didn't reckon you'd be needin' it," said Lazarus impudently. "Town's kind of crowded like, so we jest moved in."

"Who's the other hawg with ye?" asked Phoebe.

"Partner of mine," said Lazarus.

"Jest moved in, did ye?" asked Phoebe, in a voice that was almost placid. "Jest moved in and used my proppity. You got a continental gall. Before ye move out," she said, "I'll look around to see what damage you've done."

"We don't reckon to move out," said Lazarus. "We're tol'able comfortable. Mebby you didn't hear about the United States goin' and takin' what law the' was with it."

"I'm fetchin' some back," said Phoebe. "You set where you be, Bill," she said to her teamster. "I'll tend to this."

She leaped over the wheel and walked briskly to where Lazarus Ward stood with his companion. Ward extended a muscular arm across the door, barring her way.

"We don't want no wimmin here," he said.

"Mebby we do," said his unkempt friend, with an unpleasant laugh.

Phoebe marched until her body almost touched Ward's. It was as if she did not see him or he was not there, and when she reached him she lifted her heavily booted foot and stamped upon his toes. He straightened with a jerk, lifted his agonized foot with a bellow, and then doubled up with a new pain as, with all her strength, which was considerable, she thrust a small derringer into his belly.

"Back in, the both of you," she said evenly. "We'll look around."

"You tarnation hellcat!" yelled the suffering Lazarus. But he backed away and his companion backed away. Phoebe's eyes did not belong to a person who might profitably be trifled with at that moment.

She looked about the room. "Hawgs," she said tersely, "prefers hawg-pens." Without turning her head, she called loudly, "Maria!"

There was no answer. The Mexican woman had long since fled.

"Bill," she called to her teamster, and Bill came to the door, an enormous revolver in his hand. "Give me that," she said, and took from him his weapon. "You jest skedaddle back to town and fetch along a passel of the boys that's in a mind to enjoy themselves."

"Hadn't I better stay?" he asked.

"I got plenty good company," she said, waggling the revolver. "You go 'n' fetch the audience."

Bill set off in haste and in anticipation. "You men," said Phoebe, "jest back agin the wall till I'm ready fur ye. How long you been livin' in this tavern?"

"Three weeks," said Lazarus. "Listen, Phoebe; we didn't mean no real harm. A man's got to have a place to sleep. We reckoned to vamose as soon as you come back."

"Three weeks," said Phoebe, "is twenty-one days. Shut your mouth while I do some calc'latin'."

Then the door darkened and Ward's face lighted. "Grab her, Carteret," he said.

But Phoebe had wheeled. The small derringer looked at the newcomer in the doorway while Bill's revolver gave its attention to the men against the wall. She saw the beaver-hatted gentleman who had stood aside for her as she entered Solomon Warner's store.

"What," she asked, "are you doing here?"

"I live here, madam," he said politely.

"Then come right in," Phoebe said, with a sort of cordiality, "and stand alongside the other hawgs."

"But I fail to understand. You have me at a disadvantage."

"Jest where I propose to keep ye," said Phoebe, and Mr. Carteret, astonished and not at all understanding what was taking place, took his unwilling stand beside the men with whom he had been living.

"May I ask what this means?" he inquired.

"This is my house," said Phoebe. "I don't like vermin movin' in while I'm away."

"But I assure you, madam, I had no idea it was your house."

"You hain't like to forgit it in future," she told him.

And then, from town, arrived a considerable party of men and a fringe of children and dogs. With them were several of the town's substantial citizens, Warner, Oury, Kirkland— who raised the first American flag over Tucson, Julius Contzen, Paddy Burke, Guillermo Tellez.

"What's a-goin' on, Phoebe?" asked Warner.

"Kind of a barn-raisin'," said Phoebe, "only it's a house-cleanin'. These three men wants to scrub my floors and set things to rights. Solomon, send somebuddy fur three buckets 'n' water."

These things were brought, and Phoebe, placid but vigilant, spoke to the three. "Grab a pail each," she said, "and down on your marrows. No floor ever had sich a scrubbin' as this one's goin' to git."

"But, madam," Carteret started to protest.

"You have the look," said Phoebe, "of one that never done

an honest day's work. But you want to be careful of them clothes of your'n. I wouldn't see anything so purty all mussed up—not for the world. Git down and scrub," she snapped.

"I must refuse," he said. "I will pay whatever damage."

"Young fellow," said Kirkland, "if I was you, I'd scrub."

So, while Tucson looked on and encouraged with a certain ribaldry, the three men—and one of them an aristocrat whose fingers never before had been soiled by manual labor—scrubbed Phoebe's floor and her walls, and set all to rights in the little dwelling, while she watched with a housekeeper's eye and spared not her criticisms. In the end she inspected, nor was she satisfied with less than perfection. The three stood, dripping with perspiration and scrubbing water.

"Now," said Phoebe, "that's about all but what ye owe me fur lodgin'. Twenty-one days. That'll be twenty-one dollars apiece. Solomon, will ye collect twenty-one dollars from each of 'em?"

Solomon did so to an accompaniment of gleeful remarks by the audience, and handed it to Phoebe, who thrust it into a pocket.

"Now clear out," she said tartly.

Carteret, not immaculate now, but, even in this ridiculous posture, able to retain something of the mien of a gentleman, threw back his shoulders and stared at the crowd of jibing men.

"If," he said coldly, "there is any gentleman here who feels he cannot restrain his laughter, I shall be glad to discuss the matter with him." He turned his handsome face to Phoebe. "I assure you, madam," he said, "that I had no idea I was intruding upon the property of a woman. I offer my apologies."

"You already apologized with soap 'n' water," said Phoebe.

"Madam," he said, "you are one of the most remarkable women I have ever encountered. I shall hope, in more favorable circumstances, to create a more creditable impression of myself." Then he flushed darkly, pride burning hotly in his heart as he turned to the door. "I shall be glad to give of my leisure to any gentleman who regards this episode as humorous," he said coldly, and so walked erectly between their suddenly questioning eyes and passed out of the house.

"Phoebe," said Solomon, "you do beat the Dutch."

"Clear out, all of you," Phoebe said.

When she was alone, when there was none to see, she opened Peter Muncie's letter. It told in lighthearted way of his life. It thanked her humorously for her reply to his first letter. It ended on a note that Phoebe realized to be serious.

"As sure as shooting," he said, "I'll bob up in Tucson. I hope it ain't too late."

He hoped it wouldn't be too late! Suddenly Phoebe found herself thinking about her youth, and about the swift passage of years, and of how very terribly, inexorably soon, youth would have vanished. She found herself reflecting upon what was happening around her and to her, and wondering apprehensively how long, in such a grim and fearsome world, it would be before it was too late.

CHAPTER VII

Tucson was shrinking. Union men of pronounced convictions fled to Sonora. Only sixty-eight men of voting age remained in the town, and these held a convention, electing Granville Oury their delegate to the Confederate Congress, and the Stars and Bars were raised over the Old Pueblo. Of business there was none except that of providing food for the inhabitants and gambling and the purveying of hard liquors.

But food must come from Sonora or from California, and wagons and mules were necessary for its transportation. So Phoebe was not unoccupied, nor was the period wholly unprofitable to her. Such profits as she had amassed were safe in San Francisco exchange. Political changes did not affect her, for, though she was of the North by birth, her rancor ran against the government at Washington because of its desertion of Arizona; because of the massacre of its citizens that lay accusingly on the doorstep of the old government.

Her anger flared each time a party abandoned the little outpost of civilization for the dubious safety of the Mexican province or for the certain security of California. For, without realizing it herself, without ever putting it into words—even into secret words in her innermost soul, Phoebe had come to love Arizona. She had adopted it, espoused it; and every time a citizen shook the dust of Tucson from his feet she regarded him as a runagate and a traitor.

But her rage and disdain, which were acidly vocal, did not prevent her from deriving a profit from the situation.

"Let 'em go, the sneakin' galoots," she said to Solomon Warner. "A man that skedaddles hain't the kind of a one we want to stay."

"A many of them would have to stay, if it wa'n't for you," said Solomon. "It's your money carries 'em away."

"Such," said Phoebe, "as have farmed and planted in the valley. Such as have dug irrigation ditches. As long's they're fools to sell and I got money to buy, I'll keep on buyin'."

"Me," said Solomon, "I hang on to what I got. I keep a-tellin' you, Phoebe, you're too venturesome."

"Solomon," she said sturdily, "did ye ever ride down the Santa Cruz Valley when the fields was planted and the trees was bearin' fruit and cattle was scattered over the hills and desert, fattenin' on alfilaria and wild buckwheat and mesquite beans? You seen it then. You seen what it could be. I don't set up to be no prophet, but I'm a-seein' it like that agin. Wars don't last forever. This one's a-goin' to come to an end some day, and then folks'll be flockin' to the West agin. When they come, I calc'late to be ready fur 'em."

"When they come! If they come!" said Warner.

"It's why," she said, "I'm buyin' every acre of ranch land in the valley I kin contrive to pay fur. Injuns kin steal stock, they kin massacre settlers, they kin raid 'n' plunder, but there never was an Injun that could dig up an acre of land and carry it off on his pony. The land'll be there, rich to grow crops. The water'll be there. And I kin wait."

So, unaided, forgotten, Tucson remained a little Gibraltar in the desert, impregnable to Apaches, who, firm in the belief that it was their prowess that had driven out the white man, rode recklessly with arrow and lance and firebrand throughout an empire. To the very rim of the village they rode—and men who lived upon the outskirts fixed small mirrors to the ends of poles and shoved them out of their narrow doors of mornings to serve as periscopes before they dared emerge after a night of sleep.

Then, in February of 1862, Captain Hunter, sent thither by that Baylor who, a little later, was deprived of his office for slaughtering nearly a hundred Indians by putting within their reach bags of poisoned flour, arrived before what was left of the city walls with two hundred Texans and a Confederate flag. But their stay was short-lived and the life of the South in Tucson was brief; for on the 20th of May came the advance guard of the California Column—that body of troops raised on the coast to wrest from Jeff Davis the great territory between the Colorado and El Paso.

Tucson seethed with rumors. The Confederates were about to make a levy upon property; the Unionists, advancing from Tucson, had orders from Washington to embark upon some sort of reign of terror. Not that a reign of terror did not exist.

"If 'tain't one thing, it's another," Phoebe said, but with no air of complaint. "If the South don't take our proppity and the North don't chase the South away and hang a lot fur traitors, and these gamblers 'n' border ruffians that runs the

town don't murder everybody and steal all they got, then the
Injuns do it wuss and more painful."

"I hear there was a battle up north around the Pima vil-
lages," said Solomon, "and the South got licked. I dunno what
I hope. God knows we're getting no protection from these
Texans of Hunter's. Mebby Union troops'll do better by us."

"They can't do wuss," said Phoebe. "I been sleepin' with a
gun so long I'll bear the prints of it to my death. How long's
it been since you left this store, Solomon?"

"Seems as though I don't remember what it looks like outside, sleepin' on the counter with one eye open. If I was to shut
both of 'em for a minute, I wouldn't have a pound of flour
or a pair of pants left in the place."

"I got two men guardin' my corral night 'n' day," Phoebe
said. "Robbin' 'n' murderin' is the main business of this
town."

Which was true. Decent citizens and indecent citizens were
molested and plundered in broad daylight with none to hinder
or to rebuke their assailants. Murder went unpunished. There
was not, as Phoebe said, "enough law to swab a smoothebore."

Oury came into the store, armed as if in a hostile country.

"Just got news from the North. Battle up around El Picacho.
Twelve Union men licked fifteen Confederates. Killed two
and took three prisoners."

So was announced the one and only engagement of the
war to take place on Arizona soil.

"The Californy column'll be marchin' in any day, and
Hunter'll be clearin' out," said Solomon.

"And what'll happen to us who have declared for the
South?" Oury asked.

"That includes everbuddy," said Phoebe. "I don't calc'late there'll be a general massacre."

"It might be safer if we cleared out."

"To where?" asked Phoebe. "I'm sick 'n' tired of folks skedaddlin'. Scarcely anythin' else has been goin' on for years, seems like."

"But why do we stay at all?" Oury asked.

Phoebe seated herself on a flour barrel and kicked its staves with the heels of her boots.

"Because we're that kind of people," she said.

She had uttered a great truth, a truth which was making of the United States a great nation—which was carrying it from Atlantic to Pacific—across mountains, arid plains, great rivers. Which was persisting in spite of savages, hunger, hardships until it should establish and conquer the land and make it safe and habitable for a less sturdy breed who were to follow. Because there were that kind of people! Because there existed a blood that was not tame—that was driven restlessly through the veins and which could not be content in peace and quiet, but must march on and ever on until it had done the work appointed for it.

"We're fools," said Oury.

"The's folks born to be preachers," Phoebe said. "The's others born to be gamblers 'n' doctors 'n' farmers 'n' politicians. The's folks born to be most anythin' you kin name, and then the's fools like us. One fool like us is wuth a thousand wise men fur the job of work we're doin'."

"Is it worth doing?" Oury asked.

Phoebe kicked her flour barrel again before she replied. She lifted her pointed chin, and her eyes looked far beyond the

walls of the cluttered store in which they were. What she saw
was not apparent to the men who talked with her, nor did she
ever speak of the vision that came to her. Solomon Warner
who knew her best in those days would not have described her
as a girl with quick imagination. He would have told the
enquiring that she was hard, practical, cold-blooded. He
might even have said that she was masculine, bold, an oppor-
tunist. He would not have credited her with a plan, with
foresightedness, with eyes which, unaccountably, mysteriously
were able to peer down the years and to see a future dreamed
of by few. What she saw on that day, perched upon her flour
barrel has never been disclosed, but if her eyes shining, and
her brown cheeks flushing, and her shoulders setting proudly
were any indication, the scene the eyes of her mind rested upon
was splendid and glorious.

"Is it wuth doin'?" she demanded. "I'm sayin' to you now
that nothin' ever done by men is more wuth doin' than what
we're a-hangin' around to git done. And it'll git done." She
paused and closed her eyes and said a thing that astonished
them and made them think. "And," she said solemnly, "I
thank Gawd I'm a part of it."

The two men stared at her as she lowered herself from the
barrel and walked out of the door.

"I never see sich a gal!" exclaimed Warner.

"Maybe," said Oury gravely, "none of us ever did." He was
an educated man, a thoughtful man. "I wonder," he asked,
"what people thought of Joan of Arc? I wonder what those
close to them thought of the great women of the past generations? I wonder what Phoebe Titus would be in other sur-

roundings. Solomon, I've an idea we've been sitting cheek by jowl with no ordinary personage."

Phoebe made her way down the littered street, past boiling, broiling gambling house, past mescal shops. She threaded her way through a population of unsober soldiers, indecent Mexicans, women who were adjuncts of the saloons. But none accosted her or molested her. In some way she had set the seal of her personality upon that community, and it avoided giving her offense. It remembered how she had recovered her savings from the gambling house of the Mexican, Kee-soos. It recalled how she had taken her home back from Lazarus Ward and Jefferson Carteret and their ruffianly companion. Somehow people who meddled with Phoebe not only caught a tartar but caught one who had a faculty of making them ridiculous. Even the lowest marauder fears ridicule even more than death.

For a moment she paused to speak to little, malformed Estevan Ochoa.

"See," said the little fellow, "I learn for spik Ingleese. I learn for because I damn 'appy for spik Ingleese wit' you."

"Now, that's nice," Phoebe said. "That's awful nice, Estevan. But you learn less damn and more good words. It ain't polite to say damn to a lady."

"I nevair spik it some more," said Estevan. "You got pie?"

"Come to my house," said Phoebe, "and I'll put some flesh on those poor little ribs of yours."

"*Gracias,*" he said delightedly, and then he cocked his head and listened. Phoebe listened also, for a voice that she knew was speaking in its lazy, drawling way inside the house before which they stood.

"They laugh at you, Lazarus, because you permit them to do so. A gentleman does not permit himself to become an object of ridicule."

"They laugh behind your back."

"But never to my face," said Carteret. "You note, my friend, that they never laugh to my face."

"Some fine day," Lazarus said, "I'll git that consarned gal where I want her."

"Not you, Lazarus. Not you. But I—I am lonesome here. There are few diversions for a gentleman. There is no society— no drawing rooms, no white linen and gleaming silver and sparkling wine. No lovely ladies. But one must have his diversions, and this Phoebe would undeniably be worth a second glance if she were decently clothed. Leave her alone, Lazarus. Because I shall amuse myself with her. It will be a pleasure to tame her, Lazarus."

"Don't bite off what ye can't chaw."

"She has never met a gentleman," Carteret said. "And even my enemies—of which there have been many—do not deny that I have a way with the ladies. I'm offering you a little wager, Lazarus. She'll be crawling to me, begging for a kiss, before another year has gone."

Phoebe listened. She paused a moment before she brushed Estevan aside and walked with ominous directness to the open door and entered it, and stood, slender, supple, straight, to look at Jefferson Carteret with inscrutable eyes. And Carteret returned her gaze boldly, with a humorous lifting of the eyebrows.

"You seem to have overheard a private conversation," he said.

"It's the nineteenth of May," said Phoebe.

"I believe so, madam."

"You've got a year to make good your brag," she said. Then she turned on her heel and strode from the room and into the street.

"Now, what did she mean by that?" asked Carteret.

"I reckon," said Lazarus, "that I'd ruther be somebuddy else besides you."

That was the nineteenth of May in the year 1862. On the next day Colonel West led the advance guard of the California Column into the Old Pueblo and flung to the glittering spring sunshine the Stars and Stripes. For Tucson and Arizona the war was at an end.

Phoebe stood by the roadside and watched the soldiers enter the city. For some reason, she was glad. Though she had carried resentment against the government that had abandoned Arizona, she was glad. Perhaps it was because it felt more homelike to see fluttering the flag to which she was accustomed.

But she did not speculate upon flags or patriotism, for riding toward the end of the column was a tall, slim young man, with an angular, handsome, humorous face. And this young man was peering about him with what seemed to her to be eagerness. He was a sergeant. His uniform, worn and dusty, became him, and he sat a horse with ease—commendably, because unconsciously. She stood tense and still, but concealed beneath the grimness of her face and the controlled waiting of her eyes was a tumult such as she never had known. It was a strange, even an unwelcome, sensation. It made her knees tremble. And then the eyes of the slim young sergeant met her eyes and his face lighted and glowed.

Careless of discipline, he vaulted from his mount, and brushing aside any who stood in his way, strode with long steps to her side.

"How be ye, Phoebe?" he asked. "I told ye I'd be fetchin' up here someday."

It is Peter Muncie, she was saying to herself. Peter Muncie is here. And then she smiled. Tucson, had it been looking, would have seen such a look of womanliness, gladness, upon her face as it never had seen before.

"Seems as if I allus knew you would," she said gravely.

"Be ye glad, Phoebe?"

"I don't calc'late to be aggravated," she said.

"Was it pies ye come to git?" she asked, and was astonished at herself for even this mild coquetry.

He did not reply to it, but stood gazing down at her, and she liked it.

"I got a powerful good memory," he said, "but the' was some few pleasin' details I forgot." He paused. "You make tracks for your home, wherever it's at," he said, "because as soon as I kin contrive to get loose from this army, you're a-goin' to have a visitor."

"There'll be pie," said Phoebe.

CHAPTER VIII

PHOEBE TITUS was overseeing the proper feeding and watering of stock in the corral at the rear of her adobe house. With her orders snapping in their ears, her Mexicans moved more spryly about their tasks than it was in nature for a Mexican to move; and little, hunchbacked Estevan Ochoa grinned from his point of vantage to see his indolent relatives so driven.

"It is better even," he said, "than when dancers, with music and clowns, come from Sonora."

"If your uncles see you laugh at them," she replied, "one will lay a belt across your bottom."

"Not across me," he said impishly. "It is evil luck to beat a hunchback. They have fear."

"Well, I haven't," Phoebe said, "so you better behave yourself."

"The Americano with the beautiful coat walks past many times with his eyes on this *casa*," said Estevan. "If there is a moon and it is night, and if he has a guitar, I theenk he would sing the serenade." He pointed his sharp chin at the heavens and raised his thin voice in a comical travesty of a lover under a balcony.

"Angel de amor, tu pasion no la comprendo. Si la comprendo, no la puedo espresar," he sang, but maintained a watchful eye upon Phoebe's movements.

"The Señor Carteret?" asked Phoebe.

"Si."

She frowned and pressed her lips together. Why should Jefferson Carteret choose this part of the town for his strolling? And especially now. Especially now that Peter Muncie had come back in a uniform from California. She had a very shrewd idea that Peter would not be pleased to discover Carteret in that neighborhood. And what could the man be wanting?

Presently she left the corral and went into the house, but she could not be quiet there. If Carteret were prowling around, she wanted to know the purpose of it. So she went to stand in her doorway. She saw him turn the corner and come sauntering toward her, and then his eyes rested upon her slender figure as it leaned against the hot adobe, and he swept his broad hat from his head with a gesture he had brought from distant, courtly Virginia.

"Miss Phoebe," he said, "I should esteem it a great honor if you would permit me to have a few words with you."

"I heard you was prowling around," she said.

He came nearer and stood in the dust before the doorstep. She looked down at him with what may have seemed to him imperturbability, but his presence was more disturbing to her than her expressionless face admitted. He was handsome—extraordinarily handsome—and his eyelids drooped with unconscious insolence. She did not understand him. He was a representative of a life, of a society, utterly foreign to her experience. In common with her townsmen in Freeport, she had heard of the aristocracy—the slaveholding aristocracy—of the South, but it was as remote from her as was the nobility of England or France. She was not accustomed to ornate manners or exaggerated courtesies. Even his mode of speech, his correct usage of the language, marked him as foreign to anything she had experienced.

"Miss Phoebe," he said, in the manner of one paying homage, "I have sought this opportunity to offer you my apologies. I have offended you. A most evil fortune has made me appear at a disadvantage every time we have met. Yet you are the one person in this vile town in whose eyes I would like to seem no worse than I am."

"Why?" asked Phoebe tersely.

"Because," he said, "I should like to be numbered among your friends. For what has gone before—and my part in it was not attributable to ill intention on my part, but to a most perverse bad luck—I want to beg you to forgive me. Would it be possible for you to pretend that this is our first meeting, and that whatever went before has been erased?"

"No," said Phoebe.

She was not comfortable. She was intensely aware of his presence, of his handsome face, of his virility, and of those other graces and qualities which set him apart from all other men in Tucson. He aroused her curiosity, and she resented it.

"Cannot we be friends?" he asked.

"I don't want no enemies," she said. "Enemies don't pay."

"I admire you, Miss Phoebe," he said, with grave courtesy. "I admire you for what you have done and for what you are.

You and I," he said ingratiatingly, "are different from the rest
of these cattle."

"I'm different from anybody," she said. But she was vaguely
pleased, pleased that this member of Virginia's aristocracy
should include her in this difference which he claimed for
himself.

"You said somethin' about my crawlin' to ye," she said.

"I'm ashamed. I'd been drinking, Miss Phoebe, and Ward
had been jibing at me. Every man says, at some time in his
life, something he will always regret. Can't we forget all that
and be friends?"

"I wonder jest what you're up to," Phoebe said.

"I'm up to nothing but trying to make amends."

"Well," she said, "you've made 'em. Now what?"

"You are very difficult, Miss Phoebe."

"I hain't got no more time to be talkin' here," she said, and
went inside and closed the door.

Whatever had been his purpose, he had achieved a result.
He had impressed his existence upon her. Phoebe was conscious of him, conscious in a personal sort of way in which
curiosity was mixed with a queer, rather irksome sensation of
pleasure. Jefferson Carteret was a young man who seldom had
found difficulty in pleasing women. Aside from his good looks
and fine figure and courtly manners there was an intangible
something about him that attracted ladies and those who were
not ladies. Phoebe felt the impact of it as she stood in her
doorway, and was disturbed. She was disturbed because she
faced the fact, and could not deny it, that from this instant
there were two men of importance in her life, and not one.
A problem was set. She would be unable to think of Peter

Muncie now without also thinking of Jefferson Carteret; she would be unable to consider Carteret without comparing him with Muncie.

"Of all the tarnation luck!" she said testily as she went about her household tasks.

That night Peter Muncie sat at Phoebe's table. Tall, slender of hip, flat of back, he seemed to her a fine figure of a man in his weathered uniform, finishing with gusto the entire pie that she had set before him.

"I like," said Phoebe, "to see a man relish his victuals."

"I've relished a sight wuss vittles than these," Peter said, laying down the knife with which he had demolished the pastry, and fixing eyes which seemed always to be amused on Phoebe's face. That look of amusement was almost a fixed expression with him, as if the world and whatever happened in it, struck him as being just a trifle comical. "This is the fust time I ever seen you dressed like a woman. I reckon I'd 'a' come back sooner if I'd seen you this way that other time."

"I'm a-wonderin' just how much this comin' was to see me," said Phoebe, "or how much it was that joinin' the soldiers give ye a chance to go rarin' and tearin' around."

The expression of amusement in his eyes deepened and spread to his lips. "If 'twan't fur the Army," he said, "I wouldn't 'a' come, and if 'twan't fur you, I wouldn't 'a' joined the Army. Plow handles don't fit my hands wuth a copper cent. I wan't content back thar with nothin' happenin' but peace 'n' quiet."

"I calc'late ye won't never be," she said, studying his face with shrewd and penetrating eye. "It runs in my mind a woman 'ud be jest somebuddy you come back to when nothin' excitin' come to hand some'eres else."

"Wa-al," he drawled, "mebby so. But you hain't one to set home knittin' neither, Phoebe. I reckon a man 'ud just be somebuddy you kind of humored like a pet tomcat when you wa'n't busy bossin' the whole shootin'-match and makin' money out of it."

This was a strange commencement to a courtship, but they were two extraordinary people in rude and uncivil surroundings. Phoebe was more apt at uttering truths than at expressing emotions. Peter was capable of both, but he was also gifted with a certain intuition that told him when to display emotion, or when the better course was to match frankness with frankness. Nevertheless, Phoebe recognized in him something that puzzled her because it was so foreign to her own downright nature. It was an innate gentleness and kindliness—a sort of boyish sweetness that amounted almost to naïveté. It caused her to feel herself more mature than he, and protective. Yet she recognized in him a firmness and resolution, a joyous sort of fortitude, which, somehow, made the idea of protection absurd. It was given to her in that moment to understand that when he was at his gentlest he might also be at his most dangerous. This might lead men into serious error in their dealings with him.

Her eyes became blank as she compared him with Jefferson Carteret. Both were capable of stirring her—Carteret, perhaps, in a more dangerous way, because the excitement he raised was mingled with a sense of gay wickedness and a feeling of playing with forbidden fruit to one's peril.

"The' never," said Phoebe, "was a woman with so much common sense that a scalawag couldn't make a fool of her."

"Be I a scalawag?" Peter said, with a grin. "Mebby I am an amusin' one."

"I wa'n't thinkin' of you," said Phoebe.

Peter's eyes narrowed, but he did not ask the obvious question. He seldom indulged in the obvious, which may have been one reason the Apaches found him a difficult foeman in the days to come.

"How old be ye?" Phoebe asked directly.

"Twenty-eight, come July."

"I'd 'a' called ye younger," she said.

He leaned across the table. "You 'n' me," he said, "we both got one thing in mind ever since the fust time we ever see each other." He could be as direct as she was when the moment came for it. "You're a-thinkin' about marryin' me, and I'm a-thinkin' about marryin' you."

"Yes," she said frankly.

"I never set eyes on a gal I wanted like I want you. Now that I see ye agin, I want ye more'n ever."

She did not become coy or coquettish, nor did she seek to evade the issue. "Ye don't marry a man jest because ye take a sudden shine to him," she said.

"Why not?" he asked, and his question expressed him. If you wanted a person or a thing greatly that was sufficient reason for taking it—and the devil fly away with the consequences. Let tomorrow plow tomorrow's furrow.

"A body don't marry a man jest to go on a jamboree for a month or a year."

"You'd git the month or the year," he said.

"When I marry, I aim to know what I'll have to give up and what I'm likely to git fur it."

"Seems like I'd be willin' to give up a heap fur you, Phoebe."

"That's before ye git me," she said.

"I reckon I'd love stiddy and strong," he said.

"This here's Arizony," she said. " 'Tain't like marryin' back in Illinoy."

"Marryin's marryin'," Peter said.

"I got to estimate how much you'd interfere with what I aim to do."

"I hain't the demandin' kind."

"Mebby I be."

"It sticks out like a sore thumb, Phoebe, that you'd be boss of the family. That don't make me mad."

"You got a movin' foot, Peter. It hain't that you wouldn't be useful in a pinch, but when the' wa'n't no pinch you'd go a-roamin' off lookin' fur one."

"I'd allus come back," he said gaily.

She nodded. "You'd come back. I hain't a woman a man 'ud forgit. I'm studyin' if the times you stayed to home would be wuth the times you was off gallivantin'."

"You're a-studyin' suthin' else, too," he said.

"What?"

"About some other man," he said.

"I got a right to."

"To be sure," he said, and the amusement in his eyes deepened. "But Gawd help him!"

"We got to git acquainted, Peter," she said, "so we'll know if we love each other enough so's we kin endure what's got to be endured. So we kin be sure that nothin' either one of our natures forces us to do'll make the other hate him."

"I never see a woman like ye, Phoebe," he said, with a sincerity of admiration.

"Neither did I," answered Phoebe, not with vanity but with complete, introspective honesty.

"D'ye like me well enough to give me a kiss?" asked Peter.

"Yes, but I hain't a-goin' to," she said. She shook her head and squared her shoulders, and changed the subject. Peter's eyes crinkled.

"What's this here Union colonel of your'n goin' to do?" she asked. "Is he a-goin' to hang the men that went out fur the South, or take away their proppity?"

"West won't do nothin' till General Carleton comes," he told her. "He ought to be ramblin' in before long. But I don't reckon anybuddy's goin' to be hurt."

"Most of them's skedaddled anyway," she said scornfully. "I hope this here general of your'n fetches a batch of law along with him. "What's his name?"

"Carleton," said Peter.

"Will you be stayin' in Tucson a while?"

"I hear talk the's goin' to be a detachment left here. Mebby I'll be one of 'em."

"I hope it's a big one," said Phoebe.

"What you want a big one fur?"

"The more men the' is the more they got to eat. It'll fetch trade. There'll be freightin'. I got to contrive to git me a freightin' contract."

Peter's eyes were so amused now that they danced. "Makin' money comes fust with you, don't it?"

She considered that as he studied her sharp, keen face with delight. Now, as ever after, he considered her avidity to make money a comical trait. It was something he could not understand—this desire to amass property.

"Consarn," he said, "if ye hain't a reg'lar leetle pack rat."

She tried to express herself, but not yet had that terse clarity developed in her speech which one day was to be so characteristic of her.

"Take pa," she said. "He was one to set and set 'n' fish. But his stummick turned agin 'em fur eatin'. I calc'late I'm sim'lar about makin' money."

"If you 'n' me was to marry," asked Peter, "would ye reckon to set me to work stiddy, doin' the same thing over 'n' over every day?"

"I'd try to control ye," she said.

"I got a notion," he said gaily, "ye'd find ye bit off more'n ye could chaw. But it 'ud be kind of distractin', watchin' ye try."

She got up from her chair and walked across the room to the window, through which she looked out upon the night—which was not night but another more beautiful and glamorous day. The moon did not blind one nor burn. Though Phoebe saw the phenomenon she could not put it into words—the selective power of the moon. Selective power such as artists use. It omitted and it accented. The sun overdid things. It knew no restraint and poured its hot rays through the loose fingers of a prodigal. But the moon used taste and judgment. Even filthy, crumbling, sunbaked Tucson was given a fictitious, eerie loveliness by lunar artistry. She stood gazing out upon this nightly amelioration of squalidness with her straight, flat back turned to Peter. Then she turned and stepped across the room to her Sharps rifle that hung upon the wall. She wanted to express something. She was full of it, but she could not translate her feeling into suitable words. It was as if she had been vouchsafed a vision—a moment of inspiration. It was given to her to see the importance to Arizona, to the frontier, to the future of the land, of such men as Peter Muncie. They were an essential breed. The Sharps rifle stood for them, as, possibly, the plow or the ox yoke stood for men and women like herself. The rifle must make it possible for the plow to tear its furrow in the virgin soil. In themselves these men were unique, useless for any other end. But their restlessness, their recklessness, their revolt against all restraint and tethering made it possible for the plodders to plod and for the builders to build. It was upon their rifles that a future was to be erected.

All she said was, "I hain't belittlin' sich as you. You hain't got no call to belittle sich as me. Gawd he made Arizony hard to git, but wuth the gittin' of. It's fur you and your like to git, while folks like Warner 'n' Oury 'n' me keeps and builds."

"Does it fetch ye any closer to marryin' me?" he asked.

"We hain't a-goin' to speak about that no more tonight," she said, and paused. "How long d'ye calc'late to stay in the Army?"

"No longer 'n' I'm compelled. The's too much tellin' a man what to do in the Army."

"Mebby you'll find the' is everywhere," she said. "Now ye better light a shuck, Peter." She sighed. "Feels kind of good to know suthin' stands betwixt you 'n' the Apaches besides the Pimas 'n' the Papagos. It's been bad times, Peter. If it hadn't 'a' been fur them friendly Injuns hatin' the Apaches wuss'n what we do, this town 'ud 'a' been wiped out. Farmin' Injuns they be, but they're pizen in a fight."

"G'night, Phoebe," he said. "I'm kind of dubious if I'm man enough to marry ye. I reckon you're a size bigger'n me." He hesitated outside the door, and then said, awkwardly, a thing that she kept jealously in a secret treasure house until the end of her days.

"Ye make me feel," he said, "like I was alone, kneelin' out thar in the desert, a-liftin' my eyes to suthin' that makes me know I got to worship it. Though I hain't able to see it plain nor understand it, even in the moonlight."

She touched the arm of his uniform with light fingers. "We're a couple of strange people," she said, and both joy and fear were in her eyes. "But whatever comes to us on account of our strangeness'll do no lastin' harm, if we ketch 'n' hold one thing that don't never splutter nor flicker nor die out."

"D'ye mean love?" asked Peter.

She nodded. "But it'll have to be bigger 'n' deeper than most," she said, "because it'll have to endure more strain. G'night, Peter."

CHAPTER IX

Upon a ranch down the river, which Phoebe had bought from its fleeing owner, hay stood untended—and the Army needed hay. So Phoebe neglected distracted meetings of citizens in Solomon Warner's store—gatherings of apprehensive men who did not know what would happen to them when General Carleton arrived and who met rather for common comfort than to devise measures. She could do no freighting business with the military until its commander should come. But she could harvest hay, and she could sell hay because animals, even those belonging to the government, must be fed. So Phoebe set forth with a wagon and two men, against the urgent advice of Warner and Peter Muncie.

"The hosses," she said practically, "got to have fodder. If it wa'n't dangerous to git it, hay wouldn't fetch sich a price."

"What good's a price if you're layin' out on the sand with a lance through your stummick?" demanded Peter.

"What good's a stummick," countered Phoebe, "if ye hain't got a meal to fill it?"

"I never see sich a woman," Muncie said. "It's makin' money, makin' money. Seems like you're crazy over money, Phoebe."

"It's good to have," she said tersely.

"It's good to spend," Peter retorted, and therein, in these two sentences, lay the great difference between them.

Peter tried for leave to go with her, or to be detailed as escort. But that day Thomas Jeffords had come, bearing dispatches from General Canby in New Mexico, and the camp was busy with preparations for sending a column, under the guidance of this competent scout, to the Rio Grande, and the request was refused. So Phoebe, with her wagon and mules and scythes—and two men to wield them, left town in the dark of the night, lurching and creaking southward. Nighttime was the time for safe travel, because the Apaches seldom attacked before dawn. While Phoebe watched, double-barreled shotgun cradled in her arms, the men moved hay in the rich bottom land, and loaded it into the wagon. From dawn until afternoon smoke signaled from surrounding hills. The wagon was loaded high, and parched with thirst, blistered by blazing sun, they turned their mules' heads toward Tucson.

Phoebe rode beside the wagon, searching rocks and cover, hillside and desert with unwinking vigilance. She had not slept for twenty-four hours, but she was not weary. Her superb, wiry body was well calculated to sustain labor and hardship, and her fortitude of mind to hold flagging muscles to the task she set for them.

They approached a terrain grown thickly to Joshua trees, which, of all vegetation upon the surface of the earth, alone seem to have been designed by Doré as a gaunt and fitting embellishment of Hades. Weird and ghastly in the waning light, they seemed an army of skeletons of some blasted army of distorted giants—giants with outstretched, gnarled arms and awful clutching fingers.

Out of this cover, suddenly, startlingly, as if they had been created on that spot by some malignant spell, a dozen Apaches, naked, brandishing lances, bows and arrows, primitive weapons, came leaping, twisting, dodging, towards them, urged on by the squalling of their horridly painted chief.

Phoebe reined in her horse, threw the gun to her shoulders and fired once. A savage fell groveling, but the rest, yowling, filling the air with arrows, came lunging on.

"I told ye so," said the driver of the mules.

"Shet your mouth," retorted Phoebe, and reserved her second barrel until the chief, brandishing a war club and grimacing with bedaubed, inhuman features, reached a point not twenty yards from where she sat on her horse. Slowly she raised her weapon, aimed with as little tremor in her arms as if she faced a target, and pulled the trigger. The face of the Apache disappeared, became a crimson smear. His followers stopped in their tracks, wheeled and fled. It was characteristic of Indian warfare. The Apache feared readiness on the part of his victims more than death, and a setback which would have but aroused the rage of white warriors sent him scurrying. His victories must be bought cheaply. Were it not for this, had the red man been gifted with the follow-through of his white enemies and had he been capable of sustaining an attack, even in face of feeble resistance, the story of Arizona would have been darker, dreadfully more sanguine, than history's pages show it to have been.

Phoebe shrieked after the flying savages until they disappeared among the rocks and ghostly Joshuas. The driver wiped his brow.

"Gawd!" he exclaimed.

"We'll fix a notice to 'em to leave white folks alone," she said sharply. "Fetch a rope."

"What you aimin' to do?" asked the driver.

"Hang this Injun to a mesquite," she said, "and leave him to dangle a warnin'."

And so it was done. They hoisted him and tied him above the reach of coyotes or other earth creatures, but nothing could protect his body from the vultures of the air. The two men eyed Phoebe furtively. They were not gentle citizens; they were accustomed to hardship, ruthlessness, cruelty. But Phoebe's implacable face and merciless action impressed and startled them. They stared at each other as the mules surged into their collars and moved the wagon northward.

"I never see sich a dam' woman," the driver whispered to his mate.

"Me," said the other, "I'd back her agin' a mountain lion 'n' give him the fust claw."

It was moonlight when they rounded the mountain and saw the lights of Tucson before them, but the moon was low and the lofty mass of rick threw over them and the desert a blot of purple, through which they lurched and rumbled on. Riding ahead to point out the way, Phoebe became aware of motion, and her reflexes threw her shot gun into readiness.

But a small, reedy voice spoke out of the night. "*Señorita* have no fear. It is Estevan Ochoa." He spoke in his native tongue.

"What do you here?" Phoebe asked in the same language, the mastery of which had been necessary to her—indeed, had come to her by usage and custom rather than by study.

"I hear men planning that evil shall come to the *señorita*. I sleep in the shade by the mescal shop of Manuel Sais. Beside the open window they sit and talk, one with the other, and my ears are open, for they name the name of the *señorita*. This is truth."

"What men, Estevan?" she asked.

"The one with the name of him the blessed Savior lifted up from the dead."

"Lazarus Ward. And who else?"

"The gambler, Jesús."

"And what evil did they speak, Estevan?"

"That the *señorita*, for money, sold percussion caps to Captain Hunter and the soldiers of the South that were driven away. I do not understand this war. But they go to the chief of the soldiers in Tucson and have reported to him that you sell these percussion caps and other things, and that you make boast that you and ten soldiers of the South can overcome a hundred soldiers from the North. This and many other things they said, being consumed with hatred. Also it was to prevent a hiring of the *señorita* to transport from place to place food and merchandise in wagons. They also said the *señorita* would be seized and sent to Yuma, and that they could buy her wagons and mules and horses for a small price."

"Gracias, Señor Estevan," she said. "There will be many pies because of this telling."

"It was not told for pies," he said proudly, "but for friendship."

"Nonetheless there will be pies," said Phoebe—"Follow along," she said to her driver. "You're safe now." She raked her horse with spurs, so that he leaped over the uneven road, nor did she draw rein until she reached the Plaza Militar, where she slowed her mount to a walk and accosted a Mexican who was crossing the square.

"Señor," she said politely, "I seek the Señor Ward."

"He but now returned to the mescal shop of Manuel Sais," said the man. "With my eyes I saw him enter the door."

"Gracias," she responded, and walked her horse to the Calle de las Milpas, that narrow, grimy and winding street. She was behaving as those who knew her best would have predicted. There was nothing indirect or devious about Phoebe Titus. She did not hover about the edge of trouble, hesitating and planning what might be best to do. That was not her way. She was one who traveled by short, straight paths, seeking immediately the heart of the matter. If there were an emergency she did not loiter, seeking help or advice, but went to meet it swiftly and without plan. It was enough that there was an emergency. When she faced it she was supremely confident in her ability to deal with it. It was not vanity. It was something vastly greater than vanity, more admirable.

Before the squalid saloon of Manuel Sais she halted and dismounted. Then, with the shotgun under her arm, she passed through the low door into the fetid oven air of the candlelit room. It was crowded. A couple of dozen Mexicans sprawled, drank, played guitars and sang. Ebony-faced Indians squatted. The odor was heavy, sickening. At a wet table before the one window sat Lazarus Ward. He did not observe her coming.

"Lazarus," he said sharply, "I want to talk to ye."

"Go home where ye b'long," Ward said, and then allowed the lips beneath his beard to curl in a sneer. "You'll be havin' plenty to talk to, come mornin'."

"Have ye," she asked, "any idee how buckshot tears a man up?"

Jefferson Carteret turned from the rude bar, suave, polite, smiling. "Miss Phoebe," he said, "this is no place for a lady."

"I don't calc'late to be a lady," said Phoebe, "and you keep your oar out of this. . . . Be ye a-comin', Lazarus?"

"Where to?"

"When you git there you'll know," she said.

"But, Miss Phoebe—" Carteret commenced.

She silenced him. "I hain't got no reason to think you're concerned in this," she said. "Don't give me none."

"Where'd ye git the idee ye kin order me around?" demanded Ward.

"I got it packed into these here two barrels," she said. "Git up onto your hind laigs, Lazarus, and commence a-comin'. . . . No, you stay settin', Mr. Carteret. I got company enough."

"You're jest a-pilin' up trouble for yourself, Phoebe," Ward said uncomfortably. "It's said you're a-goin' to be arrested, come mornin'."

"If you want to enjoy the sight of it," she said, "you better commence to mog." She shifted her gun, and Ward arose reluctantly, with a sidewise glance about the room as if seeking help, but nobody stirred. Phoebe stepped a couple of paces into the room, so that Ward could pass through the door without coming close to her. "The' suthin' about a shotgun," she said, as he went by her and paused in the door, "that makes a body thoughtful." Then, to the room in general, speaking in Spanish, "Remain with God," she said, and there was meaning in her words.

She hooked the reins over her left arm, and so, leading her horse, urged Ward along the dark street.

"What set ye on the warpath, Phoebe?" he asked. "I hain't done nothin' to rile ye."

"Then," she said, "ye got no cause to worry."

She made him walk before her to the Calle Real, and thence to Calle del Alegria, and so across the Plaza de la Mesilla to her house, the door of which she ordered Ward to open. Then, with twin muzzles pressed to the small of his back, she made him light candles. After which she sat down, facing door and window, and laid her gun across the rough wooden table.

"If," she said conversationally, "I git arrested in the mornin' and sent off to Yuma, I'll be hung up there a long spell. It'll be onhandy. I jest can't spare the time, Lazarus."

"What've I got to do with it, Phoebe?"

"The's money to be made now, what with freightin' and sellin' supplies and sichlike, and I don't calc'late to miss the chance. Nor I don't calc'late to have my proppity seized and sold fur practically nothin'."

"Don't seem like ye kin help yourself," said Ward.

"I calc'late to help myself," Phoebe answered. "You 'n' Hoosus told them lies to Colonel West, 'n' he'll hold me till Gen'al Carleton comes. I don't count Hoosus, but you carry some weight, bein' a white man. It's funny the kind of folks carries weight sometimes. You told the colonel I was sellin' percussion caps to Hunter and takin' sides with the South."

"Hain't a word of truth in it," denied Lazarus.

"Then," said Phoebe, "ye won't have no objection to sayin' so to the colonel."

"It hain't no skin off'n my nose," said Ward.

"It's apt to be skin 'n' flesh off'n your stummick," said Phobe, moving her gun significantly. "Mebby you're a-figgerin' on Hoosus comin' here 'n' gittin' you out of this fix." She used the common English pronunciation of the Spanish name Jesús. "You ought to be smart enough, Lazarus, not to pick sich a partner. So ye don't calc'late to tell the colonel that what ye told him today was a pack of lies?"

"I didn't tell him nothin'."

"Did ye ever reflect on bein' killed, Lazarus?" she asked. "It's kind of horrifyin' to know it's a-comin' to ye. But it's a heap more harrowin' to know it's a-comin, but not know jest when."

"What ye mean, Phoebe?"

"Kin ye write, Lazarus?"

"Calc'late to."

"The's writin' things onto the table here. Be ye a-goin' to write to the colonel and own up ye told him a pack of lies about me?"

"I won't write nothin'."

Phoebe nodded. "Suit yourself," she said. "Now, sometime betwixt this and mornin', I'm a-goin to let off this here shot-gun at you. I dunno jest when. I'll wait till my finger gits to itchin'. But ye kin depend on it, you're a-goin' to git plenty buckshot. Ye kin rely on it. Mebby it'll be ten minutes, 'n' mebby it'll be two hours, but ye kin set 'n' expect it any second. And ye kin rely on it. If any of your friends come prowlin' around, it'll be then. So jest set 'n' be comfortable till I think it's the right time."

"You wouldn't never dast to do it," said Lazarus.

"The' hain't no law in Tucson," she said. "Jest keep on

thinkin' I won't shoot till ye git it. Now shet up and don't trouble me."

She sat grimly silent, glancing at him now and then. He, too, sweat commencing to roll down his face and into his eyes, maintained silence—a sort of blustering silence that persisted for fifteen minutes. Then slowly, very slowly, her hand moved down the gunstock and her finger closed over the trigger. Lazarus watched with fascinated eyes which grew larger and larger. His throat was terribly dry, but he could not swallow. Phoebe's finger curled. Lazarus could see pressure being exerted. Then she shrugged her shoulders, relaxed and sat back in her chair.

"Hain't quite ready fur it yit," she said.

Lazarus gulped. Another twenty minutes passed, and again his eyes followed her hand as it moved toward the trigger guard, as the finger tightened around the sprig of steel that would release the charge of buckshot into his body.

He yelped. "Don't ye do it! Don't ye do it!" he gasped in a hoarse, strangled whisper.

"Ye kin have a spell longer," she said. "Next time I'll probably pull harder 'n' I meant to. Ye can't allus calc'late the heft of a trigger pull."

Firmness seemed to be departing from his jaw. The lips were a bit open and his face seemed to soften and melt into new shapes as terror gripped him. Perspiration streamed down and disappeared into his tangle of whiskers.

"Honest, Phoebe, I didn't. I never told the colonel nothin'. Honest, Phoebe," he protested.

"If you're enjoyin' yourself," she said, "make the most of it."

This time she permitted a longer time to elapse before she

fingered the trigger. She shifted the gun so that its muzzle seemed to point to a spot in Ward's middle that pleased her better. "I can't spend the whole night settin' here," she said, with evidence of growing irritation. "Guess I better be gittin' it over. Brace yourself, Lazarus; here she comes!"

He could see her knuckle whiten as she exerted real pressure upon the trigger, and cried out hoarsely. It was a squeal rather than a cry. "Don't go for to do it! Don't pull! I'll write! Don't pull, Phoebe! I'll write!"

"You come clost to bein't too late," she said, wagging her head. "Grab that quill 'n' write down what I say."

She waited for him to be in readiness.

"Colonel West. There wa'n't a word of truth to what I told ye about Phoebe Titus and them percussion caps. I and a gambler Hoosus made it up to git rid of her, so as we could buy in her stock and wagons, and so as she couldn't git no contracts for freightin'. She's never took sides neither way, but minded her own business. I am a skunk and a liar." She stopped and her lips twisted. There was a gleam in her eyes that was not dissimilar to the one that lived in Peter Muncie's eyes. "Now sign it," she said, "good and readable."

He signed. She reached for the paper and tucked it into her shirt.

"The' different ways of doin' business," she said conversationally, "but the' hain't but one's worth a cuss. That's to git as much as ye kin fur what ye give, but allus deliver what ye agree to deliver. Mebby ye kin use it fur an idee. Now ye kin go to sleep, if ye want to. In the mornin' you 'n' me is goin' to deliver this here letter to the colonel."

CHAPTER X

RESPECTABLE citizens of Tucson were in a panic; disreputable citizens—the gamblers, ruffians, and riffraff—withdrew under the surface until they should discover how the wind would blow. Men disappeared in the night, never to be heard of again. Both respectable and disreputable feared lest law had come to Arizona, for if it came, it would be Northern law, and they had declared for the South. Would there be reprisals, proscriptions, seizures of property? This state of mind persisted until the arrival, early in June, of General Carleton, commander of the California Column.

A dozen men and one woman had met in Solomon Warner's store; worried men, uncertain what tomorrow's sun would bring to them. To Phoebe's disgust, they wavered, reached no conclusion. She spoke her mind pointedly, left the store, mounted her horse, which was tied outside, and on her own initiative rode to the camp on the outskirts of town and to General Carleton's tent.

"I want to see the general," she said to the sentry who lounged in an unmilitary manner outside.

"What you want to see him fur?" asked the man, with impudent lack of interest.

"'Tain't none of your consarned business," Phoebe said shortly, and then raised her voice, "General Carleton, be ye inside? I want to talk with you!"

The general, weary from riding a thirsty and inclement land, stood frowning, in the opening.

"Who are you, and what do you want?" he demanded.

"I'm Phoebe Titus," she said, "and until somebuddy better comes along, I'm representin' the territory of Arizona."

"There is no territory in Arizona."

"Jeff Davis said the' was. He proclaimed it in February."

The general's eyes narrowed as he studied her, sitting on her horse as if she had been born in its saddle. Phoebe could not tell if it was the beginning of a smile. She returned his stare, leaning sidewise with her elbow on the pommel.

"Mr. Davis hasn't the say of it," said the general. "Why is a woman representing the non-existent territory of Arizona?"

"Because," she said shortly, "I'm the best man in it."

"What do you want?" he asked.

"I want to find out what's a-goin' to be done."

"You don't talk like a Southerner," he said.

"Freeport, Illinois," she answered.

"I'm busy," he said in a sort of tentative way, as if to test her persistence.

"You'll be a blasted sight busier," she said, "if somebody don't make head or tail to what's goin' on."

"Were you one of those who declared for the South?"

"I declare for anybody that'll fetch law 'n' order to Arizony."

"Just what do you want to know?"

"The men folks has got high-strikes," she said. "Be you a-goin' to hang anybuddy or seize proppity?"

"The sentiment of this town is Southern," he said. "I'm dealing with a hostile population."

"You're dealin' with a pop'lation that's fur Arizony, lock, stock 'n' barrel. We never got anythin' from the North. The North left us in the lurch to be murdered 'n' massacreed. It was too busy squabblin' about slave 'n' free to bother with us. The pop'lation—the decent pop'lation—of this town 'ud be fur any-buddy that fetches protection from the Injuns and law 'n' order against the riffraff."

"Do you mean that the men of Tucson would turn and de-clare for the North?"

"I mean they'll declare for Arizony. All we want is to be let to work and make suthin' of this here territory. It was the blunderin' idiots in your Army that brought the Injuns down onto us, and then high-tailed out of the country, leavin' us to take care of the mess."

"Blundering idiots? Young woman, that isn't diplomatic language. You come asking favors ——"

"I'm askin' no favors. I come to tell you," she said. "I come to tell you what we want and why we want it. 'Blunderin' idiots,' I said, and 'blunderin' idiots' I mean. I don't s'pose ye ever heard of an Injun by the name of Cochise?"

"I have heard of him."

"Mebby you knew him 'n' the Chiricahua Apaches was at peace with us till that tarnation fool, Lieutenant Bascom, mur-dered his relations."

"Murdered?"

"Pinal Apaches—nothin' to do with Cochise—raided John Ward's ranch and run off stock and stole a boy. So this Bascom rides off with his soldiers to Apache Pass, and Cochise sees 'em and comes a-ridin' down, with his brother 'n' two nephews 'n' his wife, to see what soldiers is doin' there. Bascom says Cochise stole the boy. Cochise says he didn't—which he didn't— but promises to see if he can't buy him back again. So this dunderhead, Bascom, goes to arrest him, 'n' Cochise lugs out his knife 'n' slits the tent 'n' escapes, leavin' his relatives behind. Then, before you kin say 'scat,' the's plenty trouble, and Bascom up 'n' hangs Cochise's relatives. And so, havin' stirred up a war with the Chiricahuas, the Army legs it out of the country." She paused. "Ride out on any trail, general, and see the graves along it. Go seekin' a ranch house that hain't been burned. Find a mine that's workin'. Find anythin' left of all our work 'n' labor except a handful of white folks in Tucson that's afraid they'll be hung because they hoped Jeff Davis could give us the protection that Abe Lincoln wouldn't."

"I suppose you have property," said the general.

"Plenty of it."

"Which you do not wish me to seize."

She sat erect in her saddle and swept her arm around half the horizon. "I hain't worried about proppity," she said. "I'm worried about that. Take what I got and welcome, because the's plenty more to be had in them mountains and them valleys and that desert, if you'll give us law. That's all we want—law 'n' pertection whilst we're a-buildin'. We don't care if it comes from the North or from the South, so long as it lets us do our work. We hain't fur neither side; we're fur Arizony."

"What do you want me to do, Miss——?"

"Titus, Phoebe Titus. I want ye to proclaim the law. I want ye to set men's minds at rest. I want it so as we won't need but one hand for a rifle whilse we work with the other."

"What do you work at, Miss Titus?"

"Freightin'," she said.

"Well," said General Carleton, "go back and tell your men-folks that tonight I proclaim martial law. Tell them there will be no reprisals or seizures."

"Be the soldiers a-goin' to stay?"

"There will be a permanent station here."

"Well," she said, "when you got nothin' more pressin' to do, ye might see the' hain't quite so many murders 'n' robberies in town."

"Tucson shall be policed."

"Much obleeged," said Phoebe, "and now we got them things settled, we kin git down to business."

"What business?"

"Freightin'," said Phoebe. "You got to freight supplies fur your soldiers from Yuma. I got the wagons 'n' the hosses 'n' the mules."

"First public welfare and then private profit, eh?"

"What's the good of public welfare," she demanded, "exceptin' to give folks a chance to make private profit? What's a-goin' to open up this country and git the mines to goin' agin, and the ranches to raisin' grain 'n' cattle but private profit? What was it fetched the Overland Stage Route across the country, and what's a-goin' to fetch this railroad they're a-talkin' about? Private profit."

"Quite correct," said the general, "but I think I'd better attend to the law before I reach the matter of freighting supplies."

"Soldiers can't give much law, nor fightin' neither, on an empty stummick," she said. "But I won't pester ye any more today. Jest bear it in mind I got the wagons 'n' the stock—and my wagons 'n' my drivers git through. I make 'em."

"I'll warrant you do," said the general.

So, on June 8th, law came to Arizona. It was law after a fashion, martial law, but it was better than none. Citizens gathered hopefully or scowlingly about Carleton's proclamation, posted upon an ancient adobe wall:

Now, in the present chaotic state in which Arizona is to be found, with no civil officers to administer the laws, indeed with an utter absence of all civil authority, and with no security of life and property within its borders, it becomes the duty of the undersigned to represent the authority of the United States over the people of Arizona as well as those who compose, or are connected with, the Column from California. . . . The undersigned, as Military Governor, assumes control until such time as the President of the United States shall otherwise direct.

But, what did not sit so well on the stomachs even of the respectable was that something hitherto unknown and undreamed of accompanied the coming of the law—and this was taxes.

Every merchant and businessman was required to pay an occupational tax, and each saloon, mescal shop and gambling house was compelled to disgorge monthly a hundred dollars of its gains. Even the sober-minded expressed doubts if the benefits derived from law and order offset the establishment of this precedent—this eloquent, always present forerunner of civilization. Also every man over the age of twenty-one was directed to step up promptly and take the oath of allegiance to the United States on pain of being deported from the territory.

It was not until the morning of the ninth that Phoebe Titus saw Peter Muncie again. Now, as she emerged from Solomon Warner's store, she encountered him on the *Calle Real*. With an expressionless face, but amused eyes, he halted before her, not calling her by name or otherwise showing tokens of recognition.

"What's your name, ma'am?" he asked.

"You ought to know," she said.

"Not official," he answered. "I'm on a question'-askin' detail, so don't answer me back. What's your name?"

"Phoebe Titus."

"Have ye took the oath of allegiance?"

"Not yit."

"Wa-al, ye better hyper 'n' do it. What d'ye do fur a livin'? Got any occupation?"

"What if I hain't?"

"Then I got to report ye, and you'll be sent off to Yuma or some'eres."

"I'm in the freightin' business."

"Run a saloon or gamblin' hell?"

"No."

"Done any murders or committed any robberies lately?"

"Hain't found no leisure fur it," said Phoebe.

"Married or single?"

"Single."

"Plannin' on gittin' married?"

"Does the general want to know?" she asked.

"No. That thar's a kind of personal question of my own."

"Then ye better find out personal," she said.

"I aim to," he answered, but before he could continue, he

found himself confronted by a handsome young man, nearly as tall as himself, who gazed at him insolently under lazy eyelids.

"Get out of the lady's way," said Jefferson Carteret.

Pete let his eyes drop to Carteret's polished boots, raised them by degrees to his knees, to the skirts of his coat, to his waistcoat, his linen, and finally to his lips.

"Once," he said, and Phoebe noted that the amusement in his eyes had increased until it was almost laughter, "I knowed a feller that didn't mind his own business."

"Miss Titus is my business. It is the business of any gentleman to see that a lady is not molested by a drunken soldier."

"Gentleman, eh? Make a livin' at it?"

"What I make my living at is none of your affair."

"I never see a man wrong about so many things," said Peter— "D'ye know this—gentleman, ma'am?"

"I know him," said Phoebe.

"Friend of your'n, mebby?"

"No."

"But he reckons he could git to be so by showin' off and pertectin' ye from a rowdy soldier," said Peter shrewdly, and then, even more acutely, "do folks back where ye come from agree you're a gentleman, mister? Or did ye run away betwixt two days, a-leavin' a stink behind ye?"

Carteret's skin darkened as the blood surged upward. "If you were a gentleman, I'd have you out for that," he said softly.

Peter's eyes danced now. "First time I ever wished I was one," he said. "But I'll come around when I'm off duty. But I'm on duty now. What's your name, mister?"

"Suppose I decline to answer?"

"Why, then, mister, I'll enjoy takin' ye by the scruff of the neck and the seat of the pants and draggin' you to where you'll be made to answer."

Phoebe was deriving a strange enjoyment, a deep, saturnine satisfaction, from this exchange. Peter Muncie was behaving as she had guessed he would behave in any emergency— coolly, humorously, but nonetheless dangerously. Carteret debated with himself briefly and decided that he would not join issue with this tall, slender sergeant.

"My name," he said, "is Jefferson Carteret."

"Business, if any?"

"I am a gentleman. I have no occupation."

"Uh-huh. I'll put down 'teamster,'" said Peter, "because if I put down 'loafer,' you'll be chased out of the territory—and I'd hate to see ye go before we git better acquainted. Have ye took the oath?"

"Yes," said Carteret, to Phoebe's surprise.

Just why it was that unquestioning emnity had flared up between these young men at their first encounter would be a matter for savants to decide. It may have been the instinctive repellence between one with generations of ancestors who had occupied high places in society and state, and one who scarcely remembered his grandfather's name. It may, and probably was, something more animal than that; the same instinct that causes two male moose to charge each other on sight, or two bulls to lower their heads in battle for premier place among the heifers of the herd. But with the first word, the first glance, they hated.

Phoebe felt that she was at the source of it, and being

who she was and what she was, she exulted. She did not add fire to the flames (for she saw they needed nothing to make them hotter) by repeating to Peter Muncie the words she had heard Carteret speak concerning her. She held her peace and bided her time. But at the same time she felt the weight of premonition. This moment was more important than a mere encounter between rival young men. It was no mere quarrel, but the commencement of something that would live and smoulder and modify the lives of all three of them. She shivered a trifle as if with sudden chill, though the sun blazed down upon them and thermometer, had there been one, would have registered above the hundred mark.

"May I escort you to your home, Miss Phoebe?"

"Not now, nor any other time, mister," said Peter. "You hain't one I'd be willin' to see walkin' with a sister of mine. Before now I've seen men with saggin' eyelids like your'n, mister, but never a one of 'em but reckoned he was hell and repeat with the wimmin. Jest fur your satisfaction, and to kind of give ye an idee how to behave in future, I'm tellin' you I'm a-goin' to marry Miss Titus."

Carteret turned his head toward her. "Is this true, Miss Phoebe?" he asked.

"Ye kin call it almighty probable," said Phoebe tersely.

Carteret shrugged his shoulders, swung on his heel and strode away in search of shade and liquids. Peter grinned amiably at Phoebe.

"Made up your mind, hey?" he asked.

"Peter," she said, "keep your eye peeled. There walks a

man that'll do you 'n' me a meanness jest as sure's vinegar's sour."

"I never see two folks," Peter said, "that 'ud be harder to do a meanness to than you 'n' me."

"All the same, look out fur him. I got a feelin' in my bones."

Peter ignored the matter. "I hear talk," he said, "that I'm a-goin' to be detached fur scout duty."

"It'll take ye away a lot," she said, but did not refer to the extra risk of that assignment.

"But I'll allus come back," he said. and his smile felt to her like a physical caress.

CHAPTER XI

With the coming of the California Column Arizona had reason to hope; it was not to be left prostrate at the mercy of the Indians who had ravaged it and all but depopulated it. Carleton was energetic. He despatched punitive columns and established forts. His subordinates, Cremony and Roberts, fought the battle of Apache Pass—an engagement that stretched from Dragoon Springs to that ill-starred canyon through which all traffic must pass on its way from southern New Mexico into Arizona. In an engagement that lasted for days in that rocky defile and the desert on either side of it, Mangas Coloradas, great chief of the Apache tribes allied under his command—the Mescaleros, Mimbres, Mogollons and Copper Mines—joined with Cochise, terrible war chief of the Chiricahuas, and were defeated only when howitzers were brought up to blast the Indians from their positions. Carleton ordained that Fort Bowie should be erected in the pass, protecting the springs, and assuring a safe passage to soldiers, wagon trains, and emigrants through that most perilous defile. Mangas Coloradas, most splendid savage of his generation, warrior, statesman, patriot, was himself

wounded, only to recover to be murdered near the headwaters of the Gila by soldiers under the command of Captain
Shirland, after he had voluntarily placed himself in their
hands to negotiate. Carleton ordained a war of extermination.
But Cochise remained alive and ably vindictive in his stronghold in the Dragoons.

These exploits, slight as they may have been, nevertheless
promised much. And Phoebe was elated. Given protection
from the savages and the territory would yield richly of its
treasures to those who dared to ask for them. She commenced
to look to the future instead of deriving such advantage as
she could from each dawning day.

Not that Arizona was safe, nor that it would be safe for
decades to come—but something was being done. There was
at least the color of protection. And what more than this
could men and women of the pioneer breed demand of their
fatherland!

It was about this time that the habit of sententious speech
fixed itself upon Phoebe Titus. She had been a personage in
Tucson because of her deeds; now she commenced to assume
importance for what she was. She made terse observations,
uttered pithy phrases that were to be remembered and re-
peated. And men listened to her advice.

This was a prosperous year for Phoebe. Her freight wagons
ranged far and fortunately to and from Yuma, the Rio
Grande, even so far as Pete Kitchen's fortress of a rancho on
Potero Creek near Nogales, where he raised hogs, and
whence he sent hams and lard and bacon to the markets in
Tucson. She even owned a safe now, a clumsy, cumbrous
box of iron that had traveled by water from Boston to San

Francisco, and thence had been transhipped to the mouth of the Colorado, where it had been loaded upon a barge and towed up to Yuma. It had traveled the remaining two hundred and fifty miles to Tucson in a Conestoga wagon drawn by six mules.

For mules were replacing the slower oxen. Overfeeding along the trails had exhausted the grass, and grain for food had to be carried, which increased the importance of speed. So the faster animals, despite the enormous, almost prohibitive cost of leather harness, were coming into common use.

Peter Muncie, scouting with Jeffords, appeared infrequently in Tucson. He, too, had developed. He was leaner, harder, more mature, but the amused smile had not disappeared from his eyes. Hunger, thirst, constant peril, could not quench that quizzical flame. Camp, a permanent station, had been established for the troops seven miles outside the city's walls, but when he came in from duty, that ride into Tucson seemed short to him.

"Phoebe," he said on one of his brief visits, "my patience hain't wore out yit."

"If I hain't wuth waitin' fur, I hain't wuth havin'," she said.

"Be I a-goin' to git ye in the end?" he asked.

"We'll talk about that when you git out of the Army."

"I'll be free in a month. My time's up."

"Now, take cattle, Peter," she said, "they'd do well in Arizony. The's comin' a time when freightin' hain't a-goin' to pay."

"When's that?"

"When this railroad the's talk of comes through."

"You 'n' me won't live to see it."

"You 'n' me," she said, "will live to see a sight more'n jest a railroad. So," she continued with her thought, "I'm studyin' what to git into when freightin' plays out. It's a-goin' to be cattle."

"I hear tell they struck gold a couple hunderd miles northwest of here. Placer."

"From what I hear, it'll be deeper'n placer," she said. "Gold brings folks. Peter, I got to git cattle."

"Plenty in Sonora," he said.

"I don't want them spindlin', meachin' Mexican cows. I want cattle that was born 'n' bred east of the Mississippi."

"How do ye aim to git 'em?"

"I had you in mind," she said simply.

"Me!"

"You or somebody else," she said.

He eyed her speculatively. "Somebuddy else don't mean that feller Carteret, does it?"

"If I can't git you to run this here errand, I got to git the next best I can."

Peter smiled at her use of words. "Run this errand." Her idea of an errand was something measurably greater than running down to the store for a ham or a pound of butter. An errand. To ride through hostile country for a thousand miles, to the Mississippi and then beyond. To buy cattle and then drive them back a thousand miles through the lands of the Comanches, Navahos and Apaches, to Tucson. An errand of two thousand miles, with death waiting beside every mile of trail! It was not an errand, it was an epic.

"How many cows was you reckonin' on a body herdin' back?" he asked, with amusement in his voice.

"Five hundred," she said, as calmly as if she were mentioning one, and it to be driven in from an adjacent pasture.

"Mebby Carteret likes cows better'n I do," he said. "That many'll cost a sight of money."

"I'll have it when the paymaster gits here," she said.

The paymaster! Twice each year this personification of a government's bounty made his way to Tucson, and poured wealth into the hands of soldiers, teamsters, ranchers, storekeepers. Twice a year the government paid what it owed, and then there was orgy. Between these visitations the army issued vouchers, due bills, which were used as currency. Merchants accepted them; they passed from hand to hand until they were frayed and worn. But always there were those who needed gold, hard money. And these were willing to discount their vouchers—to accept ten, or twenty, or even, in an emergency, twenty-five per cent less than their face value for immediate cash. Phoebe Titus accommodated them—and it was not an unprofitable venture.

"I calc'late you're perty rich, Phoebe," said Peter.

"I'm gittin' so I'm comfortable off."

He shook his head and whistled through his teeth, staring at Phoebe's safe, bulking large in its corner.

"I wonder how money feels—bein' shut up in that box," he said musingly. "What good's it? Now if I was a dollar, Phoebe, I reckon I'd feel mighty spited to be pent up that-a-way in the dark. I'd want to be spent. Seems like the only fun a dollar has is feelin' itself bein' spent."

She wanted to explain to him, to make him see her point of view, and why the amassing of money was important in her eyes.

"Take a dollar," she said. "What kin ye buy with it?"

"A drink," he said gaily.

"Dollars hain't no good a-standin' alone, or gallopin' about alone. Ye got to herd 'em. Somebuddy's got to save 'em and herd 'em together till there's enough to use fur a purpose. It's saved dollars, herded dollars, that makes it possible to dig mines and build ships and run railroads across the country. It's different folks each savin' a little, and then gatherin' the savin's in a mess, that makes it possible to do anything big. If nobuddy ever saved nothin' big 'n' important would ever git done."

"Why should it?" asked Peter. "Hain't this country perty slick now? Proppity chokes a man and hawg-ties him. Instid of doin' what he wants to, a man with proppity has to spend his life guardin' it." He searched her face. "If ye didn't have no money, Phoebe, we could git a sight of enj'yment."

"Livin' in a hogan like Injuns," she said. "Be ye goin' to Kaintucky to git my cattle?"

"Be ye goin' to marry me?"

Through the window came the music of a bass drum and harp, the most complete orchestra Tucson afforded. In some swept shed a prosperous Mexican was giving a *baile* by the light of flickering candles. Watchful mothers or duennas squatted about the wall guarding well-behaved, bright-eyed señoritas, but each hoping behind her sharp, black eyes that some eligible *caballero* would break a cascaron over the glossy, jet hair of her charge—the cascaron was an eggshell filled with confetti, and its breaking a public declaration of honorable intention. Peter could visualize the scene; would have delighted to participate in it, and would have been welcome. He could see the hopeful, good mothers sipping *lemon-ade* and gossiping while modest daughters made merry with agile young men and thought less of marriage and children than of music and dancing.

"You'll be the first white woman ever to marry in Tucson," he said, and his eyes were gay.

"If I marry."

"We'll have to give a *baile* the like of which was never seen." He leaned toward her. "Phoebe," he pleaded, "do you love me more'n them dollars?" Then his eyes lost for a moment their glow of humor and became hard as lapis and as cold. "Or has that there Carteret come betwixt us? When I come back, we knowed we was made for each other. You knowed it and so did I."

"Nobuddy's come betwixt us," she said.

"For the fust time," he answered slowly, "I dunno if I believe ye."

He got up abruptly and strode from the low room, and when he was gone, it seemed very empty. Yet she did not call him back. She could not have called him back if the whole happiness of her life depended upon the lifting of her voice. It was not foolish stubbornness. It was not that she did not want to run to the door and implore him to return, but she could not. She could not compel herself to such a surrender. Not because she was proud. Something within her, some part of her over which she had no control, would not permit her.

She sat staring at the door through which he had passed, and hated Carteret. It was not she who had caused this thing, but Jefferson Carteret—and she had not meant to use him to arouse Peter's jealousy or to bend him to her will. It had just happened so.

She did not know that Peter searched the town for Carteret. She did not know that mere accident prevented that night the meeting of these two men—and a meeting would have meant that one of them would have been carried away from it to the new cemetery just outside the old wall. Because Carteret was absent from Tucson on some errand her affairs did not come to a climax, to a solution that night, but must await the capricious humor of the future. Had Peter met Jefferson Carteret there might have been a solution, and the life streams of many persons beside Phoebe and Jefferson and Peter have been determined in their courses.

Presently she came away from the window, snuffed the candle and went to bed, but, inured as she was to stifling heat and insects and the unbridled noises of the night, she could not sleep. She was lonely. The quarrels of the young seem so final and so blasting. For the first time in her life, Phoebe Titus knew what it meant to be alone.

In the morning Peter was gone upon some mission to the north. It was rumored he had gone toward, or even into, the fastnesses of the Tonto. And Carteret returned. Phoebe encountered him on Calle Real and he doffed his hat. Carteret did not lift his hat, did not tip it; he doffed it.

"Miss Phoebe!" he exclaimed. "This morning you dim the desert flowers. May I walk with you? I should esteem it a favor, a gracious condescension."

"Ye talk," she said, "like out of a book."

"My friends tell me," he said, and there was mischief in his voice, "that I was being searched for last night. It was my misfortune to be absent."

"Who searched fur ye?"

His indolent lids drooped even more insolently, and his full lip curled. "A Yankee soldier by the name of Muncie," he said.

"And he didn't find ye?"

"No."

"That," she said, "is how ye happen to be here today."

"Miss Phoebe, I've endeavored to be your friend."

"Did ye ever have a woman for a friend?" she asked.

"One," he said gaily. "She was eighty years old, and blind."

She appraised him with a long glance and spoke experimentally, "If I asked ye to ride back to Kaintucky 'n' buy cattle fur me, would ye go?"

"To the end of the world," he said largely.

"Hain't no cattle there I ever heard tell of," she said. "I said 'Kaintucky.'"

"Are you, by chance, serious?"

"I be."

"Setting a labor of Hercules for me to perform?"

"Don't know him or how he labored," Phoebe said. "If I asked ye, would ye go to Kaintucky 'n' fetch a herd of cattle?"

"I'll answer that when you ask it," he said.

"I calc'late you've answered before," she said. "I don't blame ye. It's a job fur a man."

"The population of Tucson is increasing," he said, "since the coming of the soldiers. It increased this morning," he added, in such a manner that she read significance in the announcement.

"Who come?" she asked.

"Lazarus Ward, for one. Back from Yuma, where you got him sent. Wriggled out of it some way."

"You're a-warnin' me?" she asked.

"I felt you ought to know."

"Been makin' threats, has he?"

"Not in my presence."

"I calc'late," she said sharply, "to be able to kill my own flies."

"But Lazarus may turn out to be a hornet."

"The kind," she said, "that don't sting unless he's one of a swarm."

"I am only striving, Miss Phoebe, to prove my friendship."

"Friendship," she said, "don't need no proof. It proves itself. I'm a-turnin' in here."

Abruptly she left him and entered Solomon Warner's place of business. Solomon was excited. Rumors of gold were coming in from the northwest. A man named Wickenberg was said to have made a strike. Someone else, up Hassayampa way, was said to have found a placer where nuggets lay on the surface, exposed like pebbles in a brook.

"Richer'n Californy!" he exclaimed. "It's a-comin'. Gold and silver and copper. There's where the future of this territory lays."

"Fools dig gold and wise folks bank it," said Phoebe. "When's the paymaster due? I calc'late he's gold mine enough fur me."

"Be along any day now. Lazarus Ward's back."

"So I hear."

"Don't forgit ye got friends if ye need 'em," said Solomon.
"I'm obleeged to ye," Phoebe said.

It was two weeks before the paymaster made his appearance, and then, for days and nights Tucson became one of the noisier, more dangerous corners of hell. It was vain to try to police its streets, for the soldiers themselves were a part of the shouting, fighting, spendthrift mob. In the midst of this, Peter Muncie returned. He returned with the light of laughter in his eyes.

"I said I'd allus come back to ye," he said without preamble. "I come to tell ye I'm journeyin' to Kaintucky."

"Be ye?" she asked.

"When I git my discharge. I'm a-goin' to buy cattle fur a crazy woman."

"I figgered I could rely onto ye," was all she said, and this was all the thanks or commendation he received for his willingness to undertake a task so vast, so arduous, so impossible of accomplishment as to make it worthy of the song of a great poet. "I'll have the money fur ye when you're ready to start."

"Be ye a-goin' to marry me before I go?"

She shook her head. "I hain't the kind of woman a man could leave to buy cattle, once he got her," she said.

"But when I come back?"

She was direct. "Whilst you're gone," she said, "I'll be buildin' a ranch house down the river. Solid like a fort, with a flat roof and a four-foot wall to shoot from behind. I calc'late we'll be able to keep the Injuns from stealin' our cattle."

"Our cattle?"

"I spoke plain, didn't I?" she asked.

Peter touched her hand gently, and she permitted it to stay within reach of his fingers. Gently! Somehow, that word associated itself in her mind with Peter Muncie. It was incongruous. Yet this restless, reckless, implacable Indian fighter was gentle. Something told her he always would be gentle, with almost a womanly gentleness, in his dealings with her. From him there would come no harsh word or sharp retort. Even when he left her to plunge into that adventure and danger which was necessary food for his soul, he would desert her gently, hoping it would not hurt her more than she could bear.

"It's time fur ye to be sayin' good night," she told him, and rising walked with him toward the door.

He took her in his arms for the first time, and she was acquiescent. Her face, lovely, wistful, very young and more girlish than he ever had seen it, looked up to him as he pressed his lips to her lips. For an instant she clung to him, yielding, yearning to yield all youth, all woman, all weakness and surrender. Had he realized it, he might have proclaimed himself victor then, might never have taken that journey worthy of an Odyssey to the lands east of the Mississippi. Had he pressed the advantage that he did not know was his, he might have wrung from her the promise to be his wife tomorrow.

But he did not know. The moment passed and she was her own woman again.

"I'll be makin' plans fur your journey east," she said.

CHAPTER XII

The paymaster came and Tucson wallowed knee deep in money. During this orgy of spending nobody cared if the current price of a paper of needles was seventy-five cents or a spool of thread a quarter, or a pound of coffee a dollar. High prices helped the quicker to empty pockets in which money burned. Faro dealers worked day and night and relays of bartenders served in saloons and mescal shops. Even among the poorer Mexicans, eking out a lazy existence in their miserable hovels of mesquite poles and candlewood wands chinked with adobe, there was prosperity for a day.

The Calle Real was choked with Conestoga wagons bringing flour from Sonora, with hay wagons fighting their way to the government corrals to feed great droves of horses and mules. The town was a roaring, jostling, carousing mob of soldiers, teamsters, gamblers, ragamuffins who boozed and sang and fought and spent.

That great battles were being fought beyond the distant Mississippi, that thousands upon thousands of young men were dying, fighting on the one side to preserve the Union and on the other to disrupt it, nobody seemed to care. News of these matters arrived as from a remote foreign land. Arizona had plenty of war of its own, fighting with unbelievable courage, clinging with incredible fortitude to its deserts and mountains. Her sons were of a breed not easy to understand in these clement days, nor could they have explained themselves, or why they found it necessary to seek out this most perilous of all frontiers and to cling to it with blind, grim tenacity.

Phoebe Titus was prompt to present her vouchers to the paymaster and to lock away the money received in her iron box until opportunity should come to forward it to California for safekeeping. Upwards of fifteen thousand dollars, the fruit of freighting and hayselling, was locked in that clumsy safe, waiting to be turned into California exchange and then to travel eastward with Peter Muncie to be transmuted into the first herd of respectable cattle ever to graze the alfilaria of Arizona's desert or to browse the succulent, fattening mesquite beans.

Solomon Warner cautioned her.

"All the town knows you got that money in your house," he said.

"I earned it," she answered, "and I calc'late I'm capable of keepin' it."

"Phoebe," he said earnestly, "you got too much ginger. You're gittin' the idee nothin' can happen to you. Young woman, you've had plenty luck."

"It wasn't luck," she said.

"Some wimmen are vain of their looks," he said. "But you're worse'n that and more foolish. You think you can tromple down the universe."

"A body kin do what they set their mind to," she said.

He shrugged his shoulders. "I hope ye don't git your come-uppance," he told her.

"When I do," she said out of an overweening self-confidence, "I won't come bellerin' around."

"Go your gait. A hard knock might change your ideas of yourself. A human bein' can't be God."

Phoebe took her precautions. She herself slept in the room with the safe while two of her Mexicans, armed, kept watch front and back by day and night. The town, it seemed to her, was too much preoccupied with its orgy to give thought to any such serious business as robbery.

She was preoccupied with cattle. Once she determined upon a project, she gave her whole mind to it. Hers was not a one-track mind; there were many branches, but she had the rare ability to utilize only one of them at a time, and to the exclusion of all else. Having made up her mind that she must look forward to a day when freighting would no longer be profitable and that cattle-raising was the occupation she should develop as its substitute, she threw herself headlong into the scheme. She talked, thought, slept cattle. She rode the lands that were hers down the river, giving thought to water, to drought, feed, to protection from the Indians. She discussed her plans with every man in Arizona who might have information to give on the subject of cows, breeds, hardihood.

Using her own intelligence, she found that, given food and water, success in this venture meant insuring the largest possible calf crop. To be certain of a crop of calves, what was essential? What age should the cows be that she meant to purchase and have driven more than a thousand miles to her rancho? Should they be young heifers? How many bulls should be provided to the hundred cows? How long did it require a calf to come to salable maturity? It was not so simple as raising wheat or potatoes. She knew Peter Muncie to be profoundly ignorant, and she must educate him, so far as she was able, before he set out upon his journey.

So accustomed had Phoebe become to the night clamors of Tucson that she fell asleep as soon as her head touched the pillow. Nor would any ordinary sound waken her. Songs, bellows of rage, screams, pistol shots, were as the ticking of a clock, so common as to have become inaudible. It had been a tiresome day, for she had been in the saddle since dawn, and she slept profoundly. Outside, in the corral at the rear and the street in front, two Mexicans did sentry-go. But their vigilance such as it was proved futile.

Two hours after midnight, a cavalcade of men in high-crowned, wide-brimmed hats and ornate, jungling breeches and jackets, thundered up out of the darkness. Horses reared as they were brought to a wrenching stop. There were a couple of shots, and Phoebe awakened to find her room filled with armed Mexicans, who gave her no instant to reach for the pistol that hung at the head of her bed.

Mexican bandits! Only second to the Apaches were these desperadoes from across the border. Smugglers, robbers and murderers who came marauding wherever there was booty throughout the southern reaches of the territory. By the vague moonlight that streamed through the window, Phoebe saw their brown mustached faces and glittering metallic eyes, over which no masking handkerchiefs were tied.

Phoebe sat up in bed. "Git out of here," she said sharply. But two of the men seized her, thrust a rag between her lips, tied her securely. Then, as she watched with enraged eyes, they busied themselves with her safe. To her, it seemed with practiced skill. Presently there was a muffled roar that shook the house and caused her senses to reel. When she could see again, the door of her iron box hung crazily from one hinge and the Mexicans were stuffing the contents of the safe into bags. Then they were gone. Outside there was a clatter as they remounted, and then the diminishing thunder of hoofs as they galloped away to the eastward. She listened as best she could to determine their direction, and then gave herself wholly to the futile effort to free hands and legs from the ropes that held her helpless. She wrenched and struggled, gnawing at the rag in her mouth until blood ran down her chin. At last she gave over the effort and lay as comfortably as she could manage. Nor did she struggle again.

This was like her. It was like a saying of hers: "If ye find ye can't do it, don't try. Ye jest wear yourself out."

So she ceased to wear herself out.

It was catastrophe, and Solomon Warner had been right. She had placed reliance on Mexican laborers. Next time she would know better than that. She seldom had to be taught the same lesson twice. Doubtless her Mexican sentries were dead, a just penalty for lack of watchfulness. Rage consumed her, and humiliation. She would have to listen to Solomon Warner saying, "I told ye so." Well, he had told her so, and at last she had got her comeuppance. Better than fifteen thousand dollars was galloping toward the fastnesses of Sonora.

It wasn't the fifteen thousand dollars that she regretted. In time she could amass another fifteen thousand. But it was a blow to her pride. More than that, it was a blow to her plans. Now there would be no herd of five hundred Kentucky cattle. Peter Muncie would not start upon that incredible errand to the East. Phoebe squirmed with the humiliation of it, with rage at thus being frustrated.

A half hour she lay, an hour. Apparently nobody in Tucson had noticed the entry and departure of the cavalcade of bandits. So, chafing with impatience and rage, she lay quietly, compelling herself to lie still and relax physically, husbanding her strength against the needs of tomorrow. She would pursue. Pete Kitchen had chased Mexican bandits into their own Sonora fastnesses and made reprisal. But Sonora was not at her very door, as it was at Pete Kitchen's, whose pig ranch was close to Nogales and the border. Every hour added to the difficulty of pursuit. After a time, as morning approached, it grew darker instead of lighter. It thundered. Then, to her dismay, there was a sudden downpour, one of those torrential rains that drench the desert in summer, turning dry gulches into swirling torrents for an hour, bringing renewed life to grasses, shrubs, alfilaria, mesquite, paloverde, but washing out trail and sign with a thoroughness to make pursuit a futile gesture.

For once, it seemed, everything was against her. Luck had turned upon her whom luck had taken so long for its favorite. Even this rain, which otherwise would have been so welcome, came at a time to frustrate pursuit.

"Well," she said to herself, as she compelled her body to quiet, "that's that."

But then a thought came to her and caused her brows to

knit. How, she asked herself, did bandits from Sonora know she had money in her safe? How could word have traveled there? How, in the three days since the coming of the paymaster, could any agency have carried such news a couple of hundred miles; or how, having learned of the booty, could a troop of horsemen have traversed so much of mountain and desert in that space of time? For the thing had been planned. It was no chance foray. Never before had Mexicans raided as far north as Tucson. And they had come provided with one who knew how to blow open an iron safe. Everything pointed to careful planning. She closed her eyes and let her mind gnaw upon this point.

The deluge ceased as suddenly as it had commenced, and then with daylight came wailing as Maria, Phoebe's fat Mexican woman, burst into the room.

"Manuel lies dead in the corral!" she cried. "Juan lies dead in the street!"

Then, through terror and grief, she saw Phoebe's plight, and with trembling, clumsy fingers released her from her bonds. For minutes Phoebe could not get up, but the sobbing, wailing woman rubbed her legs and wrists until the blood coursed again, and Phoebe sprang from bed, threw on her clothing, seized her Sharps rifle, and ran to the corral, where she saddled a horse and galloped toward the Army station seven miles away. Precious hours had passed; rain had come to obliterate trails. In her head she knew she was following a hopeless quest, but she rode on.

At headquarters she told her story tersely, gave such information as she had to give, and the commanding officer made the gesture, useless as both of them realized of ordering out a troop in pursuit.

As she rode away she encountered Peter Muncie and reined in her horse.

"Wa-al," she said in a harsh voice, "you hain't a-goin' to Kaintucky."

"Why not?"

"Mexican bandits," she said, "robbed my safe last night."

"The' hain't no Mexican bandits in Tucson."

He, too, apparently, saw the point; leaped to it more quickly than she had done.

"Anyhow," she said, "the money's gone."

"Be ye sure it was Mexicans?"

"I seen their faces."

"No white men?"

"Nary white man."

"It don't make sense," said Peter. "And then come the rain. Best trailer in Arizony couldn't foller after that."

"It exasperates a body," said Phoebe, in a gem of understatement.

"What's done's done," said Peter. "If I hain't a-goin' to Kaintucky, then what?"

Her eyes glinted as she looked down at him. "If I thought you was glad," she said, "I'd let you have this whip acrost your face."

"I ain't glad, Phoebe. I'm jest askin', what now."

She compressed her lips and set her jaw. "I'll tell ye what now," she said. "No Mexican bandit's a-goin' to upset me. Nothin's a-goin' to happen that wa'n't a-goin' to. You're startin' fur Kaintucky the day you git discharged."

"It takes money to buy cows," he said.

"I'll git it. I got friends. I got proppity. I've set my mind on them cattle, and I'll have 'em." She did not stop to say good-by; she stopped for nothing, but raked her mount with spurs and galloped headlong toward Tucson. Before Sol Warner's store, she flung herself from the saddle and rushed inside.

"Sol," she said, "I want fifteen thousand dollars."

"What fur?" he asked.

"I got robbed last night. Mexican bandits."

He nodded. "The story's around. Two of your men killed."

"Fifteen thousand, they got. Will ye lend it to me?"

"What fur?"

"To buy cattle."

"What cattle?"

"Back in Kaintucky."

"What you aim to do with Kaintucky cattle?"

"Drive 'em here," she said.

"You hain't jest plain crazy," he said, "you're a ravin' maniac. Drive a herd of cattle twelve-fifteen hunderd miles. Through hostile Injun country. You wouldn't git nary a pair of horns as far as Apache Pass. What hunger 'n' thirst 'n' the road didn't kill, the Injuns 'ud git."

"It can be done," she said.

"Now, you be sensible."

"It's a-goin to be done."

"Not with my money," said Solomon. "Look, Phoebe, I'm a friend of yourn. You've jest lost a sight of money. That's bad, but ye kin earn it back. But if, on top of that, ye throw away another fifteen thousand, you'd be plumb ruined."

"Hain't my wagons 'n' teams 'n' proppity wuth that much?"

"More."

"I'll mortgage 'em to ye."

"Because I'm your friend, Phoebe," he said, "I shan't do it. Fur anythin' sensible, I'd lend ye all I got, but not for no wild-goose chase."

"All right, Solomon, I won't argy with ye. You're a stubborn man. But I'll git it."

"Who of?"

"I dunno. But I'll git it. And I'll git them cows, and I'll fetch 'em here, in spite of all the tarnation Injuns in creation. Right now you're in a place to say 'I told ye so.' Wa-al, mark my words, I'll feed them cows on my ranch down the river, 'n' I'll ride in and rub your nose in 'em."

"You never was one to listen." he said glumly.

"Folks that listens when they know they're right," she said, "is jest dumb fools."

"You're a-talkin' about beef," said Solomon, "that Tucson'll never chaw on."

"I'll fetch ye the fust steak," she said, "and make ye eat it."

CHAPTER XIII

Two days later, the cavalry returned empty-handed. The little troop of marauding Mexicans had vanished, leaving no trace of their passing. Phoebe, meantime, had attempted to tap the financial resources of Tucson, meager as they were. There was no bank, and there were few individuals in the town who could command a hundred dollars, let alone fifteen thousand. Failing to get any such sum in a lump, she endeavored to borrow it piecemeal, but without success. She even considered the arduous trip to Yuma, or to Nogales to find if Pete Kitchen had available funds. But assistance came from a source to which she had not looked, and to which she might not have applied.

Bob Crandall, proprietor of a gambling house whose doors never closed and where faro and *chusas* games entertained and mulcted the citizenry, presented himself at Phoebe's door. Crandall was one of the handsomest men ever to appear in the Southwest, a man of family and education and of courtly manners. Where he came from was known to none, nor what had excluded him from the life to which he was accustomed. Perhaps it was choice.

"Miss Phoebe," he said, "I hope I do not intrude. I heard with profound regret of your recent misfortune."

"Spilt milk," said Phoebe.

"It has also come to my ears, and if you think me meddle-some I crave your pardon, that you desire to borrow a certain sum of money."

"I been tryin' to borrow fifteen thousand dollars," Phoebe said.

"Offering, as I understand, for security your freighting equipment and ranch land."

"Yes."

"I have some surplus funds," he said. "I would prefer to loan them upon such security rather than to send them to banks in San Francisco."

"You mean you got fifteen thousand that you want to lend me?"

"That was my meaning."

"Faro," she said, "must pay better'n I guessed."

"It does right well," he admitted.

Somewhere deep in Phoebe's mind a warning bell sounded, but she was in no mood to listen. Crandall was a gambler, associating with the riffraff of the border. But against him personally she had heard no complaints. It was said that he ran a square game. She hesitated. Some instinct, implanted in her childhood, doubtless, urged her against the acceptance of money come by in such a way. But she stifled that inhibition. Money was money. Business was business. What matter who offered money or how it had been come by, when she needed it for a legitimate purpose? She did not argue with herself for many seconds.

"I take it kindly of ye, Crandall," she said.

"You will want the money at once?"

"Soon's I kin git it," she said. "But how about the papers? There'll have to be papers. Hain't nary lawyer here."

"I think I can write them out," said Crandall, "sufficiently well to make them legal."

"I'll be obleeged to ye," she said.

"It is I who should be grateful to find so safe a place to put my money," Crandall said in his courtly manner. "May I call this evening with the document?"

"I'll be waitin'," she said.

That night Phoebe slept in the room with fifteen thousand dollars in cash, but this time she did not neglect precautions. It would be for but one night, because tomorrow a wagon train was setting out for Yuma and the funds could be trusted to the express in return for San Francisco exchange. In return for the money, she had given Crandall a signed paper, crude, but nonetheless effective, pledging to him all property, real and personal, in lands, wagons, implements and animals, of which she was possessed.

Peter Muncie rode in from camp in the morning, drawing rein before her door and calling out to her gaily before he entered the house:

"Hey, Phoebe. Come look at me. I'm a free man."

"Got your discharge?" she asked.

"And ready for a new enlistment, general."

"Ye look sound in wind and limb," she said. "Peter, I got my money. Ye kin start for Kaintucky."

"Ye got the money!" For an instant the gaiety in his eyes was quenched by disappointment. "Where'd ye git it?"

"Off of Bob Crandall."

His eyes narrowed. "Bob Crandall, eh? How come ye to go to him?"

"He come to me."

"Come 'n' offered ye fifteen thousand dollars?"

"And I took it," she said. "It's money, hain't it?"

"I reckon so. But I'm a-wonderin' where Crandall got it."

"Gamblin'."

Peter shook his head. "Mebby so. But if that thar one-hoss gamblin' outfit of hisn ever got that much ahead, then I'm a Chinaman."

"Anyhow," she said, "he had it and I got it."

Peter's eyes were slits in his angular, bronzed face. "He come to you, eh? Jest walked up and offered ye the money?"

"Yes."

"Ever had any dealin's with him?"

"Nary. Hain't hardly ever spoke to the man."

"Know he's a pardner of Lazarus Ward? Know them two is thick as thieves?"

"I've seen them together," she admitted.

"Yeah. Them two and that thar Carteret."

The warning bell was ringing again in her head, but now it was too late to heed it. Even had it not been too late, she would have ignored it in her stubbornness.

"And," he asked, "ye git back a mortgage?"

"To be sure."

Peter was suspicious of mortgages and of any other legal documents for their own sake. He was suspicious of this one because of the peculiarities that surrounded its making.

"Wa-al," he said, "I reckon you know your own business,

but if this here dicker don't stink of skunk, then I hain't got a nose on my face."

"You fetch back my cattle," she said, "and I don't care how many skunks the' is around."

"It don't make no difference to me," he said, with a shrug of his broad shoulders, "only I don't want to see you thwarted. I'll git you them cattle if cattle's to be had, but it goes agin me to leave you here alone."

"I was alone before you come and I done all right," she said.

"Peter," she commenced, and hesitated, for displays of emotion, of any softness, were difficult for her to make, "I don't calc'late to ever be able to make you see things my way, any more'n I'll ever be able to see 'em your'n." She came close to him as he stood, feet firmly set upon her adamantine floor hard packed of mud mixed with the blood of cattle and cactus juice and put a slender, capable brown hand on each of his shoulders. So she stood for an interval looking up into his brown eyes, and then she drew his head downward until she could reach his lips. "There," she said presently, "is suthin' we can allus agree on."

He was moved, shaken by the fire, the tenderness, the passion of her kiss, by its promise of surrender, by its utter, unquenchable womanliness. It was the first time she ever had come to him with a caress, and it elated him.

Out of a dry throat he said, "Ye hain't all money, be ye?" And then, after a pause during which his mind and his heart were lost in contemplation of it: "So ye do love me?"

"So hard," she said, "I could die at the sight of ye leavin' me."

"And the' hain't nobuddy else? That Carteret feller?"

"Before you come," she said, "there wa'n't nobuddy. After ye go, there won't be nobuddy. I hain't got but one love to give, Peter and you got it, lock, stock 'n' barrel."

"I reckon nothin' can come betwixt us," he said, perhaps only then recognizing the greatness and the sweep of the tie that bound them together. "I reckon we're like them folks I seen in a play-actin', where nothin' could keep 'em apart but dyin', and dyin' wa'n't so bad if they could do it together."

She held his face in the cup of her hands, knowing well that this was a precious moment, a high moment, that might never again revisit them in all its beauty. She wanted to hold it, to lengthen it, to taste it to its full.

"Peter," she said wistfully, "I hain't very big, and you're mighty strong. D'ye calc'late ye could lift me up in your arms like I was a baby, and kind of hold me that way? And keep your mouth shet."

So he lifted her gently, and held her close, with her head upon his shoulder and her crisp hair unforgettably against his ear; and she clung to him, not as a woman who desired, but as a child who was comforted. Nor did either of them speak until she signified that he was to set her down again.

"I calc'late," she said softly, "there is a heaven. Now skedaddle out of here."

"The's a troop ridin' to Fort Stockton the day after tomorrow," he said as he stepped out into the night. "I'll be goin' with them."

"Ride fast, Peter," she said, "and ride fast back again."

"As fast as cattle kin be drove," he said.

It was on a Thursday and the month was October when Peter Muncie rode away to the eastward on that journey that would wind its way through Apache Pass, across New Mexico, veering upward through Texas and the country of the Comanches, following the route of the Southern Overland Trail until it should, in good time, bring him to Independence in Missouri. A part of the way he would have company. A part of that incredible ride he would make alone. He would traverse thirsty deserts, grim mountains, vast plains, on a shopping trip at the behest of a girl he loved. He was running an errand, going to the store for a spool of thread, but the store was more than a thousand miles away, and the thread, when he should obtain it, was alive, hungry, thirsty, and coveted by every savage Indian through whose territory it should pass. An errand to the store for five hundred cattle who must be driven, watered, fed and protected on the passage over half a continent. Yet neither of them regarded it as incredible, or as a task beyond human capacity to master.

Peter kissed Phoebe and rode away, and she rode back to Tucson from the camp, and knew, perhaps for the first time in her sturdy young life, the meaning of heartsickness and aching loneliness.

As she came close to the edge of the village, passing through a huddle of Mexican shanties of chinked candlewood, with only stretched oxhide for doors, she encountered Jefferson Carteret, and knew that he had been waiting for her.

"He's gone," Carteret said.

"Yes."

"And you trusted him with fifteen thousand dollars!" He laughed, and his lazy lids half covered his insolent eyes.

"I'd trust him with a million 'fore I'd trust you with a dime," she retorted.

"And yet," he said, "I'm your friend. I fancy I have done more for you than he will ever do. He couldn't have gone without my help. But then, I wanted to see him go, and it was worth the money."

"What money?"

"Fifteen thousand dollars," he said.

"What you got to do with fifteen thousand?" she asked.

"I sent it to you by Crandall. You didn't think Crandall had that much, did you?"

"Neither did I think you had it," she said.

"The remains of my fortune," he said lightly, "but yours had it been ten times as much."

"If Peter Muncie knew you done this," she said, "he'd 'a' killed ye."

"I have every hope the Comanches or Apaches will do as much for him," he said.

"What you expect to gain by it?" she asked.

"You," he said.

"You'll git paid back, every cent."

"Perhaps that won't be necessary, Miss Phoebe. There can be no debt between husband and wife."

Phoebe's fingers itched as they clutched the handle of her whip, but she did not flick the lash across his aristocratic, handsome, insolent face. She was thinking, weighing facts, estimating their importance and their effect. She was wondering if Peter Muncie would believe her when she told him she did not know this money came from Jefferson Carteret. She was wondering what would be the outcome of a duel between her lover and this young man. For somehow she knew that such a meeting would be inevitable. She was marshaling such facts as were in her possession, and standing them side by side; and she did not like them as they stood in array, for they made her seem a dupe.

"So you had fifteen thousand?" she stated more than asked.

"I had it."

"It wa'n't Lazarus Ward's?"

"He had been using some of it, but he paid it back."

"So Ward's in it, too."

"This is between you and myself, Miss Phoebe."

Then her facts added up. They made a sum, and the sight of the thing to which they added up staggered and humiliated her. She raked her horse with spurs, and Carteret remained upon his horse, lips twisted in an ironical smile, with dust swirling about his head which her mount had spurned from the roadway. She galloped headlong to Sol Warner's store and threw herself from the saddle. Solomon stood behind his counter.

"Sol," she said, "I jest wanted ye to see a dum fool."

"What ye done naow?" he asked.

"I can't prove it on him. Mebby I never kin. But, Sol, I jest borrowed, and mortgaged my proppity to do it, fifteen thousand of my own money."

"What say?"

"I jest borrowed the fifteen thousand that was robbed out of my safe," she said.

CHAPTER XIV

GENERAL CARLETON's famous order to spare no male Indian but to take captives women and children had been promulgated, giving satisfaction to inhabitants of the territory who hated the Apaches somewhat more than they did diamond-back rattlers. On both sides the war was carried on with a ruthlessness unbelievable—unbelievable especially of men of civilized race and white skin. The infamous Pinole Treaty was perpetrated in the early winter of '64—an affair characterized also as The Massacre of Bloody Tanks. Of this example of white man's superiority the Tonto Apaches were victims. This occurred some seventy miles northeast of the Pima villages where a renegade Apache named Jack induced some thirty leading men of the Apaches to come down from the surrounding hills for council, promising peace and gifts. It has been denied by historians but upon slender authority, that pinole was distributed to the Indians—pinole treated with strychnine, and that two score deaths resulted. At any rate, poison or no, the Tontos under agreement of truce were butchered to a man.

So pacification proceeded and Arizona was made more safe

for ranchers, miners, and prospectors. The aim of the white man's war was not pacification but extermination.

Phoebe Titus, following Peter Muncie's departure for the East, threw herself into the labor of developing her ranches down the river. She selected a spot for the hacienda on a shoulder of rock jutting out into the bottom lands and overlooking an area of rich soil between mountain and mountain, between canyon mouth and canyon mouth, that contained some four or five acres of land. This was to be the home ranch, the farm. Cattle, when they should arrive, were to graze on the desert and the hills, watched and tended by Mexican *vaqueros*, fattening on alfilaria and mesquite beans and grasses of infinite variety.

There was constant flow of water down the rock-studded river bed, though in the dry months it shrank to a rill. The former owners had made primitive efforts at irrigation, throwing out two moles of rock and sand into the river to form pools at either side, feeding a couple of primitive ditches, one leading through the acres on the right bank of the stream, the other through the acres on the left.

While Mexican laborers patted out adobe blocks for the walls of the house, others improved the breakwaters and widened the irrigation trenches, so that Phoebe might look forward to almost a section of rich land, abundantly watered, and capable of raising any crop her heart desired.

Though Phoebe had not sought beauty, she had found it. She could stand upon the eminence before the rising walls of the home that was to be hers and Peter Muncie's and look across the jumble of rocks that were the river bed to white cathedral shapes, wind carved, to mesas green with cacti and paloverde and mesquite greener and more luxuriant where springs oozed miraculously from the imperishable masonry of the mountainsides. There was glamour there, rude, bewildering, frightening beauty.

There was no kinship with the wooded slopes of lovely New England, nor with the lush, level farmlands of the Illinois prairies. It was another world. The one was small, restful, quieting, solacing; but this beauty of Arizona's outposts was huge, overpowering in its majesty, threatening, disturbing. Here was no peace or promise of peace. It seemed to say, "Who dares dwell here must have iron in his soul." It was the beauty of tragedy. But one could not feast his eyes upon it, sense its challenge, and ever again be content elsewhere upon the face of the earth. New England, Pennsylvania, Ohio—these were poems, pastoral poems, soothing and lovely. Arizona was a huge melodrama conceived by the hand and brain of a ruthless master.

Each man, as he worked the adobe into bricks or as he plied pick or shovel, kept one eye upon his task and one eye upon his rifle. Vigilance during every second of day or night was the price of life. Every rock, every clump of bushes, every arroyo might conceal a blood-lusty Apache.

It was a curious home-building, an eccentric striving for domesticity and that peace which all men and women must hope will spring from marriage. The whole plan was a negation of peace, an invitation to war. It was a gauntlet thrown at the feet of the Apaches. It was more fortress than dwelling, for, as the reddish walls mounted above the roof in a breastwork, Phoebe had them pierced with holes through which the defenders might fire down upon the attackers. And, once she was established there, a sentry's feet would tread that roof by day and by night, ready to give instantaneous alarm at the approach of the tribesmen from the Chiricahuas.

Yet to Phoebe it represented a home. It was there she would live with Peter Muncie. It was there their love would come to fruition, there her children would be born, for it did not even occur to her mind that there would not be children. Those were days when marriage meant children, and when children were welcome. But it was a woman of no ordinary quality who could contemplate giving birth and rearing babies on such a spot, under such a threat where she must hold her feeding child to her breast with one hand while a firearm lay within easy reach of the other hand. It did not occur to Phoebe that this was unusual, or admirable, or astonishing. It simply was what she meant to do; it was life as she chose to live it.

November and December had passed with no word from Peter, but she had expected none. She could only guess how long it would require for him to reach Independence and civilization, if he reached that objective at all. She could not estimate how much time would be consumed in traveling to Illinois or Kentucky, or how much the war would delay his comings and goings. She was not so sanguine as to hope that it would be a matter of a day to find and purchase a herd of five hundred cattle. But she hoped. She hoped that two months might find him back again in Independence with his charges, ready to join with some California bound wagon train. After that it was a matter of luck how long it would be before he appeared at Tucson at the head of his herd.

Her business was to have all in readiness for him. House,

farm, corrals, crops planted, rude, handmade furniture in place to welcome his arrival.

Frequently she found it necessary to ride into Tucson, which was restive under the coming of the law, but more especially under that unpleasant but always present companion of the law known as taxes. General Carleton had ordained a tax of five dollars a month upon all merchants, a hundred dollars a month upon all bars, but sales of forage, subsistence stores, fruits and vegetables to the Army were exempt. But Tucson did its best to get its own back. Old Bill Bowers sold a single load of barley ten times to the quartermaster by the simple expedient of having it weighed, heading for the government corral half a mile away, but making a detour back to town to have the same load weighed and paid for once more. He disappeared and never was heard of again. At a camp near Maricopa the soldiers built a stone corral out of rocks that were delivered and weighed in with the hay, but though Phoebe joined Arizona in laughing at these practices, she had no part in them. Her hay wagons were loaded with hay alone. She had no scruples against demanding any price her services or wares would bring, but having agreed upon the price, she made exact and honest delivery.

"I calc'late," she said, "I own a part of this here govamint. It hain't sense to cheat myself."

This saying was uttered in Solomon Warner's store and in the presence of Lazarus Ward, who sneered.

"If I owed fifteen thousand dollars," he said, "I figger I'd git it as quick as I could, and any way I could."

"What're quartermasters for," asked Jefferson Carteret genially, "if not to be cheated? They do enough robbing them-selves."

Phoebe disregarded Carteret, but spoke directly to Ward.

"Suppose I owe fifteen thousand," she said, clipping her words, "what's it to you?"

"Nothin' at the minnit," said Ward.

"What news from your cattle?" Carteret asked.

"They'll be startin' before now."

"You had word? A letter come through?"

"No."

"Then how can you be certain they are on their way?"

"I know the man I sent for them," she said.

"You'll never see hide nor hair of them cows, nor the feller ye sent fur them," said Ward. "Nor of the money neither."

Phoebe eyed him as if he were unclean. "You hain't able to understand a man that don't give a darn for money, be ye?"

"Never was one," Ward said.

"There's one," said Phoebe. "If he's alive he'll turn up with them cows." She paused and stared at him. "And if he hain't alive, it won't be on account of Injuns. It'll be because he was waylaid."

"Meanin' what?" growled Ward.

"Jest what you think I meant," said Phoebe.

"If you wa'n't a woman," he blustered.

"It won't be long," she said, "before I have a man willin' to answer fur whatever I say. And mebby to ask questions I hain't had time to ask."

"May I ask, Miss Phoebe, what questions you would like to have answered?" Carteret wanted to know.

"If the time ever comes for askin' 'em," she said, "they'll be asked emphatic."

"You're hintin' at suthin, Phoebe," said Solomon Warner. "A man wouldn't dast to hint. Fust time ever I heard ye makin' stock of bein' a woman. If ye got anythin' to say, why don't ye come out and say it? You got plenty friends."

For once, in the irritation aroused in her by the assumption of these men that Peter Muncie had absconded, she had allowed her tongue to wag too freely. But she was not one to draw back, let the consequences be what they would. She could not retract what she had said nor withdraw her unwise, veiled accusation.

"Fur once," she said, "I wish I was a man."

"You claim," said Carteret softly, "that you have a man to answer for what you say. That should content everybody. If I am affronted, you supply someone from whom I can demand satisfaction."

"And who'll give it," said Phoebe grimly. She sensed a certain fatality in it all, an inevitability. She had a strange feeling of being not a deliberately acting human being but as if she were an agent speaking as some superior directed her, a puppet moved by strings held in invisible fingers.

"We're listenin'," said Lazarus Ward.

"I've concluded," said Phoebe, "that a body that borrows her own money is a tarnation fool."

"That isn't precisely clear, Miss Phoebe. Will you enlarge upon it?"

"None of ye," said Phoebe, "that lent me that money had it to lend not till after my safe was robbed."

Ward stood tense, the fingers of his right hand spread

stiffly. Carteret's eyelids drooped still farther, and spots of white appeared at the corners of his handsome mouth. Neither spoke.

"You hadn't ought to of said that, Phoebe," said Sol Warner.

She was well aware that she should not have said it, but it had, nevertheless, been put into words, and the words could never be recalled. They were an open challenge. Here was no mere subject matter for a suit for slander. Men in Arizona did not resent accusations in the courts, and honesty was demonstrated rather by revolver shots than by sword witnesses.

"Mebby you got proofs," said Ward in a half whisper.

"Mebby I have," said Phoebe.

"I guess I'll be gittin' along," Ward said harshly. "Comin', Jeff?"

Carteret lingered a moment, smiling crookedly. "Supposing what you say is true?" he asked.

"Hush your mouth," snarled Ward.

"I talk where I please and when I please," Carteret retorted arrogantly. Then he shrugged his shoulders. "But, on reflection, I perceive I have nothing to say."

The pair walked out into the Calle Real; Solomon Warner leaned against his counter and clucked. "Wa-al," he said, "ye kind of made a mess of things."

"A body's bound to, once in a while," she said, and herself mounted her horse, and followed by a pack mule carrying supplies, set out upon the road to the rancho.

As she rode along slowly through the spring sunshine, accompanied by two Mexicans, she reflected, and having reflected she shrugged her shoulders. The thing was done. Matters had been brought to a head—but some other thing would have brought them to a head if this had not. There was destiny in it, inevitably.

A part of her way led past Papago farms and villages, and she reined in her horse to stare. Cattle with disgruntled expressions stood erect, not browsing nor grazing. For some reason they would not eat. One of her Mexicans pointed down to the alfilaria that was pushing its leaves through the soil of the desert making a carpet of green as far as the eye could reach. Then Phoebe understood the distaste of the cattle for food, for the alfilaria was covered with worms—large, green worms. But if these did not excite the appetite of the cattle it was otherwise with the Indians, men, women and children, who were roaming about, picking the worms as if they had been strawberries and eating them—and the young girls, when they had eaten their fill, strung living, wriggling worms upon fibers and put them about their necks as necklaces. It was a gala, a sort of holiday. Phoebe's stomach revolted, but she concealed her aversion and rode along, exchanging greetings with the friendly aborigines.

"A lot depends on how you was raised," she said aloud.

She rode along southward, disturbed only by forebodings. It was an hour past noon when she and her companions descended a broken, mesquite-studded slope toward the river. Another hundred yards would bring them to a shoulder of the mountain, and then a mile down the waterway lay the ranch. Their mounts took to the water, pausing to drink long of the cold, clear water. Suddenly a horse lifted his head and pricked his ears. There came faintly the sound of a shot, then a scattering of shots. Phoebe slashed her horse with the spurs and plunged over rocks and gravel to a more secure footing on the earth above. The shots came from the ranch, and shots from the ranch could mean only an attack by Apaches.

Followed by her Mexicans, she urged on her mount. Now shrill, savage cries reached her ears. She veered to the left and forced her horse up a steep incline, so that she might come in toward the ranch house from higher land at the rear. From her parapet roof a brisk fire was being maintained by the defenders, but then she saw that the attack was not directed against the house itself but against the corral. As her eyes took in the scene, she saw savage horsemen drive half a hundred head of stock into the open and stampede them down the valley. Phoebe halted, threw her heavy Sharps rifle to her shoulder and fired. Her Mexicans yelled and fired. The Indians, waving rifles and bows defiantly, galloped down the valley. Phoebe fired again and saw an Apache fall from his horse. Then Indians and stock disappeared from view in a rolling cloud of dust.

CHAPTER XV

PHOEBE, raging, spurred down the hillside past the ranch house. On the bottom land she found herself alone. The Mexicans had no stomach for pursuing half a hundred Apaches. At the wrecked corral she stopped, realizing that to pursue was futile, for there were no horses, no mules. As she sat her saddle, furious at the depredation, furious at her hands for lack of vigilance or cowardice, the men left the safety of adobe walls above and came down to her. But they might better have remained in hiding, for she gave them the edge of her tongue in short biting sentences, so that they squirmed and wriggled and called falteringly upon favorite saints to witness that they were men and had done their best.

It was not alone the loss of close to fifty head of stock which, in the present state of her affairs, was no light thing. It was the reflection that she had not been able to defend her property; that the Indians had the best of her. It was galling to her pride.

Remembering suddenly the Indian who had fallen under her rifle, she rode along the valley. There he lay in the midst of a thicket. Not dead, for she could see the heaving of his chest.

He was naked, save for high moccasins with upturned toes, a cloth about his middle, a band about his straight black hair. His body was daubed with vermilion and ocher and ashes. He seemed to have been shot through the thigh, and at every throb of his heart, blood spurted from the wound. She frowned down upon him. Even through the war paint it was apparent that he was very young. One of her Mexicans rode up, stared down at the prostrate savage and leaped from his saddle. He raised his rifle as if it had been a plunger, to crush the wounded boy's skull with its butt.

"Stop it!" Phoebe commanded.

Just why she was moved to mercy she could not have explained. The young Apache was a thief, a member of a band of thieves and murderers. Had their places been reversed, he would have shown no forbearance. But he lay there so young and so helpless, and, after all, Phoebe was a woman.

"He's just a boy," she said.

"Boys become men," said the Mexican.

She tossed down a strap. "Tie this tightly about his leg above the wound. Lest he die of the bleeding."

"He is an Apache," replied the Mexican.

"Nevertheless, tie the leg," she commanded.

Scowling, reluctant, the *vaquero* obeyed. Phoebe watched to see that the task was performed as it should be performed. "You, Juan, lay him across the horse. It is a command."

Not gently, they lifted him and flung him head downward across the saddle. Phoebe took the reins in her hand and led the horse back to the hacienda.

"Now what in tunket be I doin' this fur?" she asked herself.

At the door she compelled her Mexicans to lift down the

young savage and carry him inside, motioning to a bed, upon which they placed him.

"It is against God to save the life of this vermin," said Manuel.

"I calc'late God told ye so," said Phoebe in English. Then, in their own tongue, "Make water to boil."

"Would the *Señorita* give succor to the lizard whose bite is death?"

"Scat!" Phoebe said peremptorily.

"It will call down evil fortune on this house."

Nevertheless, muttering and scowling, Manuel obeyed. Phoebe poured mescal between the teeth of the Indian youth, and he opened eyes of lustrous black, which fixed themselves upon her in a winkless stare. He did not flinch as she washed the paint from his face, making his lack of years more apparent. A fine brow arose above the black eyes, and a straight nose separated them. It was a face that might become notable; even now, before years and experience gave them character, there was promise of dignity and intelligence.

"Jest hold still," Phoebe said, "and I'll fix ye up the best I can."

The boy did not flinch or moan as she did what must be done. It was unaccustomed work, grisly work, but Phoebe went about it as she would have gone about any other necessary task without shrinking and with sure fingers. Before she succeeded in extracting the slug, the boy was unconscious again.

"That's the best I know how to do," she said, when she was finished. "And listen, you, and you, and you. It is a guest in the house. Am I understood?"

"You are understood; but he will arise in the night and cut our throats."

"It'll be several nights," Phoebe told them, "before he gits up any interest in massacres. I must ride to Tucson. There has been a loss because of your cowardice and lack of vigilance. Many head of stock have been stolen. When I come back, if that boy has not been dealt with as you would deal with your own son, there will be backs cut to ribbons with the lash."

It was necessary to replenish the stock that had been stolen by the Indians, a severe loss at any time, but now, when Phoebe found herself in debt for a large sum, it was a calamity. She waited only for nightfall and rode out on the return to Tucson, taking, as was her custom, a different way from the one she had ridden on her journey to the ranch. It was unwise to ride the same trail twice or to form other habits which might become known to the Apaches or to possible Mexican bandits. Constant vigilance and never-ending adroitness were the price of continuing to live.

She arrived in Tucson before midnight. The town, which had been increasing in population since the coming of the Army, was as wide awake as it had been at noon. A troupe of Mexican acrobats were performing tricks on a rope in the square; gambling houses were crowded and noisy, and the stench from a dead burro whose carcass had been allowed to remain where it had fallen in the street made the night unpleasant. Mangy dogs barked at the heels of her horse as she rode to her house—the only white woman in that little city.

As she opened her door, Estevan Ochoa sidled out of the darkness.

"Happy the eyes that gaze upon thee *Señorita*," he said in his soft, youthful voice.

"My house is your house," she answered politely. "Enter."

"There is much talk of gold in the gambling houses and the mescal shops," he said.

"There is always talk of gold," said Phoebe.

"But now it increases. There is in the city a bearded one with lumps of it as great as the eggs of birds. He makes himself drunken and talks of nuggets to be picked like berries. From the north he comes, having been in that place that bears the name of Yavapai, where is a river named the Hassayampa."

"I have heard," she said without interest.

"There is more to tell. There was also talk of a man named Wickenburg, and of the famous hunter whose name is Pauline Weaver, and how they have found much gold. It is said that men gather nuggets to the value of a hundred thousand pesos in two short months."

"How does this affect you and me, Estevan?"

"It is news, *Señorita,* because the enemies of the *Señorita* listen with eyes that bulge and ears that quiver. They speak to each other with lip to ear, but the ears of Estevan are sharp. These two men make ready to go to the Hassayampa River."

"You mean Carteret and Lazarus Ward are going gold hunting?"

"It is so."

"Your news is welcome," Phoebe said.

It was welcome news, for it was not a matter of a few days to go prospecting in that distant region a couple of hundred miles to the northwestward. It would take them away from Tucson at a time when their absence would be very welcome to her. For Peter Muncie, if he came at all, should be coming at any hour. It meant that they would be absent when he came and that the moment of encounter between them would be postponed. And in those days a few months of postponement might mean anything. It also gave Phoebe breathing time. She would not have to be on her guard against them, watching them vigilantly to guard herself and her property.

"Go thou with God," she said. "One friend is better than great wealth."

Carteret and Ward outfitted at Solomon Warner's store, and Phoebe witnessed their departure, pack mules laden. Ward only scowled at her, but Carteret swept his hat from his head in salute and moved his horse nearer to where she stood.

"Behold the Argonauts," he said. "We go to seek the Golden Fleece."

"If you 'n' Ward," she said, "are goin' up to the placers, the miners better sleep on their claims."

He smiled lazily. "It's a relief to you, no doubt. Perhaps you even hope we will not come back? But we will come back, Miss Phoebe. We have a little matter of business to attend to in Tucson, and you may be assured we will give it our best attention. But we are thoughtful. You might say we are even tactful."

She made no reply, for she guessed that he wished her to make some reply.

"You see," he said, after a pause, "Muncie might come back. There is a remote chance of it. So we go away considerately in order that you may know the joys of a honeymoon. By the time we return, the blissful weeks will have ended and you will not miss him so greatly."

"It's the braggin' rooster that goes into the pot," she said, but for all that, she was relieved to see the backs of them as they rode out of town and plodded toward the gap in the hills on the road that led to the Pima villages and thence to the Salt River and the Hassayampa.

"I dunno," she said to Solomon, "that I ever wished the Apaches luck before."

The year was turning into April. Since he had ridden away in November there had been no word, no letter, no message from Peter Muncie. There was no way to tell if he were alive or dead: if he had succeeded in finding cattle and herding them to Independence; if he had started with them from remote Kansas to traverse the thousand miles between civilization and Tucson. There was no way by which news could come to her that he had passed the country of the Comanches, or the tribesmen of the dead Mangus Colorado. There were pictures she did not like to paint in her mind—pictures of Peter Muncie, young, straight, reckless with that look of tolerant amusement in his fine eyes. Pictures of that same Peter—a heap of rags and bones lying on some wind swept desert—what was left of him when savages and vultures had done their work. Sometimes she tried to figure the chances, but there was no gambler so skillful as to be able to lay odds. There were times when she almost regretted that she had sent him; when she knew that if he did not return, his death would be upon her threshold. She knew that she would have deprived herself of the one, the most precious thing that life had to offer her—and that she had done it in the hope of gain. But she knew also that if time could be turned backward she would do it again. She envied the Mexicans and their religion; she envied their simple faith that could call upon beloved saints and burn candles in the hope of Divine intercession.

"If he comes back," Phoebe said to herself often in the nighttime, "I'll never send him away again."

But even as she said it she knew that if occasion should arise, she would send him away again exactly as she had done before. She was vaguely aware that she was driven; that there resided in her some force which she could not control that compelled her. And she knew that Peter was aware of it and amused by it. It did not amuse Phoebe. She was sometimes a little afraid of it.

She asked herself the question that millions of struggling human atoms have asked since consciousness became an attribute of man.

"What's a body alive for? What makes a body do this and that?"

But that night, on the very night that followed the departure of Ward and Carteret for the Yavapai district, a scout came riding in from the East.

"Wagon train camped at Dragoon Springs last night," he reported.

"Big train?" asked Warner.

"Fifteen—eighteen wagons," said the scout, "and a hell of a herd of stock."

"Cattle?" asked Phoebe. "How many?"

"My guess 'ud be five—six hunderd."

"They'll be leavin' Dragoon Springs this mornin'."

"They was plannin' to."

"Goin' the gait they travel," Phoebe said, "they'll make one more camp."

"Likely."

"Them must be your cattle, Phoebe," said Warner, and then he asked the question that Phoebe, somehow, could not force herself to ask, "Was Peter Muncie in charge of them cows?"

"Dunno. I come through in a hurry."

"I'm a-ridin' out to see," said Phoebe.

"Come mornin'," said Solomon. "Not before. Not if I have to tie ye."

She looked at him oddly, with leveled brows. "What d'ye think could harm me now?" she asked.

But they prevailed upon her, held her impatience in check until dawn, but with the rising sun she was urging her horse eastward along that trail that had been drenched with blood, that had seen massacres, herculean labors, impossible escapes. She galloped along the old Butterfield Southern Overland way, of which it had been said that Butterfield's greatest economy was paying his stage drivers a *hundred and twenty-five dollars a month*. Because so few of them ever lived to collect a month's wages.

And presently, where the rugged mountains broke away to the level of the desert, a cloud became visible—not a cloud in the heavens but a cloud arising from the earth. A thousand hoofs shuffling in the soil of the desert made a great blur in the distance. Phoebe spurred her pony.

And then she saw the array. Spread for half a mile across the desert, glamorous as the advance of a vanguard of Egyptian chariots in battle, came the jolting, swaying clattering

Conestoga wagons, not in line, one behind the other, but spread fanwise. Even after traversing half a continent, the wheels still showed blue and the great boat bodies crimson. Dirty canvas stretched over hoops of wood showed gleaming white in the sunlight. Beneath rear axles swayed buckets of coals and of tar with which to grease complaining wheels. High at bow and stern, these wagons, identical in breed with those which had accompanied Braddock to his hour of defeat, surged forward to the conquest of a continent. If America had done nothing else for human progress for the stretching out of civilization, than the invention of the Conestoga wagon and the Concord State she would have done her fair share.

Then, behind the wagons, straggling in a reddish mass, came cattle, hundreds of cattle. And through the clear air, far to north and south, in mountain fastnesses arose columns of smoke, the signals that betrayed the presence of watchful, covetous, savage eyes.

Phoebe reached the foremost wagon and reined up beside the bearded, ragged man who rode his mare beside the yoked oxen.

"Where's Muncie?" she asked shortly.

"Back thar," he said, jerking a thumb over his shoulder and pushing back a black, wide-awake hat to mop his brow.

"Back thar," he had said. Phoebe could have sung the words. He was there. He was alive. Savagely she raked her pony's flanks and gripped him between her knees as she lunged forward headlong, and her heart was singing such a song as it never before had sung. She had known hunger of the body before, but never hunger of the eyes. And she murmured his name again and again and again as she raced to find him.

Her whole being throbbed. Her whole soul quivered with eagerness. Somewhere in her mind was a picture of loveliness; a vague, shimmering, incoherent picture of the moment of meeting again with her man. It was to be a whirlwind of rapture. The world would cease to exist save for them alone. She could feel his arms; she could feel her own tears. How utterly she would make him aware of her love and of her surrender!

"Here's your cows," he said.

"How many'd ye lose?" she asked.

"Started with five hunderd 'n' thutty-one," he said. "Got here with five hunderd 'n' six."

This was the great moment. What was happening to it? Where was the glory and the beauty? It was in her heart, she knew. It was in his heart. But it would not come to the surface and make itself theirs to use.

"They're consid'able ga'nted up," she observed.

"I've seen wuss," he said, with the amusement deepening in his eyes.

"We better keep a-movin'," she said, "if we calc'late to git home tonight."

Somehow she knew that he was humoring her, laughing gently at her. Something told her that he understood and he was amused.

"Laugh, darn ye," she said happily. "Go on and laugh till ye dum nigh split."

CHAPTER XVI

PETER MUNCIE and Phoebe Titus were alone, facing each other in the little room of her adobe house upon the Plaza de la Mesilla. After five months of separation, they were together once more, and with thick walls hiding them from curious eyes.

"Well, Phoebe?" asked Peter.

"What bargains I make I stand by," she said.

"I was plumb embarrassed," he said, "when ye made sich a fuss over me in front of all them cattle."

"I was makin' plenty of fuss inside of me," she said.

"Ye was glad to see me back again," he asked, "outside of me fetchin' them cows?"

"Peter," she said, and went to him and reached her strong, slender brown hands upward to touch his unshaven cheeks, "I was like to bust with the joy of it."

Presently he released her and stood looking down at her with that quizzical glow in his eyes. "I reckon ye be able to git your attention off of cows if ye set your mind to it," he said. "I didn't know but you'd kept yourself pent up so long you couldn't let loose if ye wanted to."

"I got our house ready for us down to the ranch," she said.

"So ye was thinkin' of me some?"

"Hadn't ye rather be showed than told?" she asked.

"Seems as if I could do with a little of both."

"You'll git what you're entitled to," she said, "and now shet your mouth while I tell ye how I talked us into a mess."

"Us?"

"You more'n me," she said. "They riled me. A body that talks when she's riled is a dumb fool."

"Who got crossways of ye, and what did ye say?"

"Carteret 'n' Ward. They let on I'd never see you nor my money ag'in. So I up 'n' busted out at 'em 'n' said it was prob'ly my own money I borrowed off'n them."

"It was them lent you the money?" His mouth was suddenly grim. "You said it was that gambler feller."

"I thought so. But it turned out to be them. So then the fat was in the fire. I as good as accused 'em of stealin' my money before Sol Warner 'n' others. They said I wouldn't dast to say it if I was a man."

"And then?"

"Then's when I got real foolish," she said. "I tole 'em I had a man would answer for whatever I said."

His eyes glowed. "Ye said that, Phoebe?"

"Right out in meetin'."

"Ye thought as high of me as that?"

"It jest kind of popped out."

"Wa-al," he said, "you got jest sich a man. Where's them two skunks?"

"Gone prospectin' up on the Hassayampa."

"Reckon they'll come back?" he asked eagerly.

"Ye kin depend on it," she said.

"So ye figger they stole your money, eh? I kind of reasoned out suthin' like that myself whilst I was a-ridin' along."

"It can't never be proved on 'em."

"I reckon to do some nosin' around whilst they're away. Mebby some Mexican'll drink too much mescal and git talkative." He paused. "Anyhow ye don't have to pay back that money."

"I borrowed it, didn't I?"

"From them that stole it from ye."

"What I borrow I pay," she said, "barrin' proof. But if I can't git proof, Peter, I calc'late to contrive to make them two furnish the money to pay themselves with."

"How?"

"I dunno. But I'll contrive it."

"I reckon ye kin," he said admiringly. And then: "Was we talkin' about gittin' married?"

"Seems as though."

"When's them festivities a-goin' to be held?"

"I'm jest as ready as I ever will be," she told him. "We got to git the cattle down to the ranch tomorrow. After that, as soon's we kin git somebuddy to marry us."

"If there hain't an Army chaplain around," said Peter, "we kin fetch up a padre from St. Xavier del Bac. I reckon you'll be fust American woman ever married in Arizony."

"Couldn't we jest git married down to the ranch?"

"If we did, we probably would both git hung to a cottonwood tree," he said. "This here town hain't had no sich excust for celebration since the fust Spaniard come."

Nor was Tucson to be denied such a pretext for a merry-making. As soon as the news became public that there was to be a wedding, the town took up the matter officially. The respectable white citizens met in Sol Warner's store, and from that moment the nuptials ceased to be a private and became a municipal affair. The elders of the people even set the day for the event.

"The's a kind of a religious taint to a weddin'," said Green Rusk. "Hadn't these here festivities ought to be kind of deecorus?"

"What ye mean is the hull town hadn't ought to git drunk."

"I hold," said Rusk, "that the gamblin' hells ought to be shet. If this here celebration's goin' to be run right, we hadn't ought to have opposition."

"What I say," declared a red-shirted miner, "is a man ought to be let enjoy a weddin' any way he's got a mind to."

"This here's a history-makin' event," said Rusk, "so the' ought to be speeches."

"What I say," argued the miner, "is we ought to start her to whizzin' at sunup and let her rip till the town's wore out."

"My people," suggested Ignacio Pecheco, "regard highly the *teatro*, also the *maromas* the walkers on ropes and the acrobats. Also the trained dogs who make the barrel to roll up a board."

"We'll git 'em," Solomon Warner agreed heartily. "And all free for nothin' to all."

"The's got to be suthin' deecorus," insisted Green Rush.

"This here fete," the alcalde said ominously, "is all a-goin' to be deecorus as hell."

"What I contend," said the proprietor of Congress Hall, "is

the saloons and mescal shops had ought to be shet up fur the day. And all drinks on the house."

"What time of day'll we hold these here nuptials?" asked the alcalde.

"The way I figger it," said Rusk, "we ought to wind up with 'em."

It was therefore determined that, as a gesture toward the religious aspect of the affair, the saloons should be closed to cash customers, but open to the public with all drinks free. Gambling houses would suspend operations. At the proper moment at the end of the day, after the performance by the Mexican troupe of strolling tragedians, the alcalde would introduce the principals in the event with a brief patriotic speech, and the chaplain would then perform his function. A feast and *baile* would follow for those able to eat or to dance.

The corral near the quartermaster's office was turned into a theater. Cottonwood saplings braced upon cottonwood saplings were to be the benches, and the tragedy was to be *Elena y Jorge*, bloody and heartrending. Bonfires would light the auditorium and a row of smoking lamps would circle the little stage. Admission fees were suspended, for on that day everything was free. It was the custom to charge Americans a dollar and Mexicans a half dollar, upon the very logical theory that Americans had more money than Mexicans.

It was a long day, for the fete commenced noisily at dawn. Tumblers, jugglers and performing dogs entertained the crowd in the public squares. At night the small boys pre-empted the front benches in the *teatro*, while fat, beaming, gossiping old Mexican women arrogated to themselves places in the rear, munching sweet quinces and smoking cigarettes as tears rolled down their cheeks as they followed the harrowing adventures of hero and heroine. Between the acts, clowns mingled with the audience to make the intermissions seem shorter, and the huge torches of wood flared and spluttered, and cast garish shadows over the scene.

Then, upon the final curtain, the alcalde made his appearance, and silence, polite and attentive, fell upon the audience.

"Feller citizens," said the alcalde, "includin' Mexicans and Injuns. This here is the most important event in the hist'ry of this here territory. I hain't castin' no slurs on our Mexican folks when I say the fust marriage of a white woman, markin' as it does the westward strides of civilization, is practically the makin' of this here city, movin' it up to the class of a metropolis. In consequence thereof, I'm gol-danged proud to interduce to this here gatherin' of patriots 'n' citizens the pair that is forthwith a-goin' to enter into nuptials with each other, our leadin' female citizen, Phoebe Titus, and him she's chose for better or for wuss, Peter Muncie. To say nothin' of the parson that'll jine 'em in lawful wedlock."

Phoebe and Peter walked upon the stage. Phoebe in a dress of white, into whose making had gone the skill of unsurpassable Mexican needlewomen, delighted to be a part in this great event. Peter, in black, with shining boots, peered with laughing eyes upon the audience, now become a congregation. The Army chaplain took his place before them, and the ceremony was conducted, responses given, a ring slipped upon Phoebe's finger. As the chaplain pronounced them man and wife the applause was deafening, pistol shots shattered the cool night air, and for an hour the bride and groom stood while all Tucson filed past them, shaking hands and congratulating.

Then a way was made for them through the crowd and they walked to Phoebe's little adobe house and crossed its threshold.

With delicacy the elders of the city had ordained that the Plaza de la Mesilla was forbidden ground to merrymakers or exuberant spirits who might be moved to prankishness. And so, while Tucson reveled, danced, gorged itself on enchiladas, frijoles, tamales, tortillas and burning chile con carne, and while scowling duennas guarded bright-eyed *señoritas* from the bold advances of American cavalrymen, Phoebe Titus and Peter Muncie entered upon a new phase of their lives; entered upon it fearlessly, with joy and with brave love.

From distant hills savage eyes peered down upon the little city; somewhere on the road to the Hassayampa Jefferson Carteret and Lazarus Ward slept under the moon; in his stronghold in the Chiracahuas Cochise considered his wrongs and planned his vengeance; far to the eastward cannon roared and men in blue and men in gray sought to tear each other limb from limb—and in a mansion in Washington a tall, stooping man with tragedy in his eyes, brooded over the carnage.

But to Phoebe and to Peter these matters were nothing—for at last they had won to each other—and the walls of their little room enclosed their universe.

CHAPTER XVII

UNDER the roof of the piazza, or gallery, of Phoebe's home ranch stretched long lines, and from these hung shreds of meat, blackening in the still dry heat. Phoebe's housekeeping had commenced. It was the season for jerking beef. On a distant mesa, sheltered from the sun by a thatched cover, sat a Papago Indian, ceaselessly watching the desert to the eastward. From that eminence a sentinel could oversee plains and hills in a great radius in which he saw none of the blazing beauty, but only a territory which Apaches must cross if a raiding party was to reach the river and the range where coveted cattle browsed. Below the ranch house on the bottom land, Peter Muncie was overseeing the repairing of the corral with ocotillo wands, each of which would presently take root and grow into a living fence of green. Invisible in the mesquite, thirty horses of the *remuda* dawdled about, waiting their turn to be ridden by Mexican *vaqueros* in broad-rimmed, conical hats, feet thrust in ornate, jingling tapadera—forerunners and teachers of the cowboys of the future. The lines of *acequias* dug by former owners, or possibly by even more remote Indian possessors, were marked by rows of willows and cottonwoods. And the gardens were green with a growing crop of beans, peas, onions and pumpkins. Upon all, the sun blazed down with a merciless heat, so that even the cattle ceased to graze at midday and became invisible as they bushed in the shade of mesquite or paloverde.

A pack train of silver-bellied mules and burros had passed through yesterday on its toilsome way from Guaymas, the nearest port on the Gulf of California bearing wares to Tucson and they had left their budget of news. A foreigner named Maximilian had landed on the eastern coast and proclaimed himself Emperor! What this phenomenon portended for the hungry peon no man might guess, save that he would take no benefit from it and might be ground into even more squalid poverty by the troubles it would bring. Poor, deluded, fatuous Maximilian, cat's-paw of a lesser Napoleon who saw in the Civil War the tying of the hands of the United States so that they could not enforce the doctrine of Mr. Monroe.

Phoebe Muncie, no longer Titus, sat by a bed in a little room, fanning the flies from the face of an Indian boy, wasted, thin, almost pallid, but conscious, now that his fever had abated. Black, uncomprehending eyes glittered as they remained unwinkingly on her face. Behind them a savage brain wondered, doubtless, for what tortures he was being saved.

"What name have you?" Phoebe asked in Spanish.

The Indian lad neither moved nor spoke.

"No harm comes to you," Phoebe said. "When the wound of the bullet is healed, there will be a horse and you may go with God."

He did not believe her; his young face, whose bones

threatened to break through the skin, was that of a wounded eagle, helpless, but unafraid.

"You are of the band of the great chief, Cochise?" she asked, and suddenly his eyes blazed, but he did not reply.

Then Peter Muncie came into the room and stood staring with that laughing light in his eyes that Phoebe loved.

"Next thing," he said, "you'll be nussin' a rattlesnake."

"He won't talk," she said.

"Neither would you," he said, "if you got it into your head you was a-goin' to git staked out and tortured." He walked closer to the bed and grinned down at the youth. "I never reckoned I'd git this clost to an Apache and both of us keep on bein' alive. If the authorities up to Tucson knowed you was harborin' an Apache, there'd be a fuss."

"He's my Injun," said Phoebe. "I shot him."

"And you'd fight the hull United States Army to keep him," said Peter.

"Let the Army ketch its own Injuns," she said.

As the hot summer days passed, Phoebe sat often beside the Apache boy. Perhaps there was as much stubbornness in this as kindness, but she was as gentle with him as if he had been an ailing white child. She was determined that he should respond to her friendship—grimly determined. If he had understood at once that she meant him no harm and had exhibited gratitude, Phoebe might have lost interest in him, but his attitude was opposition, and she could not brook opposition. She worked upon him as assiduously as a young *caballero* might make love to his sweetheart.

"Ye might 's well give up," jeered Peter. "Ye can't make a pet out of a tarantula."

But Peter was wrong.

"His name is Chie," Phoebe told him one evening. "He is a Chiricahua Apache." And after that each day she would have some titbit of information that she had extracted from her captive. "The Apaches won't eat bear meat nor port nor turkey," she told her husband, "nor anything that comes out of the water, sich as fish."

"I swan!" exclaimed Peter admiringly. "I'm a-goin' to fetch ye a Gila monster and see what ye kin pump out of him."

"I'm right curious about how Injuns do," she said, and as Chie became stronger, she talked with him more and more, and he responded with a curious freedom upon many points, but maintained a strict reticence upon others.

"They're right sociable folks amongst themselves," Phoebe told Peter. "Allus a-givin' parties 'n' dances. Take when a gal's ready to git married. Lasts four days and everybody gits invited. They pitch a teepee fur her in the middle and she goes into it all decked out in her best clothes. Then she prays a lot and does religious dances, while the folks outside have a good time. The second night the devil dancers come around all got up like wild animals. All the time the gal is prayin' 'n' dancin' inside. Then, the end of the fourth night they demolish the teepee and the gal up and runs as tight as she can toward the East. Yes, sir, and when a boy marries her he b'longs to her family, and not her to his'n. And they got one real sensible law that after a couple is married the man don't ever dast to look at or speak to his mother-in-law."

As Chie convalesced she learned from him details of tribal organization; how the center of Apache life was the family;

how chiefs arose by display of sagacity or valor. How the loose organization of the nation comprised first family, which owed a very tenuous loyalty to the band, which, in turn was a part of a tribe, which very seldom united for common action; and the tribes themselves were independent of each other, rarely combining for any object—and might and frequently did make war upon each other.

"What good's all this a-goin' to do ye?" Peter asked.

"It's jest suthin' to talk about," Phoebe said.

It was early in July that a noncommissioned officer and four troopers rode up to Phoebe's door.

"Afternoon, Mis' Muncie," the officer said. "We was detailed to come down here 'n' find out if ye had an Apache pris'ner in the house."

"What's it to anybuddy if I have?" Phoebe demanded.

"I was ordered to fetch him to headquarters."

"Ye was, was ye?" She advanced to the edge of the porch and stood grimly peering up at him as he sat his horse. "Did they calc'late a sergeant 'n' four men was enough to take an Injun away from me if I didn't want to give him up?"

"I dunno, Mis' Muncie. I jest got to obey orders."

"And what'll you do with him if I give him to ye?"

"That's fur the general to say."

"And he up 'n' issued orders all men Apaches was to be killed on sight."

"Yes'm."

"Wa-al," Phoebe said, drawing out the word, "this here's my Injun. If the gen'al wants some, the's plenty roamin' the hills. You go back, sergeant, 'n' tell the gen'al to hoe his own potatoes."

"I ain't lookin' for no fuss, Mis' Muncie."

"Hey, Phoebe," interjected Peter, "it's your say-so. But it hain't sense to buck the hull Army. Grantin' this here is your pers'nal Injun that you ketched yourself, and grantin' we could chase these here troopers off the premises, which we kin, you won't be no better off. The gen'al'll git his back up 'n' send along a troop."

"What your husband says, ma'am, is real sensible," said the sergeant.

Phoebe hesitated an instant. "Calc'late you're right," she told them. "You had a long, hot ride. 'Light 'n' eat 'n' drink, whilst we feed 'n' water your hosses."

"Thank ye kindly, ma'am."

"Ye'll find water around back, if ye want to wash yourselves," she directed. "'Twon't take long to put vittles onto the table."

Fifteen minutes later they were seated about the big table and food was before them. Peter sat with them, learning the news of the town, while Phoebe occupied herself in the kitchen, urging to greater activity the lethargic Mexican cook. Once she passed through the dining room. A few minutes later she reappeared and stood in the door. Over her shoulder could be seen the gaunt Apache boy, whom she had aroused from his bed.

"Have you strength to ride a horse?" she asked him.

"I am strong," he said.

"Wa-al, ye got to whether ye kin or not," she said in English, and motioned him to follow her.

Standing in the dining room door, she spoke to the sergeant.

"Here's my Injun," she said, "but don't disturb yourselves. Set right still." She lifted a Navy revolver from the folds of her dress.

"What's this caper?" Peter asked, but his eyes were laughing.

"The gen'al," she said, "has got plenty of war without startin' one with me. Set 'n' enjoy your vittles." She lifted her voice. "Manuel," she called, "bring a pony, a fast one, unsaddled, but with a bridle."

The sergeant pushed back his chair and started to rise; his face was grim.

"Sergeant," said Peter amiably, "I wouldn't if I was you. I know her better'n what you do. She hain't funnin'. She'll shoot."

"Mis' Muncie," warned the trooper, "this'll git ye in a peck of trouble."

"I hain't never been no place else, seems as though," said Phoebe, and then to Chie, "The pony comes. Mount and ride swiftly. The soldiers will not follow. Go with God."

Chie stepped past her into the room. He looked at the soldiers, at Peter, then turned to look long at Phoebe. Then, without a word he walked slowly, with perfect dignity, from the room. In a moment they heard the clatter of a horse's hoofs.

"I'll have to take ye to the gen'al fur this," said the sergeant in a worried voice.

"Figgered out how you're a-goin' to manage it?" asked Phoebe. She leaned against the frame of the door. "Sergeant, you don't look like no idiot. I'd say ye was average smart. Ye want to keep them stripes, don't ye?"

"Yes'm, Mis' Muncie."

"How long you think they'll stay onto your sleeve if you go back 'n' tell the gen'al a woman wouldn't let you have her Injun? The way I see it, the hull territory of Arizona'll r'ar back onto its hind legs 'n' laugh at ye fit to split."

"Yes'm, Mis' Muncie."

Phoebe tossed five gold coins upon the table. "If I was in your fix," she said, "I calc'late I'd report that whatever Injun was here had taken to the hills before you come. Save everybuddy trouble 'n' annoyance. You don't need no Injun, do ye?"

"No, ma'am, Mis' Muncie," said the sergeant.

"Eat hearty 'n' enjoy yourselves," she said. "I'll have your hosses fetched up in an hour."

When the afternoon was somewhat cooler, the little troop rode northward, the sergeant wagging his head and muttering into his beard. Phoebe watched them go with compressed lips and set jaw; Peter stood by her side, smiling broadly.

"Honey," he said, "you shore aim to git me all shot up one of these here days. Here you make a play I got to back. What if that there sergeant's got sand in his craw, eh?"

"Nobuddy," she said, "not the United States Army nor nobuddy else, is a-goin' tromplin' all over my rights."

"Jest stick to that there sayin'," Peter told her, "'n' you'll encounter plenty trouble." He held up her face for his kiss. "But I like the idea of it," he said. "I got some news from town."

"Ye don't have to be kissin' me with the cook and all lookin' on," she scolded. "What's the news?"

"Lazarus Ward's back."

"Alone?" she asked quickly, and held her breath until she heard his reply.

"Alone," he said, and she was conscious of another reprieve. Not yet would there be a meeting between Peter and Carteret.

"What fetched him back?" she asked.

"The talk around is he fetched down some samples of quartz that's so rich ye kin crumple 'em in your hands."

"Means he'll be goin' back," she said.

"The sergeant says he's aimin' to git him some machinery and freight it up."

"Buyin' and freightin' machinery costs money," she said thoughtfully. "Where's he a-goin' to git it?"

"I reckon he kin worry about that."

"What I was thinkin'," she said, pressing her lips together, "is that mebby he'd be worryin' me about it. Him 'n' Carteret 'n' that fifteen thousand I borrowed. He'll be needin' it."

"If he asks ye," said Peter with scant interest, for financial matters were something he never strove to comprehend, "tell him ye hain't ready to pay it."

"I hain't," said Phoebe. "I can't. But he's holdin' my stock 'n' wagons 'n' ranches fur security. If he pushed me, I'd have to sell suthin' and when you got to sell, it's allus at a loss."

"I got to git to town and see what's goin' on."

"I'd ruther you didn't, Peter," she said. "I'd ruther you 'n' Lazarus stayed apart. I'll have my hands full 'thout worryin' about you 'n' him. You stay right here 'n' see nothin' happens to the ranch or the stock."

He walked out and stood on the piazza looking off across

country toward the mesa upon which rested the Papago sentry. With narrowed lids, he peered intently.

"I calc'late ye won't be stirrin' this afternoon," he said, without turning his head. "Jose's signalin' from the mesa."

Phoebe stepped to her husband's side. From the tableland came a series of three flashes. Then a pause. Then three flashes.

"You ride 'n' call in as many men as ye kin git," she directed. "Fetch 'em to the corral. I'll ride over 'n' find out what's scared Jose."

"Ye don't need to," said Peter. "Nothin' 'ud stir Jose out of the shade but Apaches."

"I got to know how many, and jest which way they're a-comin' from. I hope he ketched sight of 'em when they was a good ways off."

She snatched her favorite weapon, the heavy Sharps that she had carried across the country in her father's Conestoga wagon. It carried a weight of lead, and carried it with deadly effect to an incredible distance.

"Mebby, if we got time," she said, "we kin give 'em sich a stummich ache they won't want to come here fur another meal. What ye waitin' fur?"

Side by side they ran to the corral, caught and saddled horses, and while Peter galloped off upriver, Phoebe set her horse's head toward the mesa to make sure what the keen eyes of the sentry had described.

CHAPTER XVIII

PHOEBE rode alone toward the mesa, her pony, bred and raised in the land, made its way over the boulder-strewn river bed as though it had been a grass-carpeted floor. It was a rock horse capable of traveling at a gallop where an eastern nag would have broken its legs moving at a walk. She urged him on, resting her heavy rifle across her saddle before her. Abruptly she left the river and set her pony at a hillside so rugged and steep that the tenderfoot would have thought nothing but a mountain goat could have climbed it. But the pony, picking his own zigzag path, spurning loose, rolling stones with his hoofs, testing every spot before he set his shoe upon it, scrambled up like a cat and presently reached the level plateau above. Across this, ripping her way through mesquite and cat's-claw that tore at hands and face, she galloped for a quarter of a mile to the mesa wall.

Juan, the Papago, scrambled down.

"How many?" asked Phoebe.

Juan held up all ten fingers twice, and then two fingers.

"They come slowly," he said, "keeping to the arroyos."

"How long?" she asked.

He looked up at the sun, then lifted his arm and pointed to a spot in the heavens three hours away from it. That meant that the marauders would arrive in early evening while the sun was yet above the mountains and the desert was light as day.

"Go back and watch," she directed, and herself retraced her path to the corral, there to await the coming of Peter and the *vaqueros*. Her four Papagos, farmers and horse wranglers, were there already. Splendid fighting men, who, with their kinsmen, the Pimas, had more than held their own against the Apaches, even pursuing their war parties into their own fastnesses and taking vengeance for slain men and women, destroyed crops and stolen animals. But for the Pimas and Papagos there might not have been a white man left alive in Arizona in those dreadful days of '61 and '62.

In an hour Peter galloped in with three *vaqueros*, so that there was gathered near the corral a little force of eight men and one woman.

"You're the Injun fighter of this family," Phoebe said tersely to her husband. "What next?"

"Where they headin'? For the ranch house or for the cattle?"

"Juan couldn't make out yit. They're two hours away."

Strangely—or perhaps naturally—Peter made no suggestion that Phoebe leave Indian fighting to men. As a matter of fact neither he nor Phoebe nor the Mexicans and Papagos saw in the emergency anything but a normal part of the day's work. They were there, maintaining themselves in Indian country. It was to be expected that the savages would ride in upon them. Apaches simply were one of the hazards of ranch-

ing in Arizona, as grasshoppers or the boll weevil or droughts
were to farmers or planters in more peaceful sections of the
country.

Peter went about the defense in a manner businesslike and
efficient. There was no thought of holing up in safety behind
the thick adobe walls of the hacienda, for that would leave the
ranges at the mercy of the savages and make them a gift of
the cattle that Phoebe's enterprise and Peter's hardihood had
brought from Kentucky to this distant frontier. An Indian
raid was dangerous only when it took its victims unawares.
Even preponderance of numbers seldom held the Apache to
his purpose if he found the defenders in readiness. Dearly as
he loved to slay, he was reluctant himself to be slain—not because he was a coward, but because a quick dash and a
sudden retreat was the strategy to which he had been bred.

Peter himself climbed the mesa. Juan pointed to the southwest, where, now and then, as they crossed open patches, or
were forced to abandon the concealment of valley or arroyo,
the approaching Indians came into view. They were riding
at that slow jog-trot which seems dear to the savage heart,
and which will jar the spine of a white man so that it
threatens to ram through his skull. Peter studied their direction for fifteen minutes striving to deduce the point at which
they would reach the boundaries of the ranch and pass the
guarding hills to the bottom lands along the river. There
was no need for haste for the attackers were still an hour
away.

It became apparent to him, as he scrutinized, that the
ranch house could not be their objective; they seemed to be

heading for some spot to the south of that, some opening in the hills through which they might pass.

He rejoined Phoebe.

"Where be they strikin' fur?" she asked.

"Looks to me like they would come through betwixt this mesa 'n' the hills beyond likely through what you call Bridle Creek."

"Good place to git 'em," she said practically. "Be ye sure?"

"It's how I'd come if I was an Injun," he said.

He turned and headed his horse toward the river, and the others followed, riding southward a matter of a couple of miles before the towering wall of the mesa ceased suddenly and a winding pass cut through between it and the less steep ascent of the hills adjacent. Into this canyon they turned.

"Better let 'em git in a ways," Peter said. "Leave our hosses here."

They alighted and clawed their way onward afoot, their feet sinking and slipping in the sand of the dry bed of the creek.

"Take to the rocks," Peter directed. "Don't want them Injuns to see no footprints."

Presently he found a stronghold to his liking. It was on the inner side of a sharp twist in the canyon, facing the opening, and it was thick with boulders, ocotillo, and not innocent of the terrible clawing cholla. Excellent cover and ample defense against singing arrow or flying bullet.

Peter placed his little party, six of them along the face of the slope and three a couple of hundred yards beyond, so that they could take the Apaches in the rear as the larger group fired into their faces.

"Don't nobuddy shoot till I do," Peter said. "When you hear my gun go off, let 'em have it hot 'n' heavy."

He and Phoebe settled down behind the same boulder.

"I got to git to Tucson tomorrow," she said. Her eyes were half closed. "He's come down to git him minin' machinery, eh? Minin' machinery! It gives a body suthin' to ponder about."

"The hull rumpus don't make sense to me," said Peter. "You say them scalawags stole your money 'n' then lent it back to ye. If it was me, I wouldn't worry about payin' back no sich loan."

"What I know 'n' what I kin prove," said Phoebe, "is two kinds of pigs. Minin' machinery. Set still and lemme think over what I know about minin' machinery that wouldn't do Lazarus no good."

"I got a suggestion," said Peter, with eyes that danced.

"What is it?"

"It's to keep your mind on Injuns fur a spell. The's some a-comin' round that corner by the name of Apaches."

"I'll think about them when they git here," said Phoebe. "He'll be wantin' some kind of crushin' machinery, and mebby b'ilers 'n' h'istin' machinery. Have to have it freighted to the Hassayampa. Seems like I ought to contrive suthin'."

"Fust ye better contrive to shoot ye a mess of Injuns." He leaned closer and looked at her. Her hands rested in her lap and there was no tremor visible. She breathed as normally as if she were sitting in the hacienda of a cool evening. "Hain't ye scairt none?" he asked.

"Be you?" she countered.

"I been more contented."

"Then quit thinkin' about Injuns till ye see 'em," she said, and he chuckled, reaching out to press her fingers.

"Blast me," he said softly, "if I didn't pick me a woman. Love me, Phoebe?"

"Hush. Them Mexicans'll hear."

"Hain't a woman got a right to say she loves her husband?"

"I married ye, didn't I?"

"Sometimes I git it into my head it was fur my money," he said mischievously.

"Have I acted so?"

"I dunno how wimmin that marries for money usually acts. You're the fust one ever done it to me."

"Hush your noise and watch fur Injuns," she said. "You're less nuisance that way."

"I shore respect 'n' admire ye, Mis' Muncie," he told her with mock gravity. "You hain't a woman that gabbles. You're a right thoughtful lady. Yes'm. But I do wisht you was scairt of Apaches."

"Why?"

"So as you'd kind of cling to me, hangin' your arms around my neck 'n' bellerin'. I'd admire to show ye what a hand I am at comfortin'."

"Go 'way from me. I got an idee a-stirrin' around."

His hand closed over her wrist, and she fell suddenly silent. He was listening. His ears, more alert than hers, had heard some sound down the canyon. She saw him move his rifle to readiness and make certain that it was loaded as it should be. She did the same. Then, faintly, came the sound of hoofs, and she wondered, in a disinterested sort of way, how a band of Indians, skilled in stratagem and ambush, would ride so blindly into a trap. A horse whickered, and unshod hoofs grated against the stones of the dry creek bed. Peter's rifle was sighted between two boulders. Phoebe found another natural porthole. And, as if they had been flashed on a screen, a cavalcade of naked Indians were there. They were laughing and chatting. This seemed incredible to Phoebe that merciless vermin like the Apaches could laugh, even though Chie had told her how merry they were in their own villages, at their own galas and family fetes.

Peter held his fire until the war party—and Phoebe counted a full twenty-two of them—were around the shoulder of the canyon and almost underneath the hidden, ready rifles. Then he nudged her with his elbow and grinned. She saw his hand close about the gunstock and trigger guard, and a deafening roar reverberated up and down the defile. Phoebe saw a warrior throw up his arms and fall from his horse. Instantly there were shrill cries, confusion, horses rendered unmanageable and from the rocks the *vaqueros* and Papagos poured down a rain of fire upon the milling raiders. Phoebe, too, was firing, loading, firing, loading. Frantic horses tramped wounded savages; wounded horses floundered, thrashing wildly with agonized hoofs. Taken too utterly by surprise even to fire an arrow in reprisal, the Apaches jerked at their ponies' backs and, whooping and squalling, made for the exit from the cul-de-sac in which they were caught. Now the rifles from behind them joined in the carnage. It was not battle, it was slaughter. Nor was any heart stirred to mercy. As they would have destroyed a weasel in the hen coop, potato bugs in the vines, any vermin that threatened their crops, so they destroyed these copper-colored human beings. A part of the day's work. An incident of ranching. As common a task and as necessary a task as plowing a furrow, performed by them dispassionately and efficiently.

Of the party of twenty-two, nine escaped from the trap. Thirteen lay dead in the sand or among the rocks. And the episode was ended.

"Calc'late we learnt 'em a lesson they'll remember," said Phoebe. "Here's one ranch they'll be avoidin' in future. You men pile some rocks over them corpses. Hain't no use follerin' them that got away. And don't be a-loiterin'. The's work that's bein' neglected."

They walked their horses back to the corral, where Peter unsaddled and tossed leather and blankets upon a pole placed across a corner of the blacksmith shop to receive them. Phoebe stood ankle deep in the dust, waiting for him, her eyes noting with satisfaction the smooth flow of back and arm muscles under his shirt, and the ease and sure grace of his movements. She was happy. Through her mind flitted swift pictures of her life—her girlhood in her father's slipshod store in Freeport; the gangling, uncouth figure of a man sitting on a cracker barrel surrounded by loafers while he told them comical anecdotes. Much as she disapproved of him, and of the way he interrupted business, she had been compelled to laugh. And now this man was president of the United States. It seemed absurd to her that this should be so—absurd and incredible. She recalled the long evenings of argument over selling the remnants of the store and investing what remained of their competence in horses, a Conestoga wagon and supplies and setting out across the Great Southern Overland for California. A series of flitting pictures! Then recollections of those long, weary days stretching from Independence down through Texas and across New Mexico. She could smell the iron fire-pot swinging under the rear axle, preserving live coals for the evening fire. Nights of little fires about which the emigrants huddled as the bitter winds swept across the uplands! With something of disdain she recalled the courtships of that long trail and her harsh rejection of them. She had not seen a man fully worthy of the name until her eyes rested upon a savage standing by the mail station in Apache Pass. Two men who fulfilled her ideal of what men should be—one a savage, the other her debonair husband!

But what busied her mind as these pictures flickered through it was the knowledge that she had never, from earliest girlhood, known what happiness was until now. For she was happy. Peter's nearness made her happy. The reaches of her ranch, as she sat before the hacienda and surveyed them, made her happy. Her cattle made her happy. Somehow, through trial and error, she had stumbled upon what her soul required.

"Peter," she said, "nothin' is a-goin' to compel me to sell my cattle."

"Figgerin' on whether I got a market value?" he asked. "I doubt if I'd fetch as much as five hundred cows."

"I'll keep ye both, or bust tryin'," she said. "Now, if we kin git an eighty per cent calf crop that 'ud add mebby three hundred to the herd. These hills 'n' plains'll feed ten thousand cattle."

"Who'll eat 'em?" asked Peter.

"By the time this herd gits to that number," she said, "the'll be plenty folks to eat 'em. This here war'll be over. People'll be movin' west. Look at how they're pourin' into the north part of the territory now around the diggin's! The time's a-comin', Peter, when the'll be twenty thousand white folks in Arizony."

"Shucks," Peter said.

"They'll be towns, with streets through 'em, and churches, and stores, like back in Freeport. And farmers a-drivin' in to trade. That's why I won't part with my cattle, no matter what. I got to be ready for them comin' days."

"Me," said Peter, "I'm ready fur the days we got right now. Come night and I've finished a day. That's enough for me."

"Fur a man that's dum nigh perfect," she said, "you come awful clost to bein' no good."

"So long's you love me, Phoebe, I don't give a dang."

"I got to love ye from now on, whether I want to or not," she told him.

"Jest why did ye reach that conclusion?"

"Because," she said, "unless I'm all-fired mistaken, I'm a-goin' to have a baby."

"Ye picked a quiet day to tell me about it," he said.

"I'm glad. A woman ought to have children."

"If you be, so be I," he said. He chuckled and kissed her gaily. "I don't reckon you done this from ordinary motives, Phoebe. Proba'ly it was to set an example fur your cows."

"Hush your noise," she told him, and disappeared into the house. He stood staring after her, shaking his head.

CHAPTER XIX

PHOEBE faced Lazarus Ward across the table in her little house in Tucson. The man wore a half smile of self-satisfaction that enraged her, but her lean, brown face was a mask that told him nothing of what went on in her thoughts.

"Ye fell right into it," he said gloatingly. "Nobuddy does a meanness to Lazarus Ward without gittin' his comeuppance sooner or later."

"I borrowed money," said Phoebe. "I intend to pay it."

"I want it paid now. I got to have that money to buy machinery fur the mine. I'm a-goin' to San Francisco to git it 'n' I need that money."

"It hain't handy to pay jest now," said Phoebe.

"Nothin' was said about handiness when ye borrowed it," Lazarus said harshly. "Nothin' was said about time. Ye was so anxious to git it, you didn't ask no questions. Ye wanted cattle. Wa-al, ye got 'em."

"Ye didn't think I'd git 'em through, did ye?" she asked.

"Wa-al, ye did. Hain't no use talkin' about it. I lent ye my money 'n' I want it back. You give all your proppity as security. I figger to leave fur Luma the day after tomorrow. You got till tomorrow night to pay up."

"That's how it is," said Phoebe, more to herself than to Lazarus.

"That's how it is," he said, "and it'll teach ye not to go interferin' with me."

"One of these here days," said Phoebe, "I'll find out where ye got it, 'n' then I'll interfere with ye, Lazarus."

"Ye made that talk before," he sneered. "Wa-al, ye got a husband to answer fur what ye say."

"Was you aimin' to make him answer fur it, Lazarus?"

"Jeff Carteret calc'lates to enjoy 'tendin' to that," he told her.

"To be sure. Where the's shootin' to be done, you leave it to somebuddy else."

"I don't leave collectin' my money to somebuddy else," he said harshly.

"You'll git it," she said. "Now clear out. You make the house smell kind of foul."

When he was gone, she sat for half an hour calculating possibilities. She did not blame herself. It was characteristic that she did not cry over spilt milk or take herself to task for having failed to protect herself in her eagerness to borrow money. She had borrowed it when she wanted it; had used it for the purpose she had in mind, and her enterprise had been successful. That was ample justification. Now, if trouble came of it, that was to be regretted that was all.

She would be able to get the money somewhere. Her first effort would be to borrow it. If she could not do that, she would have to find a purchaser for some of her stock and freighting wagons, for ranch lands or for cattle. To part with any of these would be a blow and a humiliation. But if she was compelled to do so, that was that. A thing that was inevitable was inevitable. But of one thing she was certain: she would not sell a cow.

She walked to Solomon Warner's store and found him in the back room, examining stock.

"Solomon," she said directly, "I'm in a pinch."

"Sorry to hear it, Phoebe. What kind of a pinch?"

"I got to have fifteen thousand dollars to pay off Lazarus Ward. He's demandin' it. He's a-goin' to San Francisco to buy minin' machinery. Kin ye loan it to me, Solomon?"

"Phoebe, if it was possible, ye could have it, and ye know it. But I hain't got it. I'm cleaned down most to the bottom of the till. Bought a half interest in a mine t'other day 'n' paid cash. I couldn't raise two thousand dollars to save my life."

"If ye hain't got it to lend, ye hain't got it to buy," she said. "I calc'lated if ye didn't feel like lendin', ye might buy some stock 'n' wagons."

"I tell ye flat, Phoebe, I hain't got it 'n' couldn't raise it 'fore the paymaster comes. I venture the' hain't nobuddy in Tucson's got that much or near it."

She stood very still. "If I can't borrow 'n' I can't sell," she said, "it looks like I'm in a fix. All I own is pledged. I calc'late he kin take the hull of it. I calc'late the hull of it's his."

"You'll have time to turn around," said Solomon. "He'll have to go into the territorial courts 'n' foreclose. By that time ye ought to have the money from some'eres."

"He won't have to foreclose nothin'," said Phoebe.

"Why not?"

"Because," she said, "what I give fur security was a kind

of a deed. If I didn't pay, then the deed was to work. If I did pay, the deed was to be give back to me."

Solomon straightened up and stared at her. "I'd never 'a' called ye sich a dum fool," he said.

"A body's entitled to be a dum fool once," she said evenly.

"It means losin' all you've worked 'n' slaved fur."

"I kin still bake pies," she said. "Wa-al, I'm obleeged to ye, Solomon. I know ye would if ye could."

All that day she combed Tucson for money. It might have been had from Pete Kitchen, but Pete was at his ranch near Nogales, protecting his hogs from Indian appetites; she might have had it from Oury, but Oury was in Yuma on business. Neither John Davis nor Mark Aldrich could raise such a sum of money. Long before sundown she realized that she was attempting the impossible. There was not so much money in Tucson. Fifteen thousand dollars could not be got by her, and years of planning and labor which had brought her lands, cattle, horses and wagons would be wasted. She would not have even as much as she possessed when she first drove into Tucson with her ailing father.

Her back was straight and her mouth grim as she returned to her little house. She would have to tell Peter that she was no longer a woman comfortably off, that by her folly and lack of foresight she had been stripped. What would he think? Upon that reflection she smiled. She knew what he would think. He would grin. His eyes would regard her with that expression of amusement that was so dear to her. He might even be pleased, because, to him, money, possessions, anything that anchored a man to one spot, that impeded his mobility, was an encumbrance and a nuisance.

But Peter was not all she had to think about. There was the baby.

She ate a lonely supper and then sat as people will sit in emergencies, whipping her tired brain to activity, hunting for some way out, hoping for an eleventh-hour miracle. After a time she went to bed, but could not sleep.

It was not yet midnight when she heard the stealthy shuffling of steps outside and reached for the revolver that hung by the head of the bed.

"Phoebe," called a cautious voice.

"What you doin' here, Peter?" she asked, sitting erect.

She padded across the room and opened the door. He lifted her, kissed her and set her down on her feet again.

"I told ye to stay to the ranch," she said.

"Business come up," he told her. . . . "No, don't light no light."

"What's the matter? What fetched ye?"

"I got some news out of a Mexican," he told her. "He come a-ridin' through with a pack train from Sonora. He kind of dropped a hint, so I come up here to find a feller."

"What feller?"

"You jest go back to bed and leave fellers to me," he said gaily.

She wanted to tell him; she wanted him to know and to comfort her. It was sweet to have someone to offer comfort and love.

"Peter," she said, "Lazarus Ward wants his money and I can't git it."

"Leave him wait then," he said.

"He won't wait. He's a-goin' to take everythin' I got to-morrow."

Peter patted her shoulder. "It hain't tomorrow yit," he said. "Don't you go frettin'. Jest you lay back and be easy." He kissed her again. "I got to go find that feller."

"Peter!"

"I may be headin' fur the ranch before dawn. Can't be wastin' time now."

Then he was gone and she was alone.

An hour passed, and she lay tense and alert. Her mind seemed to be working in a white, incandescent light. Thoughts flickered, jerking themselves from one subject to another. She never had been so awake, and it seemed to her that she would never sleep again. Vaguely she was conscious of the night sounds of Tucson: Snatches of drunken song, bellows of rage, music of guitars, raucous laughter from bars and gambling places. One might almost say the town was more quiet during the day than during the busy night.

She was not even startled by a muffled shot. One heard shots often during a Tucson night, and in the morning found bodies lying where they had fallen or been dragged. The noise in town seemed to increase, and then came a tapping against her window.

"*Señorita! Señorita!*" called an urgent thin voice.

"What is it, Estevan?" she answered, recognizing the reedy tones of the little hunchback, Estevan Ochoa.

"My eyes saw it," he said excitedly. "I lay in the open because of the great heat. There is the shot of a gun which aroused me, and there was a stirring in the mescal shop of Carillo. I go there to see. Upon the floor is a man who bleeds.

I learn that a bullet comes through the window out of the darkness."

"Who, Estevan? Who?" Phoebe cried, her heart suddenly gripped by icy fingers.

"The *Señor* Lazarus Ward," he said. "The *Señor* who is no friend to my *Señorita*."

"Ward! Shot? Is he dead?"

"That was hidden from me," said Estevan. "It was a matter the *Señorita* should know so I came swiftly."

"Did you see anyone else, Estevan? Anyone I should know about?"

"Not in that spot, not at that hour," said Estevan. "But the husband of my *Señorita*." He paused. "Not my *Señorita*—my *Señora*," he said, as he reminded himself of her marriage.

"Estevan, while I dress, catch and saddle my horse."

"I go," he said, and Phoebe dressed swiftly. Lazarus Ward was shot, possibly dead. It was the eleventh-hour miracle, but had it happened by the hand of God or the hand of the devil? Peter Muncie had come secretly to town in search of a man. Had Ward been that man and had Peter found him? And, having found him, having listened to Phoebe's confession, had he lurked in the darkness and shot him through the window of the mescal shop? She could not make herself believe that. Had it been in the open, had they met face to face, she could credit her husband with goading the man to fight, and with feeling justified in his slaying. In her grim little heart she would not have blamed him for that. It would have been his reckless way of settling a problem. But if he had fired upon an unsuspecting man through a window, then he was not the Peter Muncie she thought she knew. Not the

Peter Muncie who, she delighted to dwell upon, was the father of the child that was to come.

As she ran from the back door to the corral, dawn was breaking over the mountains. She flung herself into the saddle and dug spurs into the pony's flanks. Careless of who saw her or of what thoughts or suspicions the sight of her headlong going might arouse, she thundered through the streets and out of the city toward the south. She was looking for Peter, going to Peter, to ask a question and to demand an answer.

For an hour she rode, urging her pony as daylight increased and distant objects became visible. She stopped on an eminence and gazed about her, and as her pony stood with heaving sides, she saw two mounted figures emerge from the cottonwoods and mount a distant slope. Again she spurred forward. One of those figures was Peter—there was no mistaking his seat in the saddle, the jaunty swing of his shoulders. The other she could not identify. But there was something odd about it, about the way it rode—something not natural.

The pony settled to a long lope that closed the distance between herself and those riding men. Now they were a mile away, soon only half a mile, and then so close that the sound of her hoofbeats reached her husband's ears. She could see him turn in the saddle, rein in his horse and lay a hand on his gun.

"Peter!" she called.

Then, from a boulder-strewn slope to the left, came the explosion of a gun. She could see the man who rode with Peter jerk in his saddle, but he did not fall. Phoebe set her teeth and spurred, not toward her husband but toward the shot. Peter was doing the same. They met.

"Peter!" she cried.

"They got him," he said. "Somebody rode ahead and ambushed us."

"Who? Why?"

"You better crouch behind a rock," said Peter. "I aim to find out."

But he did not find out, though they combed the hillside. Whoever had fired that one shot had vanished as completely as if he never had existed.

"No use," Peter said. "He skedaddled."

"But who? Who is that other man with you?"

"Mexican by the name of Ignacio Sais. The feller I went to Tucson to see."

"Why, Peter—why did you go to Tucson? Who else did you see besides this Ignacio?"

"A sight of folks," he chuckled, "that didn't see me."

The pony upon which Ignacio sat stood nibbling the blossoms of a mesquite. Its rider sat very still upon its back, and Phoebe saw now why his attitude had seemed unnatural, for his arms were roped to his body and his feet tied together under the barrel of the horse. It was why he had not fallen to the ground after that shot. Peter dismounted swiftly and examined the man.

"This here Mexican," he said, "hain't no good to nobuddy no more."

"Why did you take him, Peter? What for did you tie him onto his horse?"

"Jest wanted to git him back to the ranch to ask him questions," Peter said. "I calc'late he was one of them that robbed your safe. He might have up 'n' told us somethin' we wanted to know."

"That was why you went, Peter?"

"Yes'm, Mis' Muncie, that was the reason."

"But did you make up your mind to do anythin' else after ye talked to me?"

"Nary other thing. It wa'n't a-goin' to be so simple to snake this feller out of town 'thout bein' seen."

"Did you—did you see Lazarus Ward?"

"Seen him a-settin' in Carillo's mescal shop guzzlin'."

"Is that all, Peter? You jest seen him?"

"Didn't have time fur nothin' else. I was busy keepin' out of sight."

"Somebuddy else kept out of sight, Peter."

"Who?" he asked curiously.

"The one," she said, "that shot Lazarus in the back through the winder."

CHAPTER XX

"PETER," said Phoebe, "I don't want no doubts betwixt us. I'm a-goin' to ask ye a plain question and I want a straight answer."

"Yes'm," said her husband. "Whoever it was, shore scored him a bull's-eye on this here Mexican," he added admiringly.

"Did ye bushwhack Lazarus Ward?"

He turned in his saddle and looked across at her before he answered, and her heart leaped as she saw that amused look gleaming in his brown eyes. "If I done so," he countered, "what do ye reckon to do about it?"

"I hain't made up my mind," she said.

"But ye don't favor bushwhackin'," he said.

"Nary bit."

"Wa-al," he answered, "ye kin have it carved onto my tombstone that any fellers I ever shot had a chancet to shoot back."

"Honest Injun, Peter?"

"Honest Injun."

"It didn't seem like the kind of a thing you'd do," she told him, and he was able to read her unexpressed relief and joy, and more than that that she harbored not a shadow of a doubt of the truth of his answer.

"The' hain't another woman like ye in Arizony," he said.

"The' hain't but few wimmin here," she answered tersely.

"What would ye 'a' done if I'd answered the other way?" he asked curiously.

"You're my husband, hain't ye? I love ye, don't I? But I calc'late my heart 'ud 'a' busted inside of me. Even knowin' ye done it fur me."

"I wouldn't of," said Peter. "Ye hain't the kind of body would want no profit from murder." He grinned happily. "But I'll be doggoned if I know anythin' else ye wouldn't make a profit out of."

"The'll be a muss about this here shootin'," she said musingly. "Lazarus was a hydrophoby skunk, but he was prom'nent. And him gittin' shot in the back through a winder'll kind of rouse folks."

"Let 'em rouse," he said.

"If I could git it into my head you might 'a' done it," said Phoebe, "the'll be others to think the same."

"Mebby," he said, "the' wouldn't be doin' so much thinkin' if you hadn't rode headlong out of town in the middle of the night. You're a kind of a headlong person, Phoebe. But I like it in ye. It's one of your p'ints."

"I had to git where you was," she said simply.

"Anyhow," he said, dismissing the subject, "it come at a good time for you."

"That's what a heap of folks'll be rememberin'," she said. "I'm thinkin' what's best to be done."

"Jest go along 'n' mind our own business," said Peter.

"Who d'ye calc'late shot that bullet into him?"

"I dunno. And if it's a-goin' to cause him trouble, I hope nobuddy finds out."

"And why?" she went on, expressing her thoughts.

"Jest made a strike, didn't he?"

"But he didn't have no gold onto him, from all I hear."

"He wouldn't carry his claim around on a packsaddle," said Peter.

"What 'ud be the good shootin' him for his claim? He's got a partner a-settin' on it."

"Be right beneficial to his pardner," observed Peter.

She considered that for half a mile, and then changed the subject. "Jest why was ye a-luggin' that Mexican down to the ranch?" she asked.

"This here feller that come through from Sonora with the pack train," said Peter, "he was right thirsty. And then he got real friendly 'n' talkative. Him 'n' me was doggone near relatives 'fore he got through. He kind of let drop things, 'n' so, when he went to sleep, I high-tailed fur Tucson to ketch me this here Mexican. If he wouldn't of talked no other way, I'd 'a' got the Papagos to stake him out on an ant heap."

"Ye wouldn't," said Phoebe.

"He'd 'a' told all about how your safe was robbed," said Peter grimly.

"Wa-al, he won't tell now," she said.

"That's what somebuddy figgered," said Peter. "It could 'a' been the same one that slung lead into Lazarus. Mebby the hull business ties in together."

"Jefferson Carteret's up on the Hassayampa," said Phoebe.

"Didn't neither of us see him there, did we?"

"What's best fur us to do?" she wanted to know.

"Nothin'," said Peter.

"It hain't never best to do nothin'," said Phoebe. "It's always best to do suthin'—even if it's the wrong thing."

"Wa-al," he said, with amusement, "I could take a little lope up to the Hassayampa 'n' ask Carteret where he was last night."

"I've heard wuss idees," she said. "But I'm a-thinkin' about Tucson. The'll be plenty talk. Sich friends as Lazarus's got may be a-stirrin' up trouble. I got to be in and out of Tucson, lookin' after the freightin' business. And a big share of that depends on the Army."

"I knowed business would git into this somewheres," said Peter.

"I figger," said Phoebe, "we better take the bull by the horns."

"That's whar ye allus grab him," said Peter.

"So," she said, "as soon's we kin contrive to leave the ranch, you 'n' me'll ride into Tucson 'n' ask if anybuddy's got anythin' to say to us."

"Why not just me?"

"You might git too much enj'ymint out of it," she said dryly.

"Right now I'd git enj'ymint out of fillin' my stummick with vittles," he said.

The hacienda was almost in sight, and presently they rode up to the corral gate and turned over their ponies to a Mexican wrangler. They were served in half an hour with a breakfast that Peter ate with gusto and complete enjoyment.

"Sol Warner tells me," said Phoebe, "that the's a new town up the middle of the territory. So many folks been movin' in since gold was diskivered up that way that they

picked out a place and made a town of it. He says enough
folks come in to pertect themselves agin the Apaches."

"Territory'll be gittin' overrun," said Peter.

"Somebuddy fetched a St. Louis newspaper," Phoebe said.
"I didn't git to see it, but it told about this Grant bein' made
a lieutenant general, and him 'n' Lee is fightin' each other in
a place they call the Wilderness."

"Looks to me like the No'th was gittin' the best of this
war," said Peter.

"What I can't git over," said Phoebe, "is Abe Lincoln
bossin' the hull shebang. When I knowed him he was nigh
as shiftless as pa."

Peter chewed with enjoyment. Presently he looked up and
said, "Phoebe, you're so sot on makin' money, why don't ye
git ye a gold mine?"

"It hain't my way," she said. "I know how to make money
by workin' fur it, and I aim to stick to work. The freightin'
business 'n' the ranchin' business is good enough fur me."

"But some of them mines up no'th has been givin' folks
a hunderd thousand dollars in jest a few months."

She stared at him and her lips compressed. "Gittin' restless?" she asked. "Hain't life been excitin' enough fur ye
round here?"

"I was jest a-wonderin' about it," he said.

"Wa-al, quit it."

"When be we a-goin' back to town?"

"The minnit I kin git things in shape here so as to be to
leave 'em for a spell. Mebby in two-three days."

It was, as a matter of fact, four days before Phoebe and
Peter set out once more for the adobe walls of Tucson to face

whatever conditions they might encounter there. They had ridden perhaps half an hour when an Indian, unarmed and making the gesture of peace, appeared on the top of a great boulder off to the left of the trail. Peter threw up his rifle but lowered it again.

"It's Chie," he said.

They turned aside toward the boy, who advanced to meet them. He halted, young, slender, emaciated from his wound but somehow dignified in his young gravity.

"Come," he said in Spanish.

"Where," asked Phoebe, "and why?"

"A man waits for you," said Chie, "a man with a straight tongue who will drink the same water and eat the same bread with you."

"I wouldn't trust him an inch," said Peter. "These Apaches are treacherous as snakes."

Phoebe shook her head. "Why does this man wish to speak words to us?" she asked.

"That there may be friendship between you and him," said Chie.

"Where is he?"

"There," he said, pointing off the road.

"I'm going," said Phoebe determinedly. "I don't believe Chie would do a mischief to me."

"Chie," said Peter, "if this is an ambush the first bullet is for you."

The boy smiled proudly. "Chie is a messenger," he said. "There will be no bullets."

"Anyhow," Peter said to Phoebe, "I'll have my rifle ready."

"We follow," said Phoebe, motioning the lad to precede

them. He led the way for perhaps half a mile, when he stopped in a sheltered cove in the granite hills.

"This is the place," he said. "The man will come."

And presently down the ravine rode a single native, painted with vermilion and black, and carrying a long lance in his hand. Then behind him appeared a mounted party at the head of whom rode a splendid savage only slightly painted with vermilion. His size did not become apparent until he dismounted. The paint did not distort the nobility of his features or the fine intelligence of his black eyes. In his raven hair were visible strands of white. Behind him rode another youth, of the age of Chie and two women. Phoebe recognized the Indian though she had not seen him since that day when the wagon train of which her father's Conestoga was a part had halted at Apache Pass. She had seen him for only a brief space, but his person had imprinted itself on her memory.

The women dismounted and spread blankets. The Apache chieftain sprang to the ground.

"This is the man," said Chie. "This is my father."

Phoebe and Peter dismounted and walked toward the spread blankets. The Indian, well above six feet in stature, extended his hand and smiled. There was a simplicity in his bearing, an expression so pleasant upon his distinguished face that Phoebe could not believe what she sensed to be true. It was not possible, she told herself, that here was the most feared Indian in Arizona—that this noble head had directed tortures and massacres. It was incredible that a man with a smile at once simple and genial could have upon his soul hundreds of horrible deaths. Phoebe offered her hand, which he clasped firmly.

"*Buenas dias,*" he said agreeably.

"*Buenas dias,*" she responded. "I speak to Cochise, great war chief of the Chiricahuas."

He did not acknowledge her attempt at identification, and Phoebe noted that never once during the parley was his name mentioned by himself or by his attendants. He signified that they were to be seated upon the blanket, and then he took his place between them.

"It is not the custom," he said in his own language—his words were translated by Chie—"for people of your race to give medicines and food to one of my race, wounded, who falls into their hands."

"It is my custom," said Phoebe "to do as I please in such matters."

"The boy," said Cochise, "is my son. I desired to see with my own eyes the woman, and her man, who behaved as you have done. It was a thing not to be believed, for your people kill my people wherever they see them. It is an order from your general."

"It was your people who began killing," said Phoebe.

"That," said Cochise, "is not the truth. I and my band were at peace. We brought from the mountains wood to the stone house in Apache Pass. We lived in friendship. Then came a soldier who accused me of acts committed by other Indians of which I knew nothing. This soldier seized me and members of my family. But I escaped. He took the members of my family who had done no wrong and hanged them to trees. Then there was war. It was not a war of my making."

"The truth of this is known," said Phoebe.

"I speak with a straight tongue," Cochise said quietly.

"Why should men lie? I do not understand. If a man asks
me a question to which I do not wish to give the answer, I
do not lie—I refuse to reply."

"If you do not desire war," asked Phoebe, "why do you
not make peace?"

"When a war is done, it is not an easy thing to make peace,"
he said gravely. "This—all this—was my land and the land of
my fathers. It is a good land. First come the Spaniards from
the South and between them and my people is always hatred
and cruelty. Between me and the Spaniards can never be
peace. They pay in yellow metal for the scalps of my people
as if we were vermin of the desert. Then come your people
from the North to take away from us our lands and to drive us
from our homes. The hills are ours. It is ours to be free in
the hills. But you would drive us from our homes to huddle
us in some spot which is not home and where we no longer
would be free. By what right do your people, who are very
many and very strong, seek to imprison us on reservations?"

"Many people agree that you have suffered great wrongs,"
Phoebe said. "But you have done great wrongs. From these
wrongs hatred has been born."

"And hatred," said Cochise, "lives longer than man's
memory of the causes of the hatred."

"Why," asked Phoebe, "do you not seek a council with the
general? Why do not wise men like yourself and the general
seek for a way to peace?"

"My brother, Mangus Colorado, sought a way to peace,"
said Cochise sternly. "With no weapon in his hand, he came
into the camp of your soldiers. There was no council. There

was no talk of peace. But my brother was slain by treachery. Does the wise man go to such a council?"

"There can be no agreement without a meeting," said Phoebe.

The chief shook his head slowly. His fine eyes were stern; his mobile mouth was set in determined lines. "Evil things happen to my people when they meet with your people. Would you have me eat pinole sprinkled with the white powder that kills?"

"That also was an evil thing," said Phoebe. She was finding it a difficult argument. An adroit mind was required to defend the conduct of the whites in their dealings with the red men. "But you want peace?" she asked.

"My people are warriors. Warriors live by fighting. We have no fields to till; we have no herds of cattle. The arrows of every people are pointed at our hearts. No man remembers when the Mexicans did not hate the Apaches. The grandfather of our oldest man cannot tell you when there was not war between us and the Pimas and the Papagos and the Navajos. Then your people come and they, also, make war upon us. We have never been unmolested so that we could learn how to live in peace. We must make war or starve."

"But you would be given lands. You would be given fields and cattle, and protected by soldiers."

Cochise lifted his head proudly. "We do not ask for peace," he said. "No, *Chickasaw,*" he said, turning to Peter and giving him the name which signifies "brother." "We are few. Your people are numerous as the birds that fly southward. You have wagons-that-shoot, bursting even rocks asunder. A man needs no great medicine to see the end." Then his face lighted, became friendly as he bent forward. "But between your family and my band there shall be peace. For other bands I do not speak, but between the Chiricahua Apaches and you there will be friendship."

He paused and then speaking with gravity, almost with reverence, he continued. "In the clouds, in the mountains, is a Great Spirit. In each man is a Little Spirit. In all things is a spirit, a shadow of the thing. In a pot of clay, in a pony, in a lance or an arrow there is a spirit. When a man dies his spirit travels to some Other Place. His body is buried in the ground, and with it his food and his pots and his weapons. The body becomes earth; the food and the weapons and the pots become earth. We break them before burial that their spirits may more readily escape. So, in the Other Place, the spirit of the man is joined by the spirits of the pots and the weapons and the food so that he will not be hungry or helpless. It will not be long, *Chickasaw,* before I travel to that place. I do not know," he said, and his voice became low, musing, "but it may be that there there will be peace for me and my people."

For moments he sat in deep reverie, his splendid black eyes sadly fixed upon the ground at his feet. Then he lifted his head and smiled, and none who were there could be unconscious of, unaffected by the charm and the power of the man.

"Now we speak of little things such as are spoken of among friends," he said, and with the frank curiosity and interest of a child, he asked them questions—their age, their wealth, about their house and the daily habits of the house. He answered their small questions in the same frank, open, genial manner. Phoebe, looking into his mobile face, so full of intelligence and character, could not force herself to believe that here sat the ravager of Arizona, thief, murderer, guilty of every unspeakable cruelty—according to the code of the white man. She thought of the white men she knew, and there were few who could sit beside this savage and bear comparison with him, either in person or in mind. He was, she reflected, worthy to be the leader of a people much greater, much more numerous than a band of Chiricahua Apaches. In another place, in another environment, with another pigment in his skin, he might have been one of the distinguished men of the earth.

After a time he arose and stood courteously. They also got to their feet. Cochise extended his hand and, one by one, they grasped it.

"*Chickasaw*," he said to Peter, "I have spoken. Between your family and me there is friendship."

"Chief," said Peter, "I was a soldier. I am a scout. I may be called upon to lead soldiers against you."

Cochise nodded. "But a few days ago you killed many of my young men who came to steal your cattle. That is a matter between men. If you must lead soldiers against me, that is a matter between warriors and must be done. What a man must do, he must do. If you lead soldiers after my band, I shall fight you. But when you are not leading soldiers against me, you will still be my brother."

"Chief," said Peter in English, and Chie would have found difficulty in translating his words, even had he understood that language, "I don't care how big they come in any herd, you ain't no runt."

And so they parted, Peter and Phoebe riding northward to Tucson; Cochise and his little party eastward toward those grim and frowning mountains which were to immortalize his name under the title of Cochise's Stronghold.

"Peter," said Phoebe, "we jest seen a man."

CHAPTER XXI

Phoebe and Peter rode into town, knee to knee. They rode slowly, and their progress might have been called defiant. Knowing that one or both of them might be accused of shooting Lazarus Ward, they gave Tucson ample opportunity to observe them and to take action if it desired. They were conscious of more curiosity than hostility as they dismounted before Warner's store and entered.

Solomon looked up from his work and his face was not friendly; there was no warm greeting as usual, and he stood waiting for Phoebe to speak.

"We come," said Phoebe, "to hear what folks was a-sayin' about us."

"Me," said Solomon, "I'm a-waitin' to hear what ye got to say about yourselves."

"Is Lazarus dead?" she asked.

"No. Army surgeon cut out the bullet. He's bein' nussed by a Mexican woman. He's like to die."

"Gives me time to turn around, anyhow," said Phoebe.

"It come in almighty handy fer you," observed Solomon coldly.

"No denyin' it," Phoebe said, "and that's why we're here. You think one of us shot him?"

"That's how it's bein' talked around." Solomon wiped his hands carefully on the seat of his trousers and leaned against a barrel. "I'm waitin'," he said. "You 'n' me has been friends 'n' pardners, Phoebe. Knowin' ye as I did, I couldn't credit you'd do a murder fur money. I been tryin' not to b'lieve it."

"Ye kin keep on not b'lievin' it," said Phoebe tersely. "We can't prove it, now, but neither of us shot Lazarus or had anythin' to do with his shootin'."

The merchant scrutinized her face; it was grave, earnest, and her eyes met his with perfect honesty.

"Ye give me your word fur that, Phoebe?"

"I give ye my word, Solomon."

His stiff attitude relaxed and his austere face softened. "That's plenty good fur me," he said. "But the way you went a-thunderin' out of town looked mighty bad—that 'n' the fix ye was in."

"I don't pay my debts with bullets," said Phoebe.

"Folks git desp'rit," Solomon said.

"I hain't the desp'rit kind," Phoebe told him.

"Who d'ye calc'late done it?" Solomon asked.

"Is that there mine of his'n rich?"

"If the samples he showed told the truth," he said, "the's a sight of gold in it."

"Got a pardner, hain't he?"

"His pardner's up on the Hassayampa."

"See him there?" asked Phoebe.

Solomon nodded at that.

"The reason," Phoebe said, "that Peter was in town that

night was he got word about a Mexican who knowed all about the time my safe was robbed. Peter got holt of this Mexican and was draggin' him down to the ranch to make him talk. Had him roped on top of a hoss. Somebuddy dry-gulched him. The feller that did it would 'a' had time to shoot Lazarus and then go ridin' after Peter."

"You got it set in your mind that Lazarus 'n' Carteret stole your money."

"And lent it back to me," she said.

"Seems like ye ought to find out if Carteret stayed on the Hassayampa," said Solomon.

"We aim to," Phoebe said.

"What be ye a-goin' to do now?" Solomon asked.

"Ride around town fur an hour or two and give folks a chance to look at us," said Phoebe, and Peter grinned.

"I better see a few folks," Solomon said, again wiping his hands on the seat of his trousers. "Don't want the riffraff organizin' a necktie party."

Solomon made no ado about accepting her bare word for her innocence, and she accepted it as the natural thing without thanks. It would not have occurred to her to do otherwise. She had made a statement, unsupported by evidence it is true, but a positive statement. That anyone should doubt her given word was a thing that never entered her mind.

"I got business to do while Lazarus is mendin'—if he mends," she said. "Mebby I got to ask your help."

"I hain't able to help ye with money, Phoebe."

"'Tain't money. Lazarus, if he gits well, won't do no tradin' with me."

"What tradin'?"

"What did he come down here fur?"

"To collect from you."

"And to use the money buyin' machinery fur his mine. Wa-al, I jest as soon sell him that machinery."

"Ye hain't got no machinery."

"I was in the freightin' business when the troops were drawed out of Arizony," she said. "I made consid'able money haulin' away from Arivaca 'n' Tubac and one place 'n' another, when folks was abandonin' the country. Supplies 'n' machinery. The' was machinery at the Santa Rita, the Cerro Colorado, the Sopori, and it hain't rusted to dust. It was me done most of the freightin'. The's owners 'ud sell it cheap."

"What d'ye want me to do?"

"Talk to them that's talked to Lazarus. Find out what he calc'lated to buy."

"We kin find that out."

"I figger, knowin' where some of that machinery is, I kin buy it from Eastern owners fur junk prices. What with the war 'n' the Injuns 'n' all."

Peter stood eyeing his wife with twitching lips. "I thought we come up here to tromple down a charge of murder," he said, "but here we be makin' money."

"You tromple the murder," Phoebe said. "I'll make the money."

"It's a gamble," said Solomon.

"What I'm hopin'," said Phoebe, "is that if Lazarus finds he kin git what he wants cheap, he'll buy more'n he kin afford. I want you should do the dickerin', Solomon. He won't have no money, but ye kin agree to take my debt to him—'n' his note fur the rest. But the note's got to be secured by his mine."

"She thought this here all out," said Peter admiringly, "whilst we was crouchin' behind a boulder ambushin' a war party of Apaches. Never see sich a woman fur lettin' her mind wander. Apaches 'ud keep most folks busy 'thout projectin' around how to squeeze somebuddy in a deal."

"I'll help ye however I kin," promised Solomon.

She turned to Peter. "We better go out now 'n' give Tucson a chance," she said.

"Think the Army'll meddle in?" asked Peter.

"Carleton's off in New Mexico, 'n' what few soldiers is around here is busy," said Solomon. "I don't figger the law— what there is of it—'ll take no hand. It's Ward's friends."

"I wisht I knowed how long he was a-goin' to take to git well."

"If he gits well," amended Peter.

"I'd kind of hate to see him die," Phoebe said. "I want to see little Estevan Ochoa. I never knowed a child who gits to see so much."

"I'll be stirrin' around myself," said Solomon. "I better see Oury and some of our friends, jest in case."

They stepped out into the brilliant sunshine; as it beat down upon the ancient yellow adobe, it was blinding to eyes emerging from the shade of the store. They stood for a moment adjusting their eyes to the light. A dozen men were straggling toward them down the Calle Real.

"Here," said Peter, "comes trouble."

"Bob Crandall ahead, hain't it?"

Peter nodded. "Now, you leave me handle this," he said gaily. "I hain't much of a fist at money makin', but this here's more in my line of work. Mebby you better git back inside."

She only drew a little apart from him, so that they would form two targets instead of one. Peter, whose weapon was a carbine, shifted it into the crook of his arm and leaned against the wall as the straggling little mob approached and halted.

"We heard ye was in town," said Crandall.

"We come in broad daylight," said Peter.

"We're friends of Lazarus Ward."

"I reckon he'd be proud to know it," Peter said, with irritating irony. "What's your plans?" He stepped forward a step and looked down at them. "Don't bunch together, boys," he said genially. "Spread out so as I kin watch everybuddy's hands. Now, what was it you wanted to see us about?"

"We don't have to tell ye that."

"No, ye don't have to tell us that. Lazarus Ward's been shot. Some of ye, mebby, thinks we done it. Some of ye knows well we didn't. What my wife 'n' me is curious to know is what ye aim to do about it and when ye figger to set things to whizzin'."

"Respectable citizens of Tucson is sick 'n' tired of shootin's 'n' murderin's," said Crandall righteously.

"When did any respectable citizen speak to one of you to tell ye them sentiments?" asked Peter. "Now there ye be, all messed up with war paint. Why don't one of ye move fur a gun?"

"We jest come to warn ye," said Crandall. "Public sentiment is agin ye. This here town don't tolerate folks that bushwhacks a man to git out of payin' a just debt."

"Nobuddy knows how just it was better'n you, Crandall," Peter said. Phoebe glanced at him and saw how he was enjoying himself. This was a situation made for him. There was danger. Before him, threatening him, ready, if his alertness waned for a second, to take his life, were nearly a dozen of the most disreputable and dangerous men in Tucson, and he reveled in it. Incidents such as this were what he was made for.

"We're orderin' ye to keep out of Tucson," said Crandall.

"I swan to man!" admired Peter. Suddenly his face changed. It was no longer youthful and genial, but grim and set and purposeful. "Now I'm a-goin' to speak my piece," he said. "I'm a-goin' to speak it right out. A while back my wife's safe was robbed. You know who done it, Crandall, and some of them with ye knows, because they was there. Ward 'n' Carteret planned it. Now Ward's layin' with a bullet hole in him. I didn't put it there, nor my wife. But Crandall knows who did, and what fur, and when I git around to provin' it, you'll be danglin' from a mesquite for the buzzards to eat. You come a-surgin' up here to make a play. Wa-al, make it quick or tuck your tails betwixt your laigs 'n' scoot. If ye don't make it pronto, I'll make it fur ye. Shoot or skedaddle, because about the time I count up to ten, I'm a-goin' to start shootin' myself."

"You can't run it over us like that," Crandall said savagely.

"Linger around," said Peter gaily, " 'n' you'll find out." He shifted his carbine to a position of greater readiness. "Who's a-goin' to be the fust to run?" he asked. "Yo're all yaller dawgs, but I'd admire to see who's the yallerest."

A whiskered individual in the front rank was the first to turn. In the beginning, he walked slowly, but he did not like to have his broad back turned toward Peter's gun. He started to walk more rapidly, and then broke into a run. Another followed, and another.

Peter laughed aloud. "Good-by, fellers!" he called. "Come back the day you git some sand in your craws!"

Crandall was last to go. Walking slowly, he sought to save his face.

Peter fired one shot. It struck in the dust between Crandall's feet, and the gambler's dignity deserted him. He darted around the corner like a frightened rabbit, just as Solomon Warner, Oury and three other businessmen of the town came up the street armed with shotguns, rifles, pistols.

"Ye missed the party, gentlemen," Peter said, "but ye hain't too late to drop in some'eres 'n' have a drink. I done talked till I'm thirsty."

"Young man," said Oury, "this matter is serious. We do not know you well, but we do know your wife. You have been charged with a shooting. Warner has your wife's word for it that you are innocent. Her word is good enough for all of us. But this sort of thing has got to be stopped in Tucson."

"I'm in favor of it myself," Peter said amiably.

"The simple word of your wife is enough for her friends, who know her, but it is not and will not be enough for strangers. Ward has friends, and all of them are not among the riffraff. The town will be taking sides. There is apt to be trouble. I want to urge you to go back to your ranch and stay there until things quiet down."

"You forgit, Oury," said Phoebe, "that I'm in business here."

"If I were you, I would neglect my business for a while," he said.

"It takes more'n a wounded skunk to make me neglect what I got to do," said Phoebe. "And I got pressin' business."

"Phoebe, I wisht you'd show a mite of discretion," admonished Sol Warner. "Your friends can't see no harm come to ye, and we don't want this here to turn into no general shootin' match."

"I don't want to discommode you men none," she said, "but so long's I'm alive, I calc'late to come to Tucson, and stay in Tucson, whenever I figger it's necessary. And it's necessary right now."

"My wife," said Peter agreeably, "is talkin' fur the fambly. Much obleeged to you men fur hornin' in on this here." He placed his arm about Phoebe's shoulders and drew her to him. "She's in a condition jest now where she's got to be humored."

Solomon Warner's eyes opened wide. "Ye mean she's a-goin' to have a baby?" he asked.

"Sich," said Peter, "is the case."

"Feller citizens," said Sol, "I move we step into my store and hold a public-spirited meetin'. Doggone! A white woman's a-goin' to have a baby in Tucson! That kind of makes it a cat of another color. You mog along home, you two, and walk careful. It kind of devolves upon us to take steps."

The men filed into Warner's store. Presently they emerged and walked to the square of the Plaza de Armas, whose high and thick adobe walls now had practically disappeared as Tucson expanded with a rapidly increasing population. They walked to a conspicuous place and affixed a notice to the wall. It commenced formally, "To whom it may concern," and then followed the names of twelve men, all undesirable citizens.

"If Phoebe Titus or her husband is shot or otherwise molested, the twelve men named above will be taken outside the city limits and hung by the neck, and no questions asked."

It was signed, "The Committee, Solomon Warner, Chairman. Granville Oury, Secretary."

Following this, they marched into the nearest bar and refreshed themselves. When they emerged there was a considerable knot of inhabitants, white and saddle-colored, discussing the pronunciamento in whispers.

CHAPTER XXII

PHOEBE's freight wagons ranged southern Arizona. Their wheels rutted the sands as far south as Army posts on the Rio Grande, Yuma, and even to Carleton's headquarters in New Mexico. These were active and prosperous days. New residents, miners, prospectors, gamblers, emigrants were increasing the population of the state so that there were emerging sections here and there strong enough to protect themselves from Indian depredations. The new city of Prescott in the north was booming, and here the flimsy territorial government established its seat. Tucson attracted the notice even of the church, and Bishop Lamy journeyed down from Santa Fe to be received under triumphal arches of cottonwood, to make his progress through a furbished town decorated with paper flowers and finest Spanish shawls which had been handed down to the faithful from generation to generation. There was a tiny building, enlarged by loving hands, to do service as a church under the urging of *Señor* Vicario Machbeuf, who inveighed in it against murder and evil living until his flock found it necessary to guard him as he walked abroad and to set a protective guard about the church at night as he heard confessions.

232

Because Tucson was the distributing depot for the Army in Arizona its streets were jammed with mule trains from Sonora; with hay wagons, with Conestoga wagons ending their three months' journey from Independence with wares and merchandise from the East. But still the law remained aloof, or if it made its appearance it was crude and ineffective. There was civilized activity, but little civilization—and as for the softening influence of women, there was none. Aside from the Mexicans and Indians there was no woman in the region except Phoebe Muncie. And in her influence Phoebe rated more upon the masculine than upon the feminine side.

While Lazarus Ward lay between life and death, burning with fever and in delirium, Phoebe bustled about tirelessly. It was a breathing spell; it was a space in which to rectify her mistake—though she would never admit that it was a mistake. Given a few months more, and her earnings from the freighting business would enlarge themselves to a sum capable of repaying Lazarus Ward what she owed him. But she rebelled against using good, hard-earned money for such a purpose. Believing, knowing in her heart, that Ward had loaned her money stolen from her safe, she burned to discharge the debt in some manner painful to the debtor.

"Peter," she said one afternoon—it was following an electrical storm which had washed gully and arroyo and quenched the thirst of vegetation so necessary to her ranging herd of cattle, "he'll be comin' to Tucson. He's got to come."

"Carteret?"

"Him," she said. "He's got to come to find out why Ward don't turn up with minin' machinery."

"Let him come," Peter said.

"This hain't," she said slowly, "no country fur a baby to be born in without a father."

"Ye figger I hain't as good a man as Carteret?"

"Bullets hain't got no judgment," she responded. "I got a kind of a superstition about that man. If he comes, you 'n' him is bound to meet."

"I reckon. It's been brewin' fur a long stretch."

She sighed; then she shrugged her strong, slender shoulders. "Lightnin' hits where it hits," she said fatalistically. "Wa-al, anyhow, I got most of that machinery bought 'n' stored in Tucson. Engines, small b'ilers 'n' what not."

Peter's eyes lit with amusement. "Must be consolin'," he said. "If ye lost a husband ye got a b'iler."

"The hull kit of it," she said, "didn't cost me but a mite more'n five thousand—not countin' the haulin'. It's wuth, put down in Tucson, five-six times that. I wonder when Ward'll be able to dicker?"

"Mebby Carteret'll git here to do his dickerin' fur him," Peter said. "I jest heard down to the store that Lincoln was nominated agin fur President."

"Ye can't," said Phoebe sententiously, "tell by the looks of a frog how fur he kin jump."

"I'm a guessin', Phoebe, that the No'th is goin' to win this here war. Grant's closin' in on Richmond, and that crazy feller Sherman is gittin' the best of it down in Georgy. When peace comes a sight of folks is goin' to head West."

"Mebby an army of 'em, if what you hear's true. Mebby that army'll be headin' into Mexico unless suthin' happens to Maximilian before then. I wisht you'd go down to the ranch, Peter, 'n' stay till Warner'n me kin git this machinery deal finished up."

"Jest what you aimin' to do, Phoebe?"

She hesitated a moment before replying, because it was not easy for her to disclose plans even to one she loved and trusted. She was to keep silent until after she had acted—and to keep silent then.

"I aim," she said, after a moment, "to git me a gold mine."

"Thought you didn't want nothin' to do with mines."

"It depends on who owns 'em," said Phoebe.

It was in late August that she held another conversation with Solomon Warner.

"I hear tell Lazarus is mendin'," she said.

"I was in to see him," Solomon told her. "He's turrible weak, but it looks like he'd pull through."

"The minnit he's able to do business," Phoebe said, "I want ye should git at him. And the's suthin' else, Solomon. Don't say nothin' about freightin' them things."

"He won't never hire you to do it."

"He will," said Phoebe, "if the' hain't nobuddy else'll do it. And the's nobuddy but you'n' me kin handle that much weight."

"I'm in business to make money, too," Solomon said seriously.

"You do like I ask," she said, "and you won't lose by it. You'll make."

Warner, whose business had spread over the territory even as Phoebe's had done, nodded his head. He was a man of importance now. Throughout the southern part of Arizona his name was known, and he was habitually addressed now as

Don Solomon. "That's good enough fur me," he said. "But hain't ye forgittin' his pardner?"

"When a rattlesnake's buzzin'," she said, "ye hain't apt to overlook he's around."

"I'll tend to it," he said.

Phoebe rode out to the corral to give orders about her stock; she inspected such freight wagons and Conestogas as were in town waiting for a cargo or undergoing repairs. She interviewed the quartermaster; she had interviews with other individuals who were receiving merchandise or freight. It was a busy day. She encountered friendship and black looks, for the town was divided. Men muttered as she passed but there was no open hostility, and she went about her affairs without apprehension, for that notice signed by Warner and Oury made her safe. The men to whom it had been directed knew it was not to be trifled with.

In these days, despite Phoebe's condition, she was much in the saddle. The ranch could not be neglected, and, too, she wished to keep Peter away from town as much as it was possible to do, for he was not one to step aside from trouble or to listen to subdued mutterings without demanding explanations. There was a certain tension. Her cattle were doing well in their new environment and her *vaqueros* reported that a satisfactory calf crop was promised.

The days at the ranch were the pleasant ones; and the long evenings with Peter were times she was not to forget so long as she lived. The expectation of fatherhood had not altered him; he was no gentler with her than he had been, and no less amused by her absorption in business. He humored her as he would have humored an eccentric child, and she delighted in it, though she never told him so. For the most part, he did the talking and she the listening. He was voluble. He loved the sound of his own voice and delighted to put his thoughts into words. Nor was he ashamed, as she was, to express openly his affection for her—even in the presence of servants. This embarrassed her and she bickered with him, but she would not have had him change for any possession the gods could offer her. He teased her, irritated her, drew sharp retorts from her which delighted him beyond measure. And, as yet, he gave no signs of restlessness. For these she had watched vigilantly, and against them she had fought with every weapon at her command. Sometimes she was even grateful for Carteret, for somehow she knew that so long as that threat remained, horses could not have dragged him from the vicinity.

Twice the Army had sought his services to lead parties on forays into enemy country, and twice he had declined. But there would come, she knew, a time when he would not decline.

"He'll go. He'll be wanderin'," she said to herself, "but he'll come back. I'll do so that he won't be able to stay away."

This fear she never expressed to him. It had not been mentioned between them since their marriage, until he referred to it one evening as they sat looking out over the hills.

"Before we was married," he said, "you used to be concerned about my wanderin' off."

"I was," she said.

"Seems like the' hain't no danger of it," he told her. "I'm right contented. You're a mighty int'restin' woman, Phoebe. And even if ye was dumb, you're perty to look at. And even if ye was humbly, you'd be all a man could ask. Seems like I love ye more the longer I live with ye."

It made her shy when he spoke openly of love, for to her love was a secret thing, to be entertained only in the silent heart and never brought out into the light of day.

"I wonder which it'll be?" he mused.

"It'll be a boy," she said positively.

"Mebby you got word," he suggested teasingly. "Mebby a lettle bird whispered to ye."

"It'll be a boy because I got my heart set on a boy," she said. "I set for hours 'n' say over 'n' over again it's got to be a boy— Peter, be ye glad we're a-goin' to have a child?"

"A man hain't a man till he's had a baby," said Peter.

"I got to study how to do what's right by him," she said. "I wouldn't ever have a time come when he was ashamed of his ma 'n' pa."

"If ever he was ashamed of you," he said, "I reckon I'd wear out a strap on his behind."

"I don't know," she answered. "Bein' ashamed is suthin' that jest happens. The' was times when I was ashamed of my pa. I didn't go to be, but I couldn't help it. He was so dratted shiftless. It hain't a child's fault if he's ashamed of his ma 'n' pa; it's their'n."

"How come it's their'n?" he asked.

"Childern starts where their parents finishes, mostly. From one generation to another, the's different ways of doin' things, 'n' the old ways looks funny to young eyes. The's a-goin' to be big changes out here, Peter, and a different kind of folks is a-comin'. Different from us. Like Poston 'n' Pumpelly 'n' Oury is different. Eddicated. And we're a-goin' to be rich."

"What's that got to do with it?"

"Our money'll give him advantages we never had," she said. "He'll git eddicated, too. Peter, I been thinkin' we got to keep abreast of him."

"Ye mean you 'n' me got to git eddicated?"

"Yes, Peter."

"Out of books?"

"The' hain't no other way."

"I couldn't read no book," he said earnestly. "It 'ud give me stummick ache."

"I hain't no fist at readin'," she said, "but I kin read every book in the world if I got to."

"It 'ud be a sight easier on everybuddy," he expostulated, "if you'd forgit about givin' him book-learnin'."

"I got plans fur him that needs book-learnin'," she said.

"Mebby you want he should go to Congress?"

His eyes brimmed with merriment as she flushed, and he realized that he had struck the target fairly in the bull's-eye. And from that day on he referred to his son-to-be as the Senator.

"If Abe Lincoln could git to be President," she said sharply, "I calc'late a son of mine kin git to Congress, or even be a jedge."

Not even Peter realized the ambition that burned in Phoebe's breast—ambition for herself and Peter, and now ambition for the child who would be with them in a few short months. It was a grim ambition, coupled with a confidence in herself and her powers. Peter would have been uneasy could he have known the resolution that possessed her to make her menfolk lift themselves by their bootstraps.

Next day, Phoebe and Peter rode to town. Their journeys now were not the circuitous, watchful journeyings they had been. For they rode no longer in fear of their nearest neighboring enemies, the Chiricahua Apaches. Cochise had taken their hands in friendship. He had called Peter "chickasaw." There was a pact between them—a pact which bound no other band of Apaches, not the Jicarillas, or Copper Mines, or Coyoteros, who lived up near the headwaters of the Salinas. But other bands were unlikely to be raiding so near to Cochise's Stronghold.

Phoebe went at once to Solomon Warner. "Any news?" she asked.

"I seen him yesterday," he said. "We talked it all out. I give him a list of machinery 'n' guaranteed it was in prime shape."

"Is he a-goin' to buy?" she asked anxiously.

"He acted right eager," said Solomon, "but like you told me to be, I was offish about sellin' unless I could git gold."

"Did he mention what I owe him?" she asked.

"To be sure."

"How much you ask him?"

"We went over the list, 'n' what it would cost in the East, 'n' how much it 'ud cost to git it here. It run high. I told him I'd sell what was there for forty thousand."

"How much did he offer?"

"Twenty," said Solomon. "But we come to terms on that, splittin' the difference at thutty."

"Make the deal tomorrer," said Phoebe. "Take my debt to him 'n' a note fur the rest. But make him give ye a deed to the mine, like he made me give a deed to all my proppity. Was freightin' mentioned?"

"No."

"It will be," said Phoebe.

On the following day the transaction was completed. Ward bought the mining machinery for thirty thousand dollars, and a rare bargain it was. He turned over to Solomon, Phoebe's debt and security, and his own note, secured by a deed to the mine.

"I calc'late him 'n' me's almost even-Stephen now," Phoebe said, "but I like to come out a leetle mite ahead."

"It hain't all clear sailin' yit," said Solomon. "He's got a partner."

"But one partner kin bind another in sich a transaction," she said.

"That's the law," agreed Solomon, "but the law don't cut sich a wide swath hereabouts."

"This time," she said, "the law's got me back of it."

With this saying, she walked out of the store and mounted her pony. She rode down the street toward the quartermaster's office, but before she reached it she saw approaching her a man upon a tired horse, leading a pack mule. Weary as was the horse, indicating a long and arduous journey, the man rode jauntily. Even at a distance she recognized the set of those shoulders, even though they were not encased, as she had last seen them, in the dandified garments of a gentleman from the South. Her hand twitched the reins sharply and her surprised horse reared. She quieted him with difficulty and rode straight ahead. In the narrow street she would pass the approaching man so closely that their knees would almost touch.

But before she reached him he halted, swept his weathered hat from his head in an elaborate bow

"A good afternoon to you, Widow Muncie," said Jefferson Carteret.

"You'll find I'm no widow," she retorted.

"By this time tomorrow you will be, ma'am," he said, and dropping his insolent eyes from her face, he urged his horse past her and down the street.

CHAPTER XXIII

Estevan Ochoa rapped timidly upon Phoebe's door, and she, waiting for Peter Muncie to return from the post where he had gone to renew acquaintance with the soldiers with whom he had once ridden, bade him enter. Estevan had increased his stature but little in the years since Phoebe had first seen his big, hungry eyes staring at her pies. His sharp, wizened face appeared older and his fine eyes were keener, but his pitiful shanks were as thin and his back as crooked as they had been on that day which had brought into his starved life someone to admire and to revere.

"*Señora,*" he said excitedly, "the man is here."

"Carteret? I saw him."

"Then the *Señora* knows. He sits now in the gambling house of Crandall and they talk with heads together. I could not listen. But all Tucson knows why he has come."

"He has come for many reasons," Phoebe said.

"The chief of them," said Estevan, "is to kill the *Señor* Peter. So the people are saying. They gather in certain places and talk of this killing as they would talk of a fiesta or a *baile*. Men tell each other it will be a thing to see. Some say that the *Señor* Peter has run away."

"He has not run away," said Phoebe.

Estevan smiled. "I only report what is being said. For myself, I made a disrespectful sound and said that the *Señor* Peter did not run away, because, first, he is a man of courage, and second, because you would not permit it. I made it clear that you would not permit yourself to be so shamed."

"So Carteret went to Bob Crandall's place. Not to see Lazarus Ward. A body 'ud think he'd go to his partner first."

"He is with the *Señor* Crandall. Then he goes to eat and drink and be until morning in the house of Dolores."

"How do you know this, Estevan?"

"Because it is his custom. It is known. I, also, go to the house of Dolores, for there is kindness there and food. And because I am small and have a crooked back they make no account of me and do not guard their tongues. When the *Señor* does not wish to be seen in Tucson he goes secretly to that place and remains in hiding."

"Do you mean, Estevan, that Carteret has been in town before and I did not know it?"

"That was what the women at the shop talked," said Estevan.

"When?"

"They did not say, and I dared not ask questions. But, if the *Señora* desires I will find out."

"You must not go near those wicked women," said Phoebe.

"You are sure," asked Phoebe, ignoring Estevan's philosophy, "that Carteret had been in Tucson secretly before today?"

"It is assuredly so," said Estevan. "I will find out on what day. Let not the *Señora's* conscience be troubled. I shall take no harm from Dolores. There I am not regarded as a man but as a creature to whom a bone is tossed."

"I'd have thought," Phoebe said, "he'd have gone first to see Lazarus."

Her face, with its golden-brown skin, its high and prominent cheekbones, its inward-pointed brows and straight line from jaw-corner to chin, seemed very young in spite of its gravity and the depth of apprehension in her eyes. It was a spirited face, an alert face with something about it that made one think of the face of an ancient imperious elfin Egyptian queen upon some coin unearthed from the ruins of a dead civilization. There was there, oddly enough, the imponderable something called for want of a better name breeding. Though she came of no high lineage but of the people. There was that look which one associates with aristocracy—though she numbered no aristocrat among her ancestors. It may well be that the features of aristocracy come down from the first of line, rather than that they are developed by generations of authority and position. It is to be remembered that she could forget in that moment her own gnawing anxiety and think of one so inconsiderable as little Estevan.

"What's a-goin' to become of you, you pore leetle skeezicks?" she asked, half to herself. "What's a-goin' to become of you in sich a place?"

Estevan never had troubled to ask what would become of him, or what life held for him. He was as he was. And there were the saints, who might very properly be relied upon. So he made no answer, being able to think of nothing suitable to reply.

"You can ride a horse," Phoebe said.

"Si, *Señora*."

"Who can ride a horse does not need strong legs," said Phoebe in Spanish. "God has seen fit to give you intelligence. Would it please you to go to my ranch to learn about cattle? And someday to be my right hand?"

"It would please me, *Señora*."

"Then it shall be done," said Phoebe. "Now go quickly, Estevan. Let no action of the *Señor* Carteret escape you. Then to herself: "Drat it, what for do men have to fight?"

She sat down to wait, and it seemed to her that there had been much waiting in her life—waiting for Peter Muncie. She had waited for him to return after he had first passed through Tucson; she had waited for him to bring her cattle; she was waiting for him to return now to face this inevitable thing that had been hanging over her head for so long—this meeting with Jefferson Carteret. It had to come now! It had to come now, when she was about to have a baby! It had to come when she was bending every energy and every adroitness of her mind to completing a trade that would save her from the results of her last headstrong venture. Tonight or tomorrow, her husband would encounter Carteret, and one of them would die. There was no escaping from it. Fate had taken these two men and jostled them against each other for some hidden purpose of its own, making them enemies. And now one of them must die.

If it should be Carteret Phoebe would feel no repugnance for her husband. The fact that he had taken a human life would arouse no aversion. In this fortunate event all would go on as before, and tomorrow would become but a remembered episode. But if Peter Muncie died, what then? She was appalled by the vision of endless loneliness that spread itself before her—of interminable years alone, without Peter; of days and nights and nights and days stretching on over the horizon of time through which she would exist but not live. If Peter Muncie died she would cease to be a woman, for she knew that no man could ever take his place—that she never would be able to tolerate another man in her life. That was how she loved him, profoundly, jealously, exclusively. He was her man, and failing him there could be no other. That is what his death would mean to her—the end of her life. All that would remain would be a human body and a human brain compelled to continue a grim, cheerless, lonely routine.

She even resented the baby. If Peter died, she did not want the baby, because it was his. If she could not share it with him, it was not worth having. For the first time in her life she became acquainted with stark terror.

And then she heard a horse's hoofs upon the sun-baked earth, and Peter dismounted and entered gaily.

"Peter," she said, "he's here."

"So I hear tell," he said, and she turned her eyes full upon his face in a sort of startled surprise, for he had spoken casually, as if the matter were of no importance.

"I met him face to face," she said, "and he called me Widder Muncie."

"What d'you care?" asked Peter. "It wa'n't so, was it?"

"It mustn't be so."

He walked to her and put a lean, powerful hand on each shoulder. "Is that there how ye really feel?" he asked.

"It's how I feel."

"If I was to let this feller kill me, it 'ud upset ye?"

"I probably wouldn't be able to die," she said. "That 'ud be the wust of it—to have to go on livin'."

"You pick the durndest time for tellin' me you're fond of me," he said ruefully. "Now why can't ye out with it pleasant evenin's when the moon's a-shinin' and we kin kind of revel in it? Seems to me like the only times ye git to lovin' me fit to bust is jest when I'm a-goin' to git shot at. Where's this feller at?"

"Estevan says he's in Bob Crandall's. He's supposed to be goin' to Dolores' after."

"The idee bein'," asked Peter, "that he's goin' to attend to the matter of makin' ye a widder tomorrow?"

"Yes."

"Who give him the right to pick his time?" Peter asked. "Takes two to make a bargain. Bob Crandall's, eh?" He kissed her and grinned down into her face. "Guess I'll be a-walkin' over that way," he said.

"No, Peter. Not now. Tomorrow."

"When you go makin' a business dicker," asked Peter, "do you let the other feller pick his time 'n' place 'n' advantage?"

"Wa-al," he said, "this here's durn nigh as important as business."

She saw that amused look in his eyes and knew that he was enjoying himself, looking forward to this adventure, and that no doubts assailed him as to its outcome. He had no question whatever, she could see, as to what would happen. It was unthinkable to him that anything could happen to him.

It was his fight. She would not tolerate his interference with a transaction of hers; therefore she must not meddle in this matter which was peculiarly his. This was a thing he knew and understood and was adapted for. It was the sort of event for which he had been created—and she must keep her hands off. Even though it was in her behalf that he fought, as her husband assuming responsibility for accusations she had made, she must not advise nor interfere.

"Would ye like to kiss me once more before ye go?" she asked steadily, and he did so. Then she walked with him to the door.

"Good luck to ye," she said, and stood in the doorway looking after him as he walked toward the Calle Real. Once he turned and waved his hand, and then he disappeared around a corner.

She could not go with him. She could not be at his side now, nor share his danger. Nor could she bear to be alone. She thrust on her black wide-awake hat and followed the way he had taken—not to dog his steps to Bob Crandall's but to go to Solomon Warner's, where there would be company; where Solomon would be; where she could wait for the news to come.

She was conscious as she walked that life in Tucson had been curiously arrested. The town was still, with an unnatural stillness. Even the scavenger dogs were not nosing in the rubbish, and ragged Mexicans who usually sprawled, faces covered with broad hats, asleep in the dust and the sun, were invisible. Now and then the fat cheeks and beady eyes of a Mexican woman peered affrightedly from the opening where a window should have been. On the main thoroughfare, commonly crowded at this hour with wagons, oxen, military equipment, burros, belled and laden, were only knots of men in earnest conversation, their faces turned in a common direction. It was as if the whole town were poised, waiting. It was an ominous lull. Every human being in the streets stood ready to duck at an instant's warning into some doorway. And, as Phoebe passed, shoulders erect and face expressionless, they gazed at her in silence. She was embarrassed by it, because she knew she was a part of the tragedy. Her every movement and expression would be remembered and discussed and recounted, and she resented it. Her face hardened and her chin set with determination.

She skirted the carcass of a mule, dried and shrunken, which had lain where it fell for weeks, and presently came to Solomon Warner's doorway, which she entered, to find the room occupied by half a dozen of Tucson's better citizens. Solomon was there, and Oury and Lizard and Shelby and Jesús Elias and Ortiz. Silence fell as she came through the door. She walked to the counter before anyone spoke. It was Solomon who first found his voice.

"How be ye, Phoebe?" he asked uncomfortably.

"Reasonable," she answered. "Got any of Pete Kitchen's hams?"

"Eh? What say?"

"I want a Kitchen ham, if ye got one," she said.

"You—you come in here fur a ham?" Solomon asked unbelievingly.

"I calc'late ye kin hear," she said tartly.

"Listen, Phoebe, d'ye know what's goin' on in this town? D'ye know where your husband is?"

"I most allus know where my husband is," she said.

"But say, Phoebe—" He looked about him helplessly at the

other men. "Mebby ye hain't heard. Mebby ye don't know Carteret's in town."

"I seen him," said Phoebe. "I met him kerslap, face to face. He called me Widder Muncie. So my husband jest stepped over to tell him it wa'n't so."

"Then ye know them two is gunnin' fur each other?"

"To be sure," said Phoebe—"It's a middlin-sized ham I want. I need a paper of needles, too." They could not see that the knuckles of her hands were white as she clenched her hands in her pockets; nor could they know that her heart was standing still as she waited for some sound to tell her the affair had reached its climax.

"Mrs. Muncie," said Oury, "I think you fail to understand. Your husband and Carteret are looking for each other. There will be a killing."

She turned to him a serene face. "To be sure," she said, "Peter's practically forced to do it. Nobuddy'll hold it agin him— And, Solomon, I kin use a spool of white, about sixty. I do wisht somebuddy 'ud move that mule's carcass in the street."

"But, Phoebe," said Shelby, "hadn't ye ought to kind of be prepared? I mean if it didn't come out that way."

She smiled very slightly as she looked at him exclusively. "Ye hain't very well acquainted with Peter, be ye?" she asked.

Then, over the flat roofs of the adobe town, reverberating down its sordid, meandering, narrow streets, came the sound of a shot. Then a pause—and then two more shots. After that, silence. The faces of the men turned as one toward Phoebe, and they stared at her stonily. She felt as if a hand of fire was reaching inside her and squeezing her heart, but these men should never know.

"Well, Solomon," she forced herself to say, "that's over. Gimme my ham. Peter'll be hungry fur his supper."

But in her soul, her tortured soul, she was saying, "Wa-al, ye wanted a show—so I give it to ye. . . . Peter. Peter. Oh, come hurryin' to me, Peter."

They were staring at her incredulously, but she did not care. Out there somewhere Peter was alive or Peter was dead. She did not know which and she was not certain she wanted to know. It was over, as she had said. Whatever had happened was beyond recall. It now belonged to the past. And possibly she, too, belonged to the past, for if Peter were dead she also was dead. It was odd to stand there not knowing if he were alive or dead.

"I'll go and find out," said Oury.

"Ye needn't to," she compelled herself to say, but he did not heed her. He walked to the door and stepped out into the late afternoon blaze of sunshine. Now she would have to know. The news would be brought to her. Oury would bring it. She could not avoid learning the news. Silence fell. How long it persisted she never knew, but it was broken by Oury, who lunged through the door.

"It's all right, Phoebe," he said. "It's all right. He's coming down the street."

"Peter?" she heard herself ask.

"Your husband," said Oury.

She turned abruptly to Warner, and this time her voice was not so docile to control, for she was striving to hide joy rather than terror and agony.

"It takes ye a sight of time to git down one ham," she said—and then Peter was standing in the door. It was Peter. It was true. It was her husband standing there, uninjured, squinting a little as he strove to adjust his eyes to the shade of the room. She felt light as air. She was in the grip of a great elation, a tremendous upsurge of joy and relief, but nobody must know. None of these strange, curious, friendly eyes must see. Peter was coming into the store. He was close to her. She spoke to him.

"You took a mite longer'n I figgered you would," she said. "Let's be gittin' home."

And so, side by side, carrying a Pete Kitchen ham and a spool of thread, they walked out of the shadows of tragedy; nor did either of them hear what Solomon Warner said after they were gone. It was profane, admiring, almost awe-stricken. "Gawd, what a woman!" he exclaimed. "Nothin' but iron from topknot to gizzard."

But the iron woman walked blindly. Her fingers clutched Peter's arm so fiercely that her nails broke his skin. And she could not speak. But when they were inside their home she found her voice.

"If that," she said, "is what it's like to love, I'm glad I hain't never a-goin' to love but once."

CHAPTER XXIV

THERE are few women, fewer wives, who would not have cross-questioned their husbands until they were in possession of the minutest detail of such an adventure as Peter Muncie's duel with Jefferson Carteret, but Phoebe asked not one question. She wanted never to hear of the thing again; she wanted never to be reminded of those minutes of waiting in Don Solomon's store. That interval had seared her soul as with a branding iron, and she desired only to forget it. Until that hour she had never known she could love so fiercely; or that the loss of her husband could bring such utter destruction to her life. So she was grimly silent. Even Peter did not understand what went on inside her stoical exterior, and he wondered a little. Had it not been for the convulsive clutch of her strong fingers upon his arm he would have wondered more.

Phoebe referred to the matter but once, and that as they were about to enter the little house on the Plaza de la Mesilla.

"He is dead," she said, not as a question but as a statement.

"As a doornail," said Peter, and waited, as a man will do, for more questions, in order that he might give answers and hold himself up to the admiration of his woman. That is how all men must behave. They must have the admiration of their women even if they scorn the praise of all the rest of mankind. They must preen their feathers. They must crow a little, and the woman must not let it be seen that she knows her man is crowing. If she be wise she will not take her man down a peg but will exclaim and permit her eyes to glow. And then her husband will adore her and recognize her as a queen among women.

But Phoebe, wise wife that she was, gave Peter no opportunity to display. Indeed, she would never have known what occurred in Bob Crandall's gambling place had it not become a part of Tucson's history, a part of the saga of that town, so that it sifted in to her, point by point, detail by detail, until the complete picture was hers. But even when she knew, she did not dwell upon it.

She knew that Peter had walked down the street, not slowly and cautiously, not jauntily, but as a man moving to some purpose which was not unpleasant to him and to which he hastened. She knew that he reached Crandall's door before word of his coming had been carried on ahead to Carteret; and suddenly he had stood in the door, leaning with ease, but not with carelessness, against the jamb.

"Looking for me, Jeff?" he asked. "I hear you claim to be a widow-maker."

Carteret sat rigid, both palms pressed flat on the top of the table before which he sat. He and Peter were the only motionless men in the room; the others were squeezing their bodies against the adobe, to be as far from a line running from Jefferson to Muncie as was possible in the rectangle within the walls.

"Take your fuss outside," said Crandall.

"You takin' sides?" asked Peter.

"Not me."

"I wisht you was," said Peter. "I'd admire to make a day of it." Then to Carteret: "Move your checker, widow-maker."

"It doesn't seem like a good time for it, Muncie," said Carteret.

Scowling, inimical faces lowered at Peter from the two sides of the place. There was not a man in that company who was friendly to him; probably not a man there but would have shot him in the back if he could have done so without risk; so he was compelled to watch not only Carteret but every one of the riffraff who cowered out of the line of fire.

"I don't want it said I shot a sittin' bird," said Peter. "Git up on your hind laigs, Carteret."

Carteret dropped his hands under the edge of the table and stood up suddenly. At the same instant he overturned the table, sending it end over end at Peter's legs a dozen feet away. A shot came from the group of men against the wall, and Peter's hat jerked from his head. Then there were two shots, one from Carteret's gun, one from Peter's. Carteret pitched to the floor face down and Peter stood crouching, ready.

"The' wouldn't be many complaints," he said, "if I made this here a massacree."

He strode to Carteret, turned him with his foot. "You boys," he said to the riffraff, "kin let it leak out, if you got a mind to, that Mis' Muncie hain't a widder yit."

With which saying he backed to the door, backed out of it into the street, and then, turning, walked past groups of silent

Mexicans and Indians and a scattering of white men until he came to Phoebe.

That is the story as it came to her bit by bit; that is the picture she pieced together of the affray in Bob Crandall's gambling hell. She never spoke of it to Peter, or praised him for his conduct, or took him to task for his recklessness. The nearest she ever came to it was a saying.

"In this here kind of a country," she observed, "the's got to be two kinds of folk. The's got to be them that finds the fights, and them that clings and builds. One hain't no good 'thout the other. You 'n' me is a mated team."

It was a true saying. There must be men to find: hunters, trappers, prospectors to be forerunners, to discover the rivers and mountains and trails and wealth of minerals under the surface of the earth; and to fight for what they found. There must be others to venture in upon the heels of these first comers and to root themselves and cling in spite of adverse nature and inimical savage—and with grim fortitude to develop that which will result in civilization, in towns, in mines, in agriculture. The two are different in nature, but inseparable, each useless without the other. Finders, fighters, clingers, builders! A foundation, these, upon which the nation builds its future.

Phoebe possessed the characteristic of being able to put things behind her. When an event had transpired, that was that. It had ceased to be, become only a shadow in the memory, and she passed on to the next item in the agenda of her life. She knew that Carteret, in his arrogant, crooked way, had loved her—and that his desire for her had been at the root of his enmity for her husband. This did not sadden her. If she thought of this phase of the matter at all it was to say that he had no business to love her, and, doing so uninvited, must take the consequences.

On the day following Carteret's death, there remained but one consideration in Phoebe's practical mind, and that was the effect that his shooting might have upon her deviously conducted negotiations with Lazarus Ward. To her way of thinking, it simplified them. Carteret had been Ward's partner, and might have meddled in the transaction. Now he was dead and could no longer interfere. Lazarus Ward no longer had a partner. In the easy-going conception of property rights that obtained, Ward was now sole owner of the mine he had come to Tucson to develop. Phoebe went to see Solomon Warner.

"How you comin' with Ward?" she asked.

"He's set to buy that machinery," said Solomon, "but he's got a spite agin you, Phoebe. I can't git him to give up that mortgage. He aims to make ye pay cash fur it. He's ambitious to make ye all the trouble he kin. As soon's he kin git about, he says he's a-goin' to make you raise that fifteen thousand or he'll sell ye out."

"Spite," said Phoebe, "never put no meat on your ribs. It's a kind of an extry pleasure, like gravy on potaters. A body hadn't ought to make gravy till he's hot his meat to git the juice."

"Lazarus," observed Don Solomon, "didn't seem upsot by losin' a pardner. Funny thing, Phoebe, he hain't never accused you 'n' Peter of shootin' him. It hain't like Lazarus, even if he knowed ye didn't do it."

"Forgit about my mortgage fur the time bein'," said Phoebe,

ignoring the mention of Carteret. "You tell him you're willin' to take what cash he's got, and the mine as security fur the rest. He hain't a-goin' to be movin' around spry fur quite a spell. By that time the paymaster'll be around and the'll be money to be got at."

"Jest as you say," agreed Solomon.

"But don't let freightin' come into it."

"I'm rememberin'," Solomon assured her.

That night as they sat over the supper table eating of the ham that Phoebe had bought yesterday, Peter became solicitous. "I don't reckon all this here surgin' around is good fur ye, Phoebe," he said. "Hadn't we ought to git back to the ranch where ye kin be quiet?"

"Men is fools about wimmin havin' babies," she said tersely. "And wimmin have encouraged it. It's been a-goin' on fur a million years and a billion babies has been born. But every husband acts like it never happened before and regards himself as havin' accomplished suthin' original."

"Thinkin' about it kind of scares me," he said.

"I never see a woman I wa'n't better than," said Phoebe. "So it stands to reason I kin have a baby better. When it comes time to set and fold my hands, I'll set. But right now I'm busy, and so be you."

"I hain't got a thing to do in town," he protested.

"You're a-goin' to have. Little Estevan Ochoa says Carteret has been in town before this. What you got to find out is when. And who seen him, and what he come here secret fur."

"I been nosin' around among the Mexicans," said Peter.

"Ye picked the wrong Mexicans," she said shortly. "Next ye might try Dolores."

"Eh?"

"Don't want me visitin' there, do ye?"

"No," he answered; "and most wives 'ud feel the same about their husbands."

"I don't," said Phoebe. "The's two kinds of men: Them ye know is up to tricks and them ye never ketch at it. I'll be happier if you're one of the last. That's what a woman means when she says she kin trust her husband. She jest figgers he's too slick to be ketched."

"Honest Injun, Phoebe——"

"Don't go protestin'," she said. "Protestin' is like smoke risin' from a fire. I want ye sh'ud git this woman to talk 'n' tell ye jest when Carteret was to see her, and who else knowed he was in Tucson. I know dum well when it was, but I want to be able to prove it. What I never got through my head," she said, an instant later, "is why he shot that Mexican you was draggin' down the ranch 'n' didn't shoot you, too."

"I reckon," said Peter, with an understanding of his enemy's character which astonished Phoebe, "that he was ambitious to have me lookin' on when he done it. I'll talk to that thar Dolores, 'n' I'll set Estevan to snoopin'."

"Don't forgit to be int'rested in Bob Crandall," she told him. "He's a-wearin' the coyote skin I want to nail to the barn door."

"Crandall! Why Crandall?"

"You ketch him fur me," she said, " 'n' I'll show ye how to cook him."

But it was not to be Peter who was to give Crandall to her, nor was it her own planning or adroitness, but rather a very fat, chocolate-colored old woman who never had been considered by Phoebe as of even slight importance in her affairs. It was a matter of gratitude and of loyalty. Phoebe bestowed her bounty, when it occurred to her to be charitable, with carelessness, expecting no return. She was apt to be kind harshly, as if she were ashamed of a kindness. And having bestowed, she forgot the matter, or regarded it as negligible. For years she had been a sort of patroness to little Estevan Ochoa, and knew that he adored her. But that his gratitude and adoration should be shared by any other member of his clan she did not realize. She did not even realize that there was a clan; that the Ochoas and their blood cousins and their relations by marriage were a compact unit for offense or defense. Nor did she appreciate that because of the friendship of the Ochoas, she was regarded with favor by the decent, honest, simply religious Mexicans of Tucson. Accidentally she had builded well and had created for herself allies whose eyes were as sharp as their knives.

Peter had gone upon the errand upon which Phoebe had sent him when Estevan rapped upon her door.

"May the saints look with kindness upon this house," he said in greeting. "I come from my mother, *Señora*. She asks if the *Señora* will bring great honor upon our family by passing through our doorway and standing beneath our roof."

"Is there illness, Estevan?" Phoebe asked.

"There is no illness, but only great happiness if the *Señora* will come. Also there is one awaiting her that it may be well for her to see."

"The honor is not to you," said Phoebe politely, for she was able to be polite in Spanish where she would have been abrupt in her own language. "To be bidden to your house honors my unworthiness."

Estevan beamed as she accompanied him through the broken wall to a miserable mud house whose door was a cowhide stretched upon a frame of cottonwood poles. There was no window. The floor was earth, scuffled smooth by calloused bare feet, and of furniture there was almost none. As Phoebe entered she saw standing in the middle of the room an enormously fat woman whom she recognized as Estevan's mother. *Señora* Ochoa grinned proudly.

"This poor house," she said, "and all that it contains are yours."

"Words spoken in friendship," replied Phoebe, "are more precious than gold."

"The *Señora,*" said the fat woman, "has shown kindness to my son afflicted by God. It is an ill thing if grass grows not where the rain has fallen. *Señora,* behold the woman, Dolores."

In the shadows against the wall crouched a younger woman, lithe, not without remnants of beauty. She did not then, nor even later, when more wisdom came to her, appreciate what it meant for an honest Mexican woman, fiercely proud of her virtue and of the virtue of her children, to permit the woman, Dolores, to cross her threshold. She knew how the good Mexican mothers guarded their daughters and instructed them and sheltered them, so that they might go to their husbands in purity and innocence; she did not know that the daughters had been sent away and would not be allowed to re-enter their home until it had been cleansed of defilement.

"The woman, Dolores," said *Señora* Ochoa, "will answer

such questions as you desire to ask." She nodded her head grimly. "She will answer them promptly and without lying."

"Does she speak English?" asked Phoebe.

Señora Ochoa shrugged her huge shoulders and spread her hands. Phoebe faced Dolores over the candle.

"Was Jefferson Carteret in Tucson on the night when Lazarus Ward was shot?" she asked.

Dolores remained mute. *Señora* Ochoa shuffled across the earth floor and delivered a buffet with her hamlike hand. "Speak!" she commanded.

"He was here," Dolores whined.

"In your house?"

"In my house."

"Was Bob Crandall, the gambler, also there?"

"They talked long together in whispers."

"Saying what?"

"They spoke of the *Señor* Ward, and of gold in a belt, and of a mine."

"Which of them shot the *Señor* Ward through the window of the mescal shop?"

Señora Ochoa stood, an ominous mountain of a woman, over the reluctant Dolores. "Thou sow," she said, "well you know that you and your kind remain by the sufferance of honest wives. We permit it. If we give the word that you be driven out, there is an end of you. If twenty honest wives gather and visit your house, who is there to stop us from destroying it and driving you naked into the desert? Consider that well, and answer honestly."

"It was the tall *Señor* that was called Jeff. He returned, and there was talk and apprehension. For a thing had taken place. A Mexican named Ignacio Sais had been made prisoner and taken away upon a horse. I heard this spoken. This *Sais*"— Dolores was now speaking eagerly, rapidly—"must not be questioned. Nor must Jeff be seen in Tucson. He went out cautiously and rode toward the north. Crandall also rode, but to the south. He returned next day, much pleased, for he had shot this man Sais from ambush, so that he might not speak."

"What was the thing of which they dared not permit Ignacio Sais to speak?" asked Phoebe.

"I do not know all things," answered Dolores sulkily.

Once more the huge hand of *Señora* Ochoa descended, flinging the woman against the wall. "Speak!" she ordered again.

"It had to do with the robbing of a safe and the stealing of money. This robbery was a thing planned."

"Who planned it with Crandall and Carteret?" asked Phoebe.

"I fear him more than Bob Crandall," Dolores said. "I dare not speak his name."

"Speak it," said *Señora* Ochoa, and the huge paw lifted, in readiness to strike.

"The name is the name of Lazarus Ward," said Dolores. "I do not wish to be killed. I do not wish to be sent away to the jail in Yuma. If I tell all, will I be protected and set at liberty?"

"That will be as it happens," said Phoebe. "I am listening."

"The robbery was planned in my house. It was the *Señora's* safe. The men laughed together, but Ward laughed most of all."

Phoebe sighed with satisfaction. She beamed upon *Señora* Ochoa. "I am your daughter and you are my mother," she said. "Your friends are my friends and your enemies my enemies. Can this woman be prevented from fleeing until a day comes?"

"She will be present when the *Señora* desires her to be present," said Estevan's mother.

"*Gracias, Señora,*" said Phoebe. "There is much I must do. I may not remain longer."

"Go with God," said *Señora* Ochoa, and stood beaming in the doorway, eyes glittering with pride and pleasure, as Phoebe disappeared up the dark street. But not unguarded, for Estevan followed watchfully at her heels.

CHAPTER XXV

PHOEBE consulted with no one. There was no law to which she could apply or to which she could disclose the facts she had accumulated and demand that action be taken. Had there been law and courts, it is doubtful if she would have availed herself of their power, because her interest in the crimes of Ward and Crandall was not social but financial. She had no desire to inflict punishment; only to thwart Ward in his efforts to embarrass her, and to derive such profit from the situation as might be possible.

The ethical condition was eccentric. In Tucson, murder or attempted murder was more or less regarded as a personal matter between the parties involved. A man was supposed to protect his own life. A killer could walk the streets unmolested. But thievery, robbery, was a cat of another color. Over a stealing, it was possible to arouse public indignation. No man would rob with impunity, and an individual with light fingers was apt to find himself dangling at the end of a rope, or, at best, driven from the community. So it was upon the robbery of her safe that Phoebe concentrated.

Nor was she above trading upon her sex. The men of

Tucson would regard it as more heinous to blow the safe of a woman than the strongbox of a man, and Phoebe had no intention of letting the town lose sight of this fact when it came to the denouement.

But she did not hurry. As each year scuttled past her, she put on another layer of patience. She was learning the value of thoroughness, of planning, of preparation, and the dangers of flying at any object headlong. In this case she coveted thoroughness and finality. She meant to leave no loopholes, but when the time came, to spring her trap neatly, with tidiness and no trailing ends. It was her purpose to abolish Lazarus Ward so completely that he never would be able to annoy her again. She was tired of Lazarus Ward. It was not that she was vindictive. Phoebe never was that. But she was aware that as long as Ward continued in the locality, just so long could she expect to find him meddling in her affairs and threatening her peace of mind. He must be removed, eradicated, and she would do so as ruthlessly as if he were a coyote menacing her chickens.

Lazarus Ward was able to sit up in a chair. It would be but a few days before he would be afoot again. Peter, who was eager to get back to the ranch, urged Phoebe to act against him.

"Why don't ye upset his applecart before he gets able-bodied 'n' dangerous again?" he asked.

"It's easier," she said, "to have a man come and step in a hole than it is to dig the hole up and carry it to him." And she would not be moved.

The Ochoa clan was active among the Mexican population. Shrewd, fat *Señora* Ochoa was paying her debt to Phoebe, and she was a driving force that her family dared not disregard. She kept her heavy hand upon Dolores and mined for information among her cronies.

"Behold," she said, "one evil man of our race brings all into disrepute. It is well that we live in friendship with these Americanos, for there are many of them, and more will follow those who are here. If we live good lives and are virtuous, they will be our friends, and profit will be made from it. Therefore we should call upon the saints to aid us in bringing to justice thieves and murderers. It will reflect credit upon us all."

She paused, arms on enormous hips. "Besides," she said, "the *Señora* takes my Estevan to her rancho to instruct him how to become chief of her *vaqueros*."

It was some six days later, the time being early October, when the summer's burning heat was somewhat ameliorated, and Arizona was moving into an autumn of such weather as is to be found nowhere else upon earth, that Phoebe encountered Lazarus on the street. He was emaciated, gaunt, bearded, and he walked slowly, clinging to a cane. But his eyes glittered as they rested upon her.

"We got some business, you and me," he said in a voice he strove to prevent from becoming tremulous.

"I calc'late I'm ready to take it up," said Phoebe.

"Nothin' to take up. I want my money, or else you turn over your proppity to me, like the agreement says."

"The' may be p'ints to discuss," said Phoebe.

"What with one thing and 'nother, you've been give ample time."

"The's never ample time betwixt borrowin' money and

havin' to pay it back," she said. "But if you're anxious to git things settled, you might come to Solomon Warner's store tonight."

"What fur?"

"It's as good a place as any to do business," she said.

"I'll be there," he responded, "and you have that there fifteen thousand dollars ready for me."

She walked directly to Warner's. "Don Solomon," she said, "I want the use of your store tonight. I calc'late to settle matters with Lazarus."

"You're welcome," said Warner.

"I'd take it kindly if you was to be here. I want Oury, too, and Aldrich and Kirkland. And Guillermo Tellez and Jesús Elias. And if Pete Kitchen's in town."

"What ye a-goin' to do—hold a caucus?"

"I jest want witnesses to see all's done fair 'n' square."

"They'll be there," said Solomon, and they were there.

At eight o'clock, when Lazarus Ward stepped into the dimly lighted store building, he was surprised to see sitting about on barrels and counters so many of the responsible men of Tucson—Americans and Mexicans. Phoebe was already there, and Peter.

"What's this here," Lazarus demanded, "a town meetin'?"

"It might turn out that way," said Phoebe. "Lazarus and me," she said to the company, "has got a mite of business to git settled. Some time back I borrowed fifteen thousand dollars that I thought I was a-borrowin' from Bob Crandall. It turned out Lazarus was lendin'. I give all my proppity, ranches, stock and wagons as security—you got that paper with ye, Lazarus?"

"I got it, all right," he answered.

"Seems like Bob Crandall ought to be here," she said. "Him bein' the one that actually lent me the money. Will ye step over 'n' git him, Peter?"

"Yes'm," said Peter, with a look of pleasant anticipation. "But what if he don't want to come?"

"Fetch him," said Phoebe.

"The' hain't no need for Bob Crandall nor nobbudy else," protested Lazarus.

"Friend of your'n, hain't he?" asked Phoebe. "We kin wait a minute fur him."

After a short delay, Peter appeared with Crandall.

"What's a-goin' on here?" Crandall asked; then saw Lazarus Ward and scowled.

"It was you lent me fifteen thousand dollars," said Phoebe. "I thought 't wa'n't more'n fair if you was here when I paid it back. You lent it to me, didn't ye?"

"I done so," said Crandall formally.

"Where'd ye git that much, Bob?" she asked.

"That hain't nobuddy's business but mine."

"Know a woman named Dolores?"

"Most men in this town does," he said with a leer.

"Know her well enough to plan a murder in her house, and her in earshot?" Phoebe asked. "You 'n' Jefferson Carteret?"

"If she says so, she lies," Bob Crandall said loudly.

"Mebby she won't say so," said Phoebe, "but we kin ask her." She lifted her voice. "Fetch in Dolores," she ordered.

From the back room, the warehouse, appeared the monstrous figure of *Señora* Ochoa, pushing ahead of her the reluctant Dolores. "Here she is. She will speak. She will speak truth," said the *Señora*.

"I ain't goin' to stay here and listen to this," blustered Crandall.

"Sit down!" said Peter Muncie. "Or suit yourself!"

Crandall resumed his place against a barrel.

Phoebe addressed Dolores in Spanish. "Was Jefferson Carteret in Tucson on the night when Lazarus Ward was shot?"

"He was in my house."

"Was Crandall with him?"

"He was with him."

"Did you hear them talk together?"

"I heard them talk of how Carteret would kill Lazarus Ward. They went out, and returned, saying that Ward was killed. But there was another thing that gave them fear."

"What was this other thing?"

"That man there," Dolores said, pointing to Peter Muncie, "had made a prisoner of Ignacio Sais and was taking him to his rancho, tied on a horse's back, to make him talk."

"About what thing were they afraid he would talk?"

"About the robbery of the *señora's* strong box," said Dolores. "They dared not have the truth become known, for it was they who planned and carried out this robbery, with the aid of certain Mexican bandits."

"You heard them speak of this matter?"

"With my ears."

Phoebe turned to Crandall. "So you see," she said, "it kind of makes a difference where you got the money you lent me. That money didn't quit bein' mine when you stole it. And it didn't quit bein' mine when I borrowed it off of you. I don't know just how a woman 'ud go about it to borrow her own money."

"She lies. This kind of a woman allus lies."

"Looks like Lazarus b'lieves the shootin' part of it anyhow," said Phoebe.

Lazarus was crouching forward in his chair, his face livid and distorted with rage. "Gimme a gun, somebody! Gimme a gun!" he raged.

"Not time fur any shootin' yit," said Phoebe. "If ye hain't satisfied to b'lieve Dolores, mebby you're acquainted with a couple Mexicans named Leopoldo Romero and Solano Pecheco. . . . Fetch 'em in, Peter," she directed, and three men of the Ochoa clan roughly hauled two cowering compatriots into the store.

"They also will speak," said *Señora* Ochoa contentedly. "It has been arranged."

"Did you," asked Phoebe of the foremost of them, "take pay for aiding in the robbery of my safe?"

"We did," replied Romero through chattering teeth.

"From whose pocket came the gold?" asked Phoebe.

"From that of the *Señor* Crandall," Romero said.

"Does your companion tell the truth?" Phoebe asked of Pecheco.

"He speaks truth, as the saints hear me!"

Crandall waved his arms and shouted, "You men ain't a-goin' to believe that woman and these Mexican thieves against the word of a white man, be ye? It's a pack of lies!"

"We believe the testimony of these people, Crandall," said Oury gravely, "do we not, gentlemen?"

"We do," echoed the men who sat about in the background.

"You and Jefferson Carteret were in this thing together," Phoebe said, "but there was someone else. Mebby it might make a difference how we treated ye, if you was to tell who else."

Lazarus Ward had been husbanding his strength as he sat. His small eyes had shifted about the room, darting from man to man, burning as they came to rest on Crandall's face. Suddenly he darted from his chair, snatched a revolver from Peter Muncie's belt and fired. But as his finger closed about the trigger, Peter struck his arm upward, and the bullet splintered the ceiling above Crandall's head. In another instant Peter held Lazarus securely in spite of ravings and struggles.

"Lazarus acted mightly like he wanted to shet your mouth fur ye," said Phoebe. " 'Twan't a friendly way to behave. What was it he didn't want ye to tell?"

Crandall snarled. "It was him," he said. "Him 'n' Carteret. They planned the hull shebang. I didn't do nothin' but help 'em recruit Mexicans. He took the money. I never tetched it till he sent me to Mis' Muncie to lend it to her. That's the Gawd's truth of the thing."

Oury arose. "There is no law available," he said, "but this is a matter that cannot pass unnoticed. We should proceed formally to the organization of a committee——"

"Jest hold your hosses before ye git to committees," interrupted Phoebe. "Fust off, is it the jedgment of you men that I owe Lazarus Ward fifteen thousand dollars?"

"Assuredly not," said Oury.

"Then his mortgage hain't no good?"

"Only as good as this," replied Kirkland, reaching into Ward's pocket and extracting a paper, which he examined.

He nodded his head and tore it to fragments. "Satisfied?" he asked.

"Not yit," said Phoebe. "I got my own back, but I hain't took no skin off'n Lazarus' back. The' hain't no profit to be got from hangin's."

"What would you suggest?" asked Oury.

"Jest a final dicker," said Phoebe. "I'm offerin' to swap him two hosses 'n' rifles 'n' ammunition 'n' a bag of food for a minin' proppity he's got up on the Hassayampa. Then turn 'em both loose, head 'em east, and what happens after that is betwixt them 'n' the desert 'n' the Apaches." She paused. "I'm almighty weary of bein' irked by Lazarus."

The assembled men were hard. They stared at Phoebe with level eyes, eyes that were a little amazed. They could have hanged Ward and Crandall and slept soundly after it, but here was a hardness more adamantine than theirs.

"It's your say," said Oury, after a moment's pause.

Phoebe sighed. "I'm kind of glad," she said, "that everything come out so nice. Now I kin go back to the ranch 'n' have my baby in peace 'n' comfort."

CHAPTER XXVI

It was May. Phoebe sat in the shade of the hacienda of the ranch with a sleeping child on her lap. He was in his seventh month and his round little cheeks were brown as those of a Mexican. She was happy; she was more than happy, she was contented. As far as her eye could reach, the land was hers, rich bottom lands eager to pour into her lap gifts of grain and fruit; miles of mountainside and desert upon whose abundant alfilaria and grasses and shrubs grazed or browsed a growing herd of healthy cattle. The spring rodeo was over and the count of calves completed. It was satisfactory. As nearly as she could estimate, there had been a seventy-five per cent calf crop. She sat and considered this, planning how many heifers would be turned back to browse and to multiply; how many steers would be covering their frames with salable meat. The herd numbered close to a thousand head now. It would grow in a couple of years to two thousand, then to five, then to ten thousand herd. She liked this way of increasing her wealth.

Peter Muncie rode up big with news.

"Word jest come," he said. "The war's over. Lee surrendered to Grant at a place they call Appomattox, April ninth."

The war was over; the war that had occupied the energies of America for four long years had come to an end. Now, Phoebe saw, those tremendous energies would be released and would flow in fresher down channels of peaceful enterprise.

"It'll be the makin' of Arizony," Phoebe said.

Peter frowned. "Emigrants'll be flockin' in," he said, speaking as one who did not like the prospect.

"I calc'late," she said, "we've gone through the wust of it. We've clung to our toe-holt."

She permitted her mind to drift back over the years, back to that day when she drove tired horses hitched to a Conestoga wagon into walled Tucson—into the Old Pueblo. The promised land of California lay ahead of her then, but she never had reached it, and never regretted that she had been halted to take root in Arizona.

One wagon, a team of horses and a dying father! It seemed so long. So much activity had filled the years she felt like an old woman, until she counted her years. She was not yet twenty-five. Not yet twenty-five but she was a power in this new territory; a figure of authority and personality to be consulted and to be reckoned with.

From a penniless girl, baking pies in the blistering heat of Tucson's Plaza de Armas, she had shouldered and jostled and fought her way in an environment that would have blasted and destroyed most of her sisters, to a place where she could sit upon her own gallery and look out over more acres than were possessed by many an English Earl. She could ride to Tucson and see her teams and wagons come in and go out, carrying freight over mountain and desert to her daily enrichment. She could study reports from her mine on the Hassayampa—the Two-Horse Mine, so called from the circumstances of its acquisition, and could realize that it was increasing her wealth not by tens of dollars nor by hundreds, but by tens of thousands which were stored safely in the banks of San Francisco.

There had been suffering and hard work; there had been tragedy and peril—and there had been good fortune. None would have been more ready to admit that good fortune played its part in her success than she. But each item of good fortune had been the effect of a definite cause, the reward of bread thrown upon the water.

Where, for hundreds of miles in every direction, settler, miner, prospector heard with terror the name of Cochise, she was at peace with the great Indian. A private peace pertaining only to her and to hers. She could ride in safety where others rode in constant peril.

Before her stood a husband of whom she could be proud; a man of the frontier. In her lap slept Peter Muncie's son and hers. All these things, these riches, material and imponderable, had come to her while the land was in travail. They had been snatched out of cataclysm; wrenched from the very claws of calamity.

Peter looked down at her and smiled, and touched his son's cheek with gentle finger.

"The' hain't much more a body kin ask fur," he said.

Phoebe did not return his gaze, but peered off across the valley to the frowning mesa beyond.

"It hain't what a body asks fur," she said. "Anybuddy kin git. It takes an able person to keep. And ye can't jest keep. You got to keep addin'."

"Won't ye never be satisfied, Phoebe?"

"We're here amongst the fust," she said, "where it's rainin' treasure. Want me to put a lid over my bucket, so none kin fall in?"

She held up her son.

"There's him to think about. We got to build up a country fur him to grow in. We can't rest content. We got a hole dug 'n' the foundation put in. The' won't be no restin' fur you 'n' me, Peter, till the walls is up 'n' the roof on 'n' thatched, 'n' the furniture placed, 'n' a garden in the yard. We can't let go."

"When do we commence havin' fun?"

She disregarded that. "The war's over," she said. "Ye might say on that day Arizony was born. What went before was jest a mother's sickness whilst she was a-carryin' the child."

"The' was other news I didn't tell ye, Phoebe," said Peter. "Some actor feller shot 'n' killed President Lincoln."

She sat brooding upon this. "Pore feller," she said. "I calc'late I misjedged him. No good's a-goin' to flow from sich a killin'. He wan't one to hold malice." She moved her shoulders as if to toss off the weight of these tidings. What was done could not be mended. Then she held her son up to him.

"Him 'n' Arizony is babies together," she said. "You 'n' me, Peter, has got to help both of 'em grow up to be men. It's a task that can't noways be dodged. An infant child and an infant land," she said. "You 'n' me, Peter, 's a-goin' to be held responsible fur how both of 'em is raised. We hain't at the hind end of things, Peter. We're jest steppin' over the edge into the beginnin'!"

THE END